T0285367

CELIA IN THE REVOLUTION

CELIA IN THE REVOLUTION

ELENA FORTÚN

TRANSLATED BY
Michael Ugarte

FOREWORD BY
Nuria Capdevila-Argüelles

SWAN ISLE PRESS

CHICAGO

Elena Fortún (pen name of María de la Encarnación Gertrudis Jacoba Aragoneses y de Urquijo, Madrid, 1886-1952) is the author of the classic twenty-volume saga *Celia and Her World* (1929-1951), a work that created an essential link between pre- and post-Spanish Civil War generations of women writers. Her novel, *Celia en la revolución* was not published during her lifetime. *Celia in the Revolution* is the first English-language translation of the work.

Michael Ugarte is professor emeritus at the University of Missouri–Columbia. His works include translations and publications on modern Spanish and postcolonial literature including his translation of *Las tinieblas de tu memoria negra* by Donato Ndongo, *Shadows of Your Black Memory* (Swan Isle Press, 2007).

Nuria Capdevila-Argüelles is professor of Hispanic Studies and Gender Studies at University of Exeter, and co-director of Biblioteca Elena Fortún/Editorial Renacimiento. Her numerous scholarly books on the history of Spanish feminism have been widely praised.

Swan Isle Press, Chicago 60611
© 2023 by Swan Isle Press
© Herederos de Elena Fortún
Translation © Michael Ugarte
Foreword © Nuria Capdevila-Argüelles

All rights reserved. Published 2023.
Printed in the United States of America
First Edition
27 26 25 24 23   1 2 3 4 5
ISBN-13: 978-1-7361893-6-8

Originally published as *Celia en la revolución* by Elena Fortún with prologue by Marisol Dorao © 1987 by Editorial Aguilar; *Celia en la revolución* by Elena Fortún with prologue by Andrés Trapiello, edited by María Jesús Fraga, Inmaculada García Carretero © 2020 by Editorial Renacimiento.

Cover Photograph: Robert Capa © International Center of Photography / Magnum Photos. Courtesy of Biblioteca Regional de Madrid: Frontispiece and archival image Elena Fortún's *Celia en la revolución* handwritten manuscript (1942).

Library of Congress Cataloging-in-Publication Data
Names: Fortún, Elena, author. | Ugarte, Michael, 1949- translator. | Capdevila-Argüelles, Nuria, writer of foreword.
Title: Celia in the revolution / Elena Fortún ; translated by Michael Ugarte ; foreword by Nuria Capdevila-Argüelles.
Other titles: Celia en la revolución. English
Description: First edition. | Chicago : Swan Isle Press, 2023.
Identifiers: LCCN 2023036018 | ISBN 9781736189368 (paperback)
Subjects: LCSH: Spain--History--Civil War, 1936-1939--Fiction. | LCGFT: Historical fiction. War fiction. | Novels.
Classification: LCC PQ6611.O78 C4513 2023
LC record available at https://lccn.loc.gov/2023036018

Swan Isle Press gratefully acknowledges that this edition was made possible, in part, with grants and generous support from the following:
UNIVERSITY OF MISSOURI-COLUMBIA, RESEARCH COUNCIL
LITERARY ARTS EMERGENCY FUND: ADMINISTERED BY THE AMERICAN ACADEMY OF AMERICAN POETS, COMMUNITY OF LITERARY MAGAZINES & PRESSES, NATIONAL BOOK FOUNDATION, SUPPORTED BY THE MELLON FOUNDATION
ILLINOIS ARTS COUNCIL AGENCY
EUROPE BAY GIVING TRUST
OTHER KIND DONORS

The paper used in this publication meets the minimum requirements of the American National Standard of Information Sciences—Permanence of Paper for Printed Library Materials.

CONTENTS

	Foreword by Nuria Capdevila-Argüelles	*vii*
1	Segovia, 1936	*3*
2	Escape	*9*
3	Madrid, 25th of July	*19*
4	The Carabanchel Military Hospital	*27*
5	Executions in Madrid	*37*
6	The Refuge	*47*
7	Chamartín de la Rosa	*61*
8	Evacuation!	*73*
9	November 1936	*85*
10	February 1937. Hunger and Bombs	*93*
11	Evacuation of Madrid	*103*
12	Valencia, September 1937	*111*
13	Albacete	*119*
14	The Sail	*125*
15	November 1937	*135*
16	Barcelona, Christmas	*145*
17	January 1938	*153*
18	Totalitarian War	*161*
19	March 1937	*169*
20	The Return	*181*
21	Madrid in Spring	*189*
22	Hunger!	*197*
23	In My House We Don't Eat, But…	*207*
24	Winter. Papá	*217*
25	The War is Lost	*223*
26	Valencia	*235*
27	Juan García	*245*
28	*Adiós*	*253*

Nuria Capdevila-Argüelles

Celia Gálvez de Montalbán is to this day Spain's most beloved children's book literary character, and yet in this last novel of the renowned Celia series by Elena Fortún, Celia is no longer a little girl. She's becoming a young woman during the Spanish Civil War, and readers of all ages will be moved and inspired throughout this compelling narrative. As the Spanish Pippi Longstocking or Anne of Green Gables — and ever since she made her first appearance in the Spanish press in the roaring twenties — Celia has embarked on thrilling adventures that have been enjoyed by generations, but wartime for Celia and her family, her Spain, is utterly different. When the series began Celia was seven years old. She was a pretty girl always nicely dressed; she lived on Serrano Street, in the affluent Salamanca quarter of Madrid. A bit of a handful, she, like Fortún, loved reading and was a novelist in the making, an author's project. As a child, Celia embodied the promise of female independence and emancipation, and brought irrepressible joy and high spirits to all she did. In *Celia in the Revolution* at seventeen, a decade later, so much has changed, and yet that spirit, determination, her fierce sense of independence remain.

Elena Fortún shared that same emancipation trait and fierce sense of independence. She was a woman born in the nineteenth century, and in her youth, she had not envisioned the huge change she would experience in the Spain of the late 1920s and early 1930s. She went from being a housewife with a basic education to becoming a successful author and a woman who learned enthusiastically about librarianship, went to cultural events, earned a good living, and made the most of the feminist spaces and opportunities offered by the Second Republic in Madrid. Celia is the result of those experiences.

Yet, despite her success, Fortún was always insecure about her literary abilities. In *Celia in the Revolution*, the subjectivities of Fortún and Celia draw nearer to one another. Celia talks about writing in the press and being popular. People recognise her when she travels. The same happened to Fortún. The first-person narrator thus blends her subjectivity with her author's, narrowing the gap between them. Both belong to the losing side of the war and must leave Spain if they want to survive. Fortún feels a sense of duty to remain with her husband and look after him even though she had wanted a divorce years ago and preferred women. The responsibility to care for the masculine "other" as a mother figure will also be central to Celia's decision to leave Spain and look for her father and sisters. Neither author nor character will break the family unit.

Like her autobiographical *bildungsroman*, the novel *Oculto sendero*, with recent English translation *Hidden Path* (Swan Isle Press, 2021) by Jeffrey Zamostny, *Celia in the Revolution* remained for decades inside the closet of Spanish writer Elena Fortún (pen name of Encarnación Aragoneses Urquijo, 1886-1952). Having fled Spain at the end of the Spanish Civil War (1936-39), the "Revolution" in the title, Fortún returned in 1948, four years before her death. To bring *Hidden Path* and *Celia in the Revolution* back from her Argentinian exile at that time would have been dangerous. Both novels, one about lesbianism and one about the war, remained in America, hidden and protected. Closets serve this double purpose of hiding and protecting, and both novels remained inside until the late Marisol Dorao, an academic from Cádiz University and Fortún enthusiast, brought them back to Spain along with most of Elena Fortún's papers, now permanently in Madrid's Biblioteca Regional Joaquín Leguina.

Closets are exterior, seen from the outside, but they also offer perspective from their interior, protecting and restricting what they hide. They contain revelation, pristine meaningful discourses bound to make us question realities and principles. The poet and playwright Federico García Lorca, killed at the beginning of the Spanish Civil War and mentioned in *Celia in the Revolution*, knew this all too well. The author of *Poet in New York* created a character that was similar to him in *The Audience*, one of his last plays, and both were theatre directors. The one in the play says that, if he could, he would poison the open air, a space of artifice, lies, deceit, and violence. Only then, a performance of hidden discourses could be brought out from inside the closet, the site of truths not yet ready to be spoken out. These thoughts on performing are what narrate the silenced discourses, occurring before Lorca or Fortún achieved canonical status. Both authors had texts to hide, performed or spoken by their alter egos, and both had published widely during their lifetime.

In her first encounter with English-speaking audiences, Celia's first-person voice, Fortún's main creation, mentions Lorca's murder. This civil war murder in August 1936 was painfully emblematic, and as a chronicle of the war, this novel must include it. Contemporary readers will realize, from this and other details, that *Celia in the Revolution* constitutes a realistic account of the day-to-day of the Spanish Civil War. It is about people, daily lives, and experiences of "Totalitarian War," title of one of the chapters. We see Isabel García Lorca, the poet's sister, working with the famous Celia in a children's war refuge. We see Madrid and understand the impact of the bombs on the geography of the city. We read about *checas* and *paseos*. We feel the hunger and the cold.

While *Hidden Path* is about authorship, sexuality, and gender identity, *Celia in the Revolution* is about national identity and the Spanish Civil War, with authorship also featured. Celia, as ever, will talk about writing and reflect on Fortún's activities in the press. Whereas Fortún began writing *Hidden Path* in the mid-1930s and probably finished it between 1940 and 1945, *Celia in the Revolution* has a clear date pencilled at the end. There is no second draft or final typed version, however, which differs from what Fortún used to do with her manuscripts. She apparently lost the first version of the book leaving Spain. She also left a few handwritten pages with a detailed account of how she managed to escape via Valencia and France, thus enabling readers to see how much of her own traumatic experience she would lend to her most famous literary creation, Celia. In a letter addressed to novelist Carmen Laforet in 1948, with *Celia in the Revolution* and *Hidden Path* written and closeted, Fortún did remark that separating the author's life from his or her writing was never a good idea. During the war, Fortún wrote in the press, sharing her experience of the war effort in real time and leaving another textual mirror of Celia's hunger and terror, the bombs, and the destruction. Both author and character never abandon the habit of reading and writing. Both would need it not to just earn a living but also to make sense of the world around them and to feel accompanied.

Until what was inside the authorial closet came out, Fortún was just the name on the covers of a saga of 20 books featuring Celia, the storyteller, and her family as they lived through the troubled first half of twentieth-century Spain. Celia was, and is, famous. Fortún was not. In post-Francoist Spain, people knew about Celia but not about the author, and definitely not about her work in the press or her activities in Republican Spain. She is now not only the name behind the book series and the 1993 TV adaptation by José Luis Borau and Carmen Martín Gaite but also the author of *Hidden Path*. *Hidden Path* is arguably the most important lesbian novel written in Spanish, a sort of *The Well of Loneliness* happening between Castile and the Canary Islands. Fortún has emerged as the creator of the Spanish queer girl literary type and, crucially, as the author of one of the best novels about the Spanish Civil War, if not the best one.

Fortún's portrait hangs now in Madrid's *Ateneo*, and a library has been named after her. There is a plaque in one of the houses where she lived in Madrid on beautiful Huertas Street. Her archive, luckily, is being preserved for future generations, and all her books are enjoyed by old and young. She is back, fully here, accompanied by a generation of authors that is being recovered on both sides of the Atlantic. She continues reaching new audiences. And Celia, the most important trace she left of her own existence, is never lost in translation. On the contrary, she comes more alive than ever in this world of ours where civil wars still exist. The *belle époque* of Fernando Trueba's 1992 Oscar-winning film *The Age of Beauty*; the civil war that Hemingway and Orwell wrote about; the Spanish exile, so intellectually stirring in America; and the Francoist dictatorship constitute the historical background of the *Celia* series.

During the war, Celia writes that she is having lunch "in Aguilar's house." She is referring to Mr. Manuel Aguilar, founder of the Aguilar publishing house. He published the books that made Encarnación Aragoneses become Elena Fortún. The children of the transition to democracy, born towards the end of the dictatorship (1975), grew up when Aguilar printed the whole saga for the last time. Aguilar would then go out of business as an independent publisher and get absorbed by bigger publishing houses. *Celia in the Revolution* would not come out until 1987, years after *don* Manuel and Fortún passed away. A generation of teenagers, the same age group to which Celia belonged during the war, were then growing up without knowing much about Spain's first democratic attempt, and the war that tragically ended it, the context of Celia's childhood and teenage years. Elena Fortún finished writing the book on the 13th of July 1943, 44 years before it came out for the first time, and 76 years before it became a best-seller through its publication by Editorial Renacimiento in 2016, in the *Biblioteca Elena Fortún* series I co-direct.

Manuel Aguilar encouraged Fortún to put pen to paper and had Celia recount the war while knowing he could never publish the story during the dictatorship. He was convinced that only Fortún's and Celia's voices could tell the story with some degree of objectivity. Marisol Dorao, on returning from America with the manuscript, went to Aguilar and prepared the first edition of *Celia in the Revolution* with the editorial team, not long before Aguilar's small, independent press disappeared. Without a reasonable alternative at another press, Dorao left *Hidden Path* unpublished due to its lesbian content even though getting the last book of the *Celia* series out was vitally important to her. She, too, had grown up reading Celia's adventures. Well into the new millennium, *Hidden Path* and *Celia in the Revolution* are renowned books in the Spanish-speaking world, praised by both academic and non-academic audiences. These hitherto closeted novels have redefined not only Fortún's authorship but also Hispanic Studies, Memory Studies, and Gender Historiography.

The Spanish Civil War and the ensuing almost forty years of Francoism succeeded in nearly erasing feminist memory in Spain. And yet, after 1975, scholars were quick to declare the feminist debate open, and activists started to dismantle Francoist misogyny, but they had little awareness of a feminist legacy to support the heavy burden of undoing deeply rooted sexism. Women's rights and gender equality seemed new. Orphanhood characterized feminist debate until the new millennium.

When *Celia in the Revolution* was published for the first time, it was bound in striking cherry-coloured cloth, with beautiful illustrations by Asun Balzola. It quickly sold out and became a collector's item. In the 1980s, when the second attempt at democracy was reasonably well established, but still resting on the erasure of the experiences of Fortún and her generation, this historic story of Celia during the Spanish Civil War came out only to go back into the closet of Fortún's authorship. There was one edition only, and it was not a very big one. Celia's childhood books continued to be successful and were adapted to TV.

Hidden behind her character, Fortún was ignored because she belonged to a generation of female writers and artists turned into ghosts by the *Pacto del olvido*, "Pact of Forgetting," which became the foundation of the Spanish transition to democracy. This unwritten pact explains, in part, the nearly thirty years that separate the Aguilar edition of *Celia in the Revolution* and Renacimiento's. By the time *Oculto sendero* (*Hidden Path*) and *Celia en la revolución* (*Celia in the Revolution*) were released in Spain in the new millennium, the *Pacto del olvido* had already started to show substantial cracks, so the generation of writers to which Fortún belonged was coming back. This was not the case in the 1980s when Dorao brought the manuscript back to Spain—the wounds of the past were still too raw to be exposed and examined.

In 1981, six years before the first edition of *Celia in the Revolution* came out, Colonel Antonio Tejero's military failed coup d'etat attempt had taken place, endangering the stability of the new, second and still young, democracy. *Celia in the Revolution* begins with a coup too, which is how the civil war started. On hearing about it, in the first chapter, Celia tells her grandfather that Spain has no democratic praxis. She insists that military declarations happen all the time and that the one happening in Africa should be no surprise. While Celia seems to be aware that violence is a mechanism for political change in the Spain in which she has grown up, her grandfather sees clearly that what is starting outside the peninsula, in North Africa, is not simply another military declaration. Instead, it is the end of the first attempt at genuine democracy. Celia's grandfather had lived long enough to see it happening, and he would witness its failure.

Celia en la revolución has become the most widely read book of the *Celia* series, and now, with this first volume of the saga rendered into English, a generation of Anglophone readers will be able to meet Celia in a very different world, with a voice that transcends borders and time. In 1943, when Elena Fortún finished her draft version of Celia's war experiences, she was living in Buenos Aires, as Celia would do after the end of the Spanish Civil War. Once settled in Argentina, Fortún filled the gap between two volumes of the saga, *Celia is Now Mummy* (*Celia madrecita*) and *Celia Becomes a Governess* (*Celia institutriz*), with this war novel now lucidly translated by Michael Ugarte. While working on this English version, he, not new to the nuances of presenting female genealogies in text form, has always remembered the importance of Fortún's vivid dialogues and the visual and realistic dimension of her prose. He has also highlighted the central role of war scenarios like Madrid, Barcelona, and Valencia. Small details like the oranges and flowers in Valencia or the crisp mornings in Spain's capital matter because those reality snapshots are hugely recognisable today.

Before 1936, in weekly installments and then in book form, Celia drew young readers to her bourgeois world in Madrid, Santander, Paris, or the Cote d'Azur. Through her eyes and her first-person voice, readers became acquainted with her friends and family: her English nanny; her grandfather in Segovia; cousins Miss Fly, Pili, and Matonkikí; her brother Cuchifritín; and her sisters Teresina, a.k.a. Patita, and Mila, the beautiful baby that would grow into an androgynous vagabond girl. The endearing characters of Valeriana and doña Benita became grandmotherly figures for generations of Spanish children. We feel Celia's loneliness when her parents leave her behind in search of better economic prospects, with people who are not able to look after her properly and do not understand her imagination. We feel her despair when her mother dies giving birth to Mila at the beginning of Celia's teenage years. We worry about Celia's father and his unfruitful attempts to remain in the social class in which Celia is born and, most importantly, we always see the logic and fairness in Celia's actions, even when she is, as the nanny would say, "a very naughty girl."

Celia never tells a lie. In contrast, the world of adults appears hypocritical and painfully unfair in the books of her childhood. Beyond the adult world, there was a country living in tense modernity that would make it go from dictatorship to short democracy to war to long dictatorship, followed by another transition to democracy after 1975. Spain is always a problem in the *Celia* series, even after the family returns from exile to live in a flat divided into two opposing sides, as if the atmosphere of the war somehow prevailed there. If Spain is always seen as a problem, then it is always portrayed as a nation in transition, a nation in the process of sorting the problem out to reach some sort of solution. The only thing close to being perennial, it appears, turns out to be the voice of a girl. Celia will forever be the "I" and the eye that tells and sees the history of a family, and a nation, struggling with tradition and modernity to achieve a better tomorrow that will be forever pending. "Will I always be

Celia?", the character asks her mother in the first volume of the series, *Celia Says*. The mother's pre-war death when Celia is fifteen reads highly punitive as well as representative of the fate of that first generation of feminists surrounding Fortún, a diaspora contained in her telephone notebook. Her mother had indeed the answer, and already then, she told her daughter that yes, in one way or another, she would always *be*. She was right. Through thick and thin, Celia will always be Celia. Through Celia's fortunes and misfortunes, readers can do the same thing we do when reading *Don Quixote*: be immersed in a historical time, be part of the society living it, and join the quest for the "I" that presents a socio-historical landscape and tries to understand what a narrator could not understand as a character. Fortún wrote what she saw. That faithfulness makes it impossible for Celia to ever be lost in translation, and readers will love getting to know her in this unique book.

Beyond love for the character, why has Celia's account of the Spanish Civil War been so meaningful for Hispanic audiences reading her in the new millennium? The answer is simple: sooner or later the need to know where we come from would come back to haunt us. It has not always been easy to satisfy that need. In the process of bringing out the literature that Fortún left closeted to redimension her authorship for contemporary audiences, I have often pointed out that, while growing up in the Spanish transition to democracy after Francoism, my only connection with a narrative of Spanish 20th-century history was Celia. She connected us to the experience of growing up with our mothers and grandmothers. She signaled an opening into the past in the otherwise apparently solid and modern, yet tense, façade of the newly democratic Spain. She gave young Spaniards their history in a way *Huck Finn* could not. On a personal level, as much as I loved Holden Caulfield in *The Catcher in the Rye*, *Tom Sawyer*, or even *Colette*, they did not connect me with the past Spain that explained my present and that, as a teenager, I craved to know about. I was 15 years old when *Celia in the Revolution* came out. I knew there had been a war. My grandparents had suffered from it. There was "not enough sugar" when my mother was a little girl, and this line, often repeated, hides so much history that took my generation so long to know. My great-grandfather had been shot, but we did not talk about it. I knew Spaniards had gone into exile. Relatives of mine had gone to the USA and Argentina starting in the 1930s. We knew people in Mexico. Very vaguely, I started to understand the political dimension of the *Celia* series after reading the first edition of *Celia in the Revolution*, which hardly made it to the shops, in the local library.

Celia in the Revolution made Spaniards fathom the siege of Madrid, the hunger, and the bombs. It explains why Ferraz Street in Madrid looks so new and why the area around the Chamartín train station, where both Celia and Fortún had a house, has such a peculiar design. Tall buildings co-exist with streets that look like village roads, and detached houses with gardens and balconies from the 1910s and 20s. Celia's account of the most violent years of the twentieth century had all the answers to questions Spaniards did not dare to ask. After Franco died in 1975, Spaniards felt that the wounds of the past were better left untouched. In order to do so, obliterating the dictatorship, the civil war, and the Second Republic was fundamental for Spain's society and politics to move on in the last third of the twentieth century. What was not openly discussed in the political arena had memory closets to recess to. In a sense, *Celia in the Revolution*, like Celia herself, has always been there, waiting to come out and be read, haunting feminist historians for quite a while. This haunting quality of Celia's war testimonial is now shared with English-speaking readers for the first time.

In my foreword to *Hidden Path*, I outlined the historical dimension of the closet in which Fortún hid her best writing, this volume, and the Sapphic *Hidden Path*, texts about national and gender identity. These volumes, both now published in translation by Swan Isle Press, break the *Pacto del olvido* that tried to erase Fortún and the generation of women writers from Spanish historical memory, just like Celia's mother is removed from the plot of the saga. Now we fully understand why. Until the so-called Spanish second transition to democracy, marked by both equality legislation and historical memory legislation passed in 2007, forgetting was foundational. Wiping the slate clean after the death of Franco had tacitly signified delaying the return of the mothers of Spanish feminism and their experience of emancipation pre-1936, of war and defeat, of exile and dictatorship. Yet the time for their story would come in this new millennium, now. On leaving Spain when the war is over, and when Franco's victory puts her life in danger, Celia receives a book for her trip. Some pages are stuck together, but she is told not to separate them. Fortún will not explain this scene in full. But it is important now that readers participate in it. Fortún, too, received that book on fleeing Spain by following the same route awaiting Celia. Inside the pages, there was money for the trip. It is ironic and inspiring how, even then, both Fortún and Celia would need books to survive. They did survive within "their" books, their voices still heard and read, and they will continue to inspire young and old for generations.

CELIA IN THE REVOLUTION

Celia en la Revolución

Segovia 1936
Cap. I

El abuelito dejó el periódico
violentamente, soltó una pa-
labrota

Ferñín le miró con los ojos
redondos de asombro, y Mariu-
Fuencisla que comía su sopita
de a pucheros con su

— Abuelito, que has enseñado
a los niños?

— ¡Muy asustada estás tú! ¿tú
sabes lo que pasa? ¿ello?

Biblioteca Regional de Madrid

BIBLIOTECA REGIONAL DE MADRID

SEGOVIA, 1936

Granddad furiously throws down the newspaper and lets out a curse.

Teresina looks at him with her startled round eyes while María Fuencisla puckers her lips and sips her soup.

"Granddad! You've frightened the girls!"

"Frightened? I'm terrified! You know what happened?"

"No, Granddad, I don't."

"There's been an insurrection in Africa."

"Oh, Granddad," I say with relief. "It's not the first time. Insurrections, riots, revolutions… Same as usual in this country." I say no more; I don't want to upset my grandfather. He takes off his glasses and looks at me.

"What nonsense are they teaching you in those damn schools? Do you think they issue weapons to soldiers so they can express their opinion?… They want to bring down our government, bring back monarchies, and gun down the very people who voted for them! You think nations have armies and all those weapons to use against whoever they want? Do you believe that? … Do you?"

"Granddad, I …"

"If you believe that, you don't know anything, or else I don't know what I'm talking about." He bangs his fist against the table and curses again.

"Where is it going to end? That's what I want to know."

Granddad makes us shiver with his fists banging and the dishes and glasses jumping. Teresina looks into his face turning red, eyes filled with tears. María Fuencisla, sitting in her highchair as I feed her, turns her frightened face to look at Granddad.

"Granddad, can't you see you're scaring the girls?"

The old man takes his newspaper and shuts himself in his room. He hasn't eaten anything. Valeriana, who had set the table, places the soup on a tray along with the bread, wine, and water. She frowns at me as she goes into Granddad's room.

"Now, let's eat," I say to the girls. "María Fuencisla, a little more soup."

"No more," declares my little sister. "Granddad, look at me… bang, bang, bang…" She closes her little fist imitating her grandfather.

From his room we could hear Granddad's harsh voice accompanying Valeriana's laments; then we hear chairs moving and dishes breaking. Granddad had thrown the tray on the floor!

He does not come back to the table, and the next day, as I give María Fuencisla a bath, Valeriana says that Granddad had urged us to go to the basement because it was cooler there.

"The basement! It's a mess, full of cobwebs…"

"It's not so bad. Farruco's fixing it up, it'll look great. Just do as he says… I'll bring down Dad's straw chair, your books, and junk… and the girls' dolls… Ya know?" she whispers to me. "There's riots everywhere…"

"Really? What's going on?"

"Who knows? Some locked themselves in the schools and they're not gonna come out. Some say this, others say that, no one agrees, some even shoot people and everything, and they killed someone in Plaza Azoguejo."

It's impossible to figure out what's going on; Valeriana's information is sketchy, so I decide to stop trying to know and go down to the basement with my sisters. Teresina and María Fuencisla are delighted when they heard the news.

"We'll prepare our own meals, right Celia? And later you'll cut the material for my doll's dress and I'll sew it."

"Me too," said María Fuencisla. "I want a dress for my doll too!"

The basement is dark, and you can feel the coolness of fresh water. It smells of fresh damp clay. If only my sisters would let me fix the collar of the dresses I started yesterday. If only…

"Celia, thread my needle…"

"Mine too, mine too…"

"Not like that, the thread doesn't go through…"

"My thread too…"

Oh my! All I do is thread needles. María Fuencisla pricks her finger: there's a drop of blood and she cries out.

"It's nothing, *querida*, it's nothing."

I kiss the wound and recite a little verse, "Get better, you little frog, if not today, tomorrow." She repeats it, and falls asleep in my arms as I sing her a little song.

At midday, Valeriana brings us our lunch.

"Why don't we eat in the dining room? Is Granddad still angry?"

"No, that's not it… he's still pouting, but he just doesn't want to eat… I brought him all the newspapers I could find, and he's devouring them."

"You mean he's eating them?" Teresina was worried.

Valeriana kept on talking. "I say it makes no difference. You think he's going to solve anything? He thinks he can… and he just makes everything worse."

I want Valeriana to tell me about her fears as I feed the girls and eat a bit myself, but it's no use. She doesn't want to tell me anything, and besides, she can't make herself understood anyway.

Two more days in the basement; I'm getting used to it. I've brought books for myself and the girls. We sing while I sew… and I read to them. When they allow me, I read a novel on my own. It's about a fourteen-year-old girl, like me. She's blond too. But she lives in a castle in England surrounded by forests; she goes hunting with her father and brothers… Outside the castle there are swans in a lake. My God, what a life! In the castle there are dozens of servants and an Irish governess who saw the birth of the count. Ah, that's because Alice's father was a count.

What a beautiful name, Alice! It sounds like a flower… In another castle nearby lives a duchess who has a blind son… he writes poems. He will inherit the castles.

I can't resist the urge to tell this story, so one afternoon I tell it to Valeriana…

She is distracted as she listens and says:

"Did that really happen?"

"I don't know, maybe."

"Well, look, if it didn't happen, leave it be, and don't be disappointed, because much worse things are happening… Your grandfather is going to drive himself crazy if he isn't already; he's about to make big trouble for us."

"Why?"

I can't get through to her, but when I go up for dinner she tells me:

"Have you noticed the stairway?"

"No."

"Don't you see how dirty it is, straw, manure, and everything? It stinks."

"No, *hija*, I haven't noticed."

"Don't you have eyes? That bunch of people coming and going, they take packages, dirty up everything, and make things difficult for us…"

Valeriana's worries almost make me laugh.

"So all our problems are because the stairs are dirty?"

"No, not just that, but I think…"

For two days I hear gunshots and crashes that shake the windows of the balcony. Just now we hear something so close to us that Valeriana cries out and crosses herself. As if she were in the middle of a storm, she prays, "Saint Barbara most holy, in heaven thou art, and in the altar of the Cross until the hour of our death, amen."

Today when I get out of bed, I find out what was happening at home. According to Valeriana, Granddad's distributing all the weapons we have in the vestibule to a gang of bigshots; I don't know who they are.

"Well good luck, they're all dirty and rusty."

"The old man has been cleaning them so carefully you wouldn't believe… That's not all, he gave them your dad's rifle and shotgun, those old things, along with boxes of pistols, big ones."

"What are they going to do with all that?"

"I don't know, but those beasts with shotguns could kill your mother 'Sweet Mary Ever Virgin! Deliver us from all this!'"

"Look, Valeriana, don't get so upset and don't scare the girls. Let's have breakfast before we go downstairs."

"No, that's not necessary. Can't hear any more shots."

"Al right, then it's all done for now."

"Seems to me that now that it's over, it's just when it all starts."

At midday, as we eat, I'm surprised to see the look on Granddad. He is livid, he looks at us as if he didn't recognize us.

At the table, I say:

"Are you sick, Granddad?"

"No… I'm fine. Don't worry."

"Any word about your father?"

"No… There's no way of finding out. Here in Segovia the insurrectionists have taken over, but not in Madrid… We don't have access to news."

"He probably won't get involved," I say just to add something.

"Well, that's not right," answered Granddad.

I notice his hands shaking as he pours water into his cup; still, I try to talk, so I tell him how it was in the basement.

"We heard a mouse fall into the mousetrap; it scared us."

"He was so little, Granddad, and pretty. I wanted to come up and show you, but Celia wouldn't let me."

"My little mouse."

Valeriana added:

"Where's the mouse? I didn't see it."

"I let him go," I laughed. "Poor thing has a right to live."

"True," said Granddad. "It's a divine right."

He didn't say anything else.

In the afternoon we went out into the yard, always with Granddad; today he didn't want to let us out of his sight; he listens to us sing and play:

I spy with my little eye,
I see..
What do you see?
I see something.
What is its letter?
Starts with a "C" and ends with an "E."

"Can you eat it?"

At nighttime we go inside and wait for Granddad to come out of his room for supper. He sits on the couch with one of the girls on each knee, and I lower the lamp to arrange pieces of a puzzle that have come out from their box.

Suddenly we hear someone knocking at the door to the street. Granddad tries to listen and tells the girls to shush.

It's hot. The shutters are down in the balcony, so I get up to raise the blinds, but Granddad says:

"Be still."

I sit down. Someone is coming up the stairs… Granddad says with a voice I barely recognize:

"Celia, if something happens to me… I want you to go to Madrid with the girls… Swear that you will…"

"Yes, Granddad."

We hear steps approaching; the door opens.

"Don Juan Antonio de Montalbán."

Three tall, strange men come into our room. Granddad stands up leaving María Fuencisla alone on the couch, while Teresina tries to hide behind Granddad's legs.

"You are under arrest. Come with us," I hear as if it were a dream.

"I'll go on my own," cries Granddad. "Don't touch me, you traitors."

"No insults! The traitors are the ones distributing weapons…"

Granddad's fiery eyes accompany his growly voice; he's a man accustomed to telling people what to do. He gives his captors a lecture about the Catholic Kings of Spain, the obligations of the military, the people, but they cut him off by grabbing his hands and escorting him out the door.

His white head stands out above the insurrectionists. Their words fade as they go down the walkway. I hear the gate to the street close.

Valeriana comes in; we look at each other without speaking. Two tears stream down her face.

ESCAPE

I don't know what time Valeriana wakes me up.

"Up, up, we're leaving. Let's go, Celia… *Muchacha*, don't go back to sleep! We're off."

I sit up in bed and rub my eyes, still sleepy. I can't remember. Something horrible has happened; I don't know what… Oh, yes! They arrested Granddad!

Valeriana goes from the bedroom to the main room where there's more light. I hear voices… soft voices conversing. Who's there?

I get up and go to the door. It's Farruco, the servant, talking to Valeriana. I can make out some of the words: "Don Antolín's under arrest too… On the way to Fuentemilanos I'll catch up to you as soon as I fix this No, you're not in danger if you go alone He gave don Antolín the money…"

Valeriana is coming into the shadows of the bedroom.

"You still here? Look, we have to get the girls dressed! C'mon, *mujer*, no time to waste; we've got to get out of Segovia."

"I want to know… Why are we leaving? Where is Granddad? Are they going to arrest us too? Where are we going? To Madrid? But there's no train at this hour."

Valeriana doesn't know much either. Granddad knew he'd be arrested, so yesterday he left everything in order. Farruco and don Antolín know what we have to do.

"Farruco says don Antolín is under arrest."

"It's all the same. Just do as they say. You help María Fuencisla get dressed, and I"ll look after Teresina."

María Fuencisla is fast asleep; it's best for her not to wake up, so I carefully put on her smock, shoes too.

Teresina complains:

"I don't want to get up. I don't want to. I'm sleepy. Leave me alone, stupid."

"Shush… Be quiet… We're leaving; we're going to look for *Papá* in Madrid."

She's half convinced and lets me dress her, yawning still sleepy as I guide her little arm into the sleeve…

As soon as she's dressed, she falls asleep on the bed again; we gather her clothes and put them in a sack.

"Wouldn't it be better in a suitcase?"

"No, *hija*, for the donkey it's better in sacks."

"We're going to Madrid on a donkey?" I ask astounded.

There are no trains to Madrid, that's what Valeriana says. Besides, this is not a trip, it's an escape.

Valeriana doesn't want us to turn on the lights, so we go from room to room with lighted candles. The smell of the kerosene heater where we warm coffee and milk gives the house a new sensation. Our shadows on the walls get longer… What does this remind me of? It's something I've felt before. I don't know when. Maybe in a novel…

Farruco's worried; he comes into the kitchen and tells us:

"Aren't you ready yet? Picio's saddle is on; I've wrapped burlap around his hooves so he doesn't make too much noise."

We have to get Teresina out of bed, she doesn't want any coffee and milk. María Fuencisla is asleep in my arms when we go out to the patio by the kitchen stairs The moon illuminates the well and the façade of our house, all covered by creeping ivy.

Suddenly, I'm nervous. Are we leaving for good? I think of my books, of a box of toys my mom gave me… and of the blue dress my aunt Cecilia gave me.

"Valeriana, please. I'd like to take… hold the girl for a moment."

"Shush… There's no time."

Farruco and the donkey emerge from the shadows, moving toward us.

"No, there's no time. The stars are high; it'll be morning by the time you get to Fuentemilanos."

Valeriana grabs the little one and I get on top of Picio. His saddle is wide and comfortable… What's this lump?

"*Hija*, it's the sack with your clothes in it and some things for the trip," says Valeriana as she hands me María Fuencisla, who cuddles up into my arms. My little Fuencisla!

Teresina, half awake, is behind me. Valeriana ties her to my waste with her scarf.

Then she takes the halter and guides Picio through the only open door. The burro stumbles, almost falling.

"Whoa," says Farruco, trying to stabilize the donkey. "This damned animal can barely see."

We manage to make it to the plaza. The big house in front belongs to the Marquis of Lozoya; the lights are still on in the balcony. The marquis was Granddad's friend, but not anymore. Who are our friends now? Maybe only Valeriana and Farruco.

We go down the Azoguejo hill; the sky is covered by the Segovia aqueduct shining in the moonlight. Farruco unties the burlap from Picio's legs and Valeriana tugs at the halter. We come across a road with trees at both sides…

"*Dios*," cries Valeriana, coming to a stop. "The Civil Guard!"

Two civil guards have come out of nowhere.

"Where are you going?"

"To Otero de Herreros," says Valeriana. She remains calm. "We're bringing the girls back."

The police approach to take a look at them.

"There are three of you."

"Yes, I brought 'em with me, I told 'em in the morning you'll be with your dad for a few days, I wanna keep 'em away from this mess."

"Go along," say the police.

Picio resumes his pace… Teresina seems to be crying. She says:

"Did they want to arrest us?"

"Shush, not so loud, my little lamb. No, no one's going to arrest us."

"So why did Valeriana lie?"

"Because it's better that way. Go on now. Go to sleep on my back."

"I'm not sleepy anymore."

But as soon as I sense she's asleep, the donkey's paces make her sway. Poor thing.

The night smells like dirt and straw. You can hear the bells nearby as cows settle down to rest. Soon they'll be tied to the threshing machine or the cart. We hear the sounds of horses galloping toward us, again the civil guards.

When we come out of the shadows of the trees, they see us and halt.

"Where are you going?"

"To Otero de Herreros."

"Not that way, you can't go that way. Where are you taking the lady?"

"She's not a lady, she's a girl; she's the doctor's oldest daughter. She…"

"Alright, go ahead."

The further away we are from Segovia, the calmer I feel. We're in the middle of fields; the night sky is covered with stars that brush against the hills in the distance. You can't even hear the crickets, nothing except the sound of a distant bell. Suddenly there's a flash in the mountain.

"It's the war," whispers Valeriana. "War… May God have mercy on us. Let's pray, Celia? It's better that way; we won't fall asleep, and God will accompany us."

I think this poor woman is going to get tired soon; we have a hundred kilometers ahead of us.

"Valeriana, if you're getting tired, get on the *burro* and I'll take the reins."

"For God's sake, what are you talking about? I ain't a weakling. Just say the rosary and we'll be fine."

She feels for the rosary beads in the depths of her petticoats, although she doesn't know where they are exactly. When she finds them, she takes them out and commences:

"In the name of the Father, the Son, and the Holy Ghost. Holy Mary,

Mother of God, pray for us sinners now and at the hour of our death, amen. First mystery, Our Lord's Incarnation. Get on, there Picio! For God's sake…"

The prayer in rhythm with Picio's trots makes me drowsy. I'm nodding off, but I wake myself up so as to not let go of the girls.

The sun is rising, the stars are fading, and a pearl-like clarity takes over the mountainous horizon in the distance. Suddenly flashes of light. We hear cries and explosions far away.

Valeriana is terrified. "The war's right over there!"

You can see the first houses of a town; it's not a good idea to cross the road after we pass by the town.

Smells of dawn. The smoke of pine wood burning in the chimneys, the freshness of streams, the sweet smell of mountain pines. They're all like little devils who come to sit beside me, my heart is lit like a hearth. I can't keep myself from nodding off.

When the sun comes out, Teresina wakes up, unsettled, not knowing where she is; she's frightened.

"Have we escaped, Celia?"

"Yes…"

"Have we been arrested?"

"Don't be silly, precious. No one is going to arrest us."

"But Granddad…"

María Fuencisla is awake too; she's laughing in my arms, as if she had spent all the nights of her life on top of a donkey; she yells with glee:

"Giddy-up, burrito, we're off to Bethlehem…" like the Christmas song.

We arrive at a chapel and Valeriana decides that Picio is tired and says we should rest.

We move into the shade to avoid the burning sunlight of the Castile plains in July.

Valeriana is like our mother; she brought along chocolates for us. We gobble them up and drink water from a fountain on the other side of the road as Teresina and María Fuencisla, delighted to be in the fields, play in front of the hermitage.

The chapel is closed, but I can see the inside from a grating at the top, illuminated by the sun shining through the roof.

I can see the altar, a saint with a long beard, artificial flowers, and curved columns of a faded golden color.

"It's San Antón," says Valeriana who is also looking inside the chapel. "Saints on high, deliver us from evil, amen," and she quickly makes the sign of a cross.

"Will San Antón come with us?" asks Teresina.

"Of course he will," Valeriana replies.

"But he'll have to open the door." She takes a look at him with his long white beard and tells me, "I'm scared of him."

Later, at midday, the sun rises directly above our heads, and I hear Teresina scolding María Fuencisla:

"If you don't behave, San Antón and his long beard will come with us to make sure you stay in line."

"I don't want to…"

"Yes, he'll come, Valeriana said so."

Some women see us; they're on their way back from washing clothes in the river.

"Good day. Are you from here?"

"Just outside Segovia," says Valeriana.

"So… if you don't mind us asking, where are you going?"

"To Zarzuela del Monte, to take these girls to the doctor's house; the doctor's their father."

"You seem like nice girls," says one of the women, looking us over.

"Sure they are, upper crust," assures Valeriana.

"So what's happening in Segovia?" they ask. They look as if they want to accompany us. "They say there's a revolution."

"I ain't seen nothing," says Valeriana. "Everything's calm there."

"Calm? Well some say there's cannon fire in the Alcázar, people firing guns in the mountains, they've executed some of them."

"Rumors."

"Maybe, but last night you could hear the shots. My Juan didn't dare go out to the fields because of what might happen."

Since Valeriana pretends to be asleep, the women turn to me, and ask me how old the girls were.

"The little one, two, and this one, five and a half."

"They look older. Do they have brothers?"

"Yes, one brother, he is…"

"Really far away," offers Valeriana.

At last they leave stirring up the grass as they pass, the air smells of thyme.

"Busybodies," pouted Valeriana. "They only want to get into everything. A bunch of gossip."

As the day goes on, Valeriana gives us hard bread and ham she had wrapped in a cloth. Teresina goes to the fountain for water and fills her aluminum cup, but she comes back empty because she finds a frog.

"It was looking at me like this, like this," she says with her eyes wide open and gesturing with her hands.

We wait for Farruco who had planned to meet us at the hermitage.

"If he doesn't get here by nightfall, we'll go to Calvario de las Navas, and he'll look for us there," said Valeriana.

Then she starts talking about what happened to Granddad.

"Men always get themselves into things they should pay no mind to; they should only take care of their homes. Just take a look at what happens when two of 'em get together…don't matter if they're rich or poor, all's they do is talk about politics: the mayor this, the city council that, the elections…and some have got the gall to make fun of what the priest says in his sermons, that the friars are… that the Pope in Rome… Seems like they think they can fix the world… that they know it all…"

"Sure, *mujer*. And what about women? All they talk about is the price of potatoes and their sons and daughters…"

"That's the way it's gotta be," scowls Valeriana. "No matter what the mayors or city council does, it's not gonna fill your pots or feed your children."

"Yes, Valeriana, that's the way it is. That's why God has given us chores: women at home, men everywhere else."

Valeriana thinks about it. Then, she says as she washes María Fuencisla's face with a towel.

"It's true what you said before. You've studied a lot. But it seems to me that all those men talking about things they don't know about, they're the ones making revolutions… Women, some more than others, know how to fix things in their house. If those men have to fix the world, why don't they take lessons? That's what I'd like to know."

The afternoon gets longer; we have to move to the other side of the hermitage where there's more shade.

There's a delightful aroma coming from the herbs in the afternoon sun; it's as if all the earth was filled with incense as an offering to the heavens.

"We're close to Ávila," I say thinking about Saint Teresa.

The girls ask for water, then they want to mount Picio who is chewing on grass, then they ask for a story. They're up and about trying to relieve their boredom.

"Let's keep going," complains Teresina.

"We're waiting for Farruco; he's on his way."

When she hears this, she tells us over twenty times that Farruco is coming. Valeriana and I go to the road to see if we can catch a glimpse of him. No Farruco, but we do see something: a shepherd, or a man, selling tomatoes from town to town, and there's an ox or something on its way back to the stable.

Valeriana doesn't want us to move until nightfall.

Then she puts Picio's harness back on along with his saddlebags, and I mount him with María Fuencisla in my arms and Teresina behind me.

Valeriana, as always, takes the reins, leading us along the road in silence.

Soon the two girls are asleep and Valeriana tells me that we won't get to Calvario de las Navas until midnight.

"As long as Farruco gets here," she says this twice.

I know she's worried about Granddad, but she doesn't want to talk about it.

"I don't think anything will happen to Granddad," I say.

But Valeriana doesn't answer. Then she says:

"Let's pray for him and ask God to protect him."

"*Mujer*, I think it would've been better for us to stay home to make sure they let him go."

"No. He ordered you to go and find your father…"

When at last we see the church tower of Calvario de las Navas in the moonlight, Valeriana tugs at the reins, making Picio move along faster. God, I'm so sleepy. Valeriana helps me down; we lower Teresina to the ground fast asleep, using the saddlebags as pillows. Valeriana arranges everything to allow the girls to lie down and fall asleep. I'm sitting on the ground with María Fuencisla in my arms; soon I can't keep myself from sleeping.

Valeriana sits down beside me, making sure there are no pebbles under her. Then she takes María Fuencisla from me and says:

"Lay your head on my lap… Go on. I'll cover you with the blanket when the sun comes up; it'll be cold."

I sleep profoundly in the care of this woman, my safety net, my pillar of strength.

It seems I've been sleeping a long time when I wake up to someone's words; I don't open my eyes, just listen. It's Farruco.

"They threw don Antolín in jail, don Andrés too, and don Rodrigo, the pharmacist. I couldn't talk to any of them."

"Didn't you see don Juan Antonio?"

"Yes, sort of, I saw him at dawn when they were taking him away…"

"For what?"

"Well, I didn't want to tell you, but it's no use. They took him and Antolín. I could see the master's head above them all. He's so tall!"

"But why?"

"Well… they executed them, took them to a cliff and shot them."

"Dear Jesus," Valeriana cries out.

"Crying's no use. I just hid… I seen it all. The *Señor* said 'Long live liberty!' and then they shot 'em."

MADRID, 25TH OF JULY

We get on a bus at El Escorial; we have to stand, pressed together like sardines in a can. Before getting to Madrid they make us get out of the bus and walk.

Valeriana carries our sacks with our belongings in them and a basket she has not let go of throughout the whole journey, no matter the complaints of other passengers. I have María Fuencisla in my arms while Teresina ambles on merrily in front of us.

We rest every now and then.

"Soon we'll find *Papá*," I say to Valeriana. "And we'll get to Aunt Julia's house rested, we're sure to find him there."

Climbing up Cuesta de San Vicente to Plaza de España tired us out. Valeriana has left our bags at the entrance of a building. She looks around and says:

"Is this Madrid?"

"Yes, we're in the Palacio neighborhood."

"Well this all looks like a pigsty to me… for such a famous capital city," she says gravely.

It's true. The trees in the plaza look as though they've been ravaged by a hurricane, all those branches and leaves on the ground, and the leaves aren't dry, we're in the middle of summer! The ground is littered with papers, pages of books, pieces of lead.

I pick up one of the pieces of lead.

"It's a bullet."

"Drop that now," says Valeriana frightened.

A woman with a boy at her side who was on the same bus tells us what happened.

"They tried to take the Montaña Barracks, over there. They say troops locked themselves in and started firing from inside, but the militia's cannon fire and rifles forced them to stop shooting. They were all flattened out like dead bugs, some were dragged out right around here."

"Poor soldiers," laments Valeriana.

"What are you talking about? Poor nothing, traitors, worse than traitors, dirty blood-sucking swine, if you ask me," growled the woman.

"So who's right?" asks Valeriana.

Teresina and I want to know too. We want to be on the side of justice.

"What do you mean by that, woman?" asks another woman sarcastically. "The people are always right."

And she continues up the hill with her son in tow and glances back at us.

"Should we go on?" Valeriana asks.

When we get to Ferraz Street we get on a tram to Puerta del Sol.

Much to Valeriana's chagrin, Teresina changes seats playfully several times, and María Fuencisla whimpers sleepily.

"The poor little lamb's got to be hungry," Valeriana sympathizes. "How far have we got to go?"

The ticket collector has a slight altercation with Valeriana, who can't seem to find the coins tucked away in her petticoats.

"How much did you say it is? Does the little girl ride for free?"

"She pays too if she's older than three."

"Well, look… She's really thin. Doesn't take more space than a three-year-old."

A man on the bus solves the controversy by demanding there be less conversation and more solidarity.

With that, the ticket collector gives up trying to charge us as we arrive at Puerta del Sol.

It's hot under the midday sun; the asphalt feels like rubber under our feet. Here we wait for the tram to Goya Street. Valeriana repeats that it looks like a hurricane has blown through Madrid. Preciados Street is in disarray and the tram's rails are out of place. Our feet shuffle over the cracks on the dirty sidewalk; everything is sordid and dusty.

The only thing we see is workers and women who look distracted and do not wear anything over their heads; they look like peasant women. The stores are half closed, everything looks filthy and sordid.

"How sad to see Madrid like this!" laments Valeriana.

There are few cars except for one or two driven by people who don't know how to drive; there are rifles poking out the windows.

Some of the tram passengers are armed workers pointing their rifles up toward the sky.

"Who is stronger," asks Teresina, "the tram riders or the other ones?"

Valeriana whispers to me:

"I think there's a revolution here too."

"Of course, *mujer*! They told us so in El Escorial."

"Men are nothing but brutes. God, just brutes!" snarls Valeriana.

We get on the tram. It's unbearably hot. I try to lower the curtain over my window, but the ticket collector stops me.

"Not allowed."

"But the little girl is suffocating. She's sweating."

"Let her sweat. There's no harm in it."

The man calls me *tú* instead of *usted*; he's condescending and insulting, but I don't say anything. If only I could find some of my school classmates. They'll think I'm a little worker girl traveling with her mother. I don't know why I'm embarrassed.

"What a trip! It's been five days since the morning we left Segovia."

Suddenly an abrupt stop and bells make me snap back to reality. Two men get off, one of them pushing the other one.

"Look, broken glass from a bullet shot," Valeriana whispers to me. "Don't say anything. Look at the hole in the broken window. Will we get there soon?"

Finally we arrive. We step down with all our belongings. I'm the only one who knows the way. María Fuencisla tries to keep her little feet moving with me as I take her by the hand.

The street we're on is empty; it doesn't look like the one I lived on a year ago.

"Here it is." The door is not locked, and when I open it we feel a fresh breeze from inside.

I ring the bell; it's loud, but no one answers. Finally someone opens the peephole.

"Who is it?"

"Is doña Julia Gálvez here?"

"Who is it?"

"Celia. Tell her it's Celia."

We hear rustling behind the door and Aunt Julia's voice:

"Open the door, Mari, it's my niece. Open."

There they are, all of them, and Auntie so surprised to see me.

"What are you doing here in the middle of the summer? Lord, this is crazy, and you've brought the girls and everything. Madrid is no place to travel to right now."

I kiss her, but she's so astonished and nervous, it seems she's annoyed to see me.

"As soon as all this madness is over, we're going to the mountains for the summer. I'm all packed… But why have you come? Your father isn't expecting you at all. We let him have the house on Chamartín in exchange for the one in the mountains. He's fixing it up for the winter. This is all so unexpected!"

Aunt Julia doesn't invite us in, not even to sit down, as if she's hoping we leave.

"Auntie, we had no choice. Don't you see? We had to go to El Escorial on a donkey."

"Good God, like gypsies. Why didn't you take the train?"

"There are no trains, Auntie."

"Please, ma'am, no need to make a fuss over us," says Valeriana. "Please tell us where the *señor* is, and we'll be off."

"Your *Señor*," Aunt Julia interjected sarcastically. She turns to me and says,

"Your father is out of his mind, this morning he went to the mountains with Gerardo's hunting rifle. He says the fascists are all hiding in the mountains. Why does he get himself into things that he can't do anything about?"

"Well, *Señora*," Valeriana insisted again. "Don't get upset on our account, we can sleep anywhere, I'll take care of the girls. And don't worry about the cost, I have my savings…"

But Julia did not let her finish:

"Be quiet, woman, don't be a chatterbox. No one's talking about costs or inconveniences. It's just that you should not have left Segovia where everything is in order, the right people are in charge now. Don Juan Antonio is probably concerned about your safety."

"Well, don Juan Antonio's not around anymore — they executed him."

"My God!"

Teresina tugs at my dress, she's looking at me with her round eyes wondering what's happening.

"Never mind, little one."

We're in the inside of Auntie's house; Valeriana is insufferably hot so she takes off her dark scarf, showing the white streaks of her disheveled hair.

"Auntie, the girls have not eaten anything since yesterday."

"What about you?"

"We can manage."

Aunt Julia changes her disposition after the initial shock and shows us some tenderness and sympathy. I don't know why she was so upset.

The dining room door is half open and our table is ready. The room is fresh and breezy. María, the servant, brings out the dishes and serves us. I fall asleep on the chair next to the balcony.

Eight days have passed, and things seem to have gotten back to normal. Valeriana takes the girls for afternoon walks, she's carrying María Fuencisla, and Teresina grabs her skirt as they stroll along the dusty walkway, they never go too far. Cousin Gerardo, the one I didn't see the first day we arrived, has appeared without telling us where he's been, always locked in his room. Aunt Julia and I sew and talk next to the balcony. Maybe Auntie knows what has happened in Segovia, but I don't think I ever will, just like I don't know what's

23

going on in Madrid.

At night I hear isolated gunfire: screams and things passing by under the balconies and fading, leaving something tragic in their wake.

"This morning we found three men shot dead in that corner of the street," Aunt Julia says to me. "I don't know what's going to happen, all this for not having faith in God."

The girls are hot in the afternoon hours, and they're bored; I don't know what to do to amuse them. Aunt Julia naps, and Gerardo is still in a bad mood.

"You need to sleep, girls," I say to my sisters. "Shut your eyes and sleep."

Sometimes I get them to rest by cuddling up in the rocking chair in the dining room with María Fuencisla in my lap; I sing to her softly.

On the street there is absolute silence with occasional interruptions of passing trams. Between the shades I can see the street covered by a furious sun, like fire, burning up the dusty walkways.

This is the revolution. I imagined revolutions with people yelling in the street, men climbing up streetlights and trees demanding their enemy's heads, banners, passionate speeches by people on balconies yelling and gesticulating. Maybe I've seen these things in pictures of the French Revolution. But here, there's nothing but silence, dust, dirt, heat, and men in streetcars with rifles. But they don't attack, they're just defending us against a mysterious enemy hidden in the earth. No one is repairing buildings or fixing streets; maybe no one is working in factories either. The workers have headed for the mountains to fight against the fascists, others walk in the streets with their rifles loaded. I wonder who among them goes around killing in the night. I also wonder who they kill.

A splashing sound coming from the bathroom interrupts my reflections. Terrified, I leave María Fuencisla asleep on the dining room couch. This takes a few minutes because I don't want to wake her. Then I rush to attend to Teresina.

From the door to the hallway I see her playing with the faucet.

"What are you doing, girl?"

"Come see, it's flowing down the drain. Look, look how it flows."

It's Gerardo's necktie going down the drain; I manage to save it by grabbing the end. It's red, and the water in the sink is tinged with a rose color.

"What on earth are you up to, silly? What are you doing?"

Teresina is upset as she covers her eyes with her hands. She says:

"I was washing Gerardo's neckties; he said they were dirty."

Her explanation worries me.

"Neckties? Is there another one?"

"It's over there," says Teresina.

"But Teresina, dear, what a stupid thing you did! What will Aunt Julia say?"

The phone rings but no one answers. I go toward the phone with Gerardo's bloody tie in my hands. Aunt Julia says:

"Yes, it's here. Comrade Antonio, you say? You mean don Antonio Gálvez? … No, not the same names. I'm his sister… What? Military hospital?… What?… Injured? You say he's injured? My God, what madness!… Room 22 of the central hospital? Is it serious?… Lord… Lord…!"

Auntie hangs up and looks at me, she's pale.

"Your father's been shot; a bullet went through his lung. We need to go to the hospital now. This is madness!"

THE CARABANCHEL MILITARY HOSPITAL

Every morning at eight thirty I get on a streetcar at Plaza Mayor. I'm looking for the statue of Felipe IV and his bronze horse. It looks as though an earthquake has torn everything up, it's all uneven, the statue is dismantled, covered with dust and dirt.

I'm not wearing a hat or beret; I'm dressed in espadrilles and a percale smock that I made in Segovia. In an oilcloth bag, I've got everything I need to spend the day in the hospital.

Everyone is poorly dressed, maybe because they don't want to get their nice clothes dirty, or because we've all become paupers. I don't know.

The streetcar goes from Plaza de Toledo to the bridge over the Manzanares. When I get there, I see people gazing at the river, chatting, and pointing toward the other side.

I gaze too, but I'm not sure what the attraction is. A man says curtly: "Over a hundred fish today."

Everyone approaches the river shore to take a look.

"Where? Can you see them from here?

"Yesterday there were twelve."

"I didn't see them."

Everyone is talking. I figure out that they're referring to those who were executed last night.

They're all looking for something; I, too, get as close as I can. Yes, over there I can see a dark pile… I can see the whiteness of their faces. My God, so many.

"Deader than doornails," says a fat woman with a striped apron, smiling as she crosses her hands over her belly.

"They're fascists… bloodsuckers!"

At the entrance to the Carabanchel road, two armed workers and a woman dressed in military garb tell us to get off the streetcar.

"Show us your papers."

I hand her my hospital card, my student I.D. and my national I.D. One of them looks at it and shows it to his comrades, spelling out the letters with difficulty.

"You can go," he says, proud of carrying out his noble duty with such military efficiency.

One night, as I return to Madrid, I see these same officials who make us show our papers. One of them says to a streetcar passenger:

"You're ordered to stop. Come with us to the commissary."

One man is so nervous that he scares me. There he remains with the officials as we get back on the streetcar. The conductor says to him:

"That guy's gotten himself into trouble."

One woman laughs but the rest of the passengers continue in silence as if we were on our way back from a funeral.

Few people traveling on streetcars talk to each other these days. People prefer to keep their thoughts to themselves.

When we begin the ascent up the Carabanchel hill, we're happy to see street vendors selling peppers, tomatoes, and lettuce. It seems everything is normal.

The further we go, the landscape turns arid, yellow, and dry: the smell of dried grass and the stench of rotting meat.

At one point the ticket collector says:

"Military Hospital."

I get off; this is where the road to the hospital ends. Another streetcar will take me to the hospital. It only takes a few minutes, but since there's just one car and the driver is taking a refreshment break, it takes longer than a few minutes. So I decide to walk the remaining distance.

As I walk by those low houses, taverns, and indistinguishable stores, the smells are stronger.

"What a stench!" I hear a woman say as she covers her nose. If they don't bury the ones in the gutter, everyone's going to vomit.

There are probably dead bodies close by. I don't want to think about it. As I pass a tavern, I hear someone say:

"Those are the ones they executed yesterday; they're still in the ditch… You'd think they'd bury them."

There is the fence that surrounds the hospital. There's always a lot of cars in this area.

The spacious, cool hallway is a relief from the heat outside. Men from the town with rifles and dressed in military garb, the ones they call the militia, are guarding the premises. There are more than twenty of them sitting down or walking around, six or eight are women; each of the militiamen carries guns in holsters.

The concierge, a fat man in a uniform, speaks with them. I show him my card and he lets me by. He's a horrid man; I'll say why later.

As I pass through the hallway to the garden, I smell the disinfectants. The flowers are irrigated, the floor and staircase are clean. It's like being in another world.

Papá is on the first floor. He's waiting for me, looking at the door. He's sitting, four pillows at his back so he can breathe comfortably.

"Daddy! Could you sleep last night? I've brought some lemon powder you can mix in water… and newspapers, and a clean shirt."

I place it all on the bed, and Father caresses my head; he looks at the paper. As soon as he reads it, he gets upset.

"Those traitors had help! They had help!" he cries.

But I'm used to his indignation and his desperation, his joys too. Without listening, I prepare the basin to wash his hands and face, comb his hair and help him put on his clean shirt.

Later I'll have to negotiate for ice. The hospital personnel don't want to be bothered, they don't listen to me, always complaining.

The nurses… where are they? I go into the hallway, tired of calling for them.

"Don't bother," a woman in the adjoining room says. "Don't bother, they won't come. Only the male nurses are here because they fired the nuns; it's much worse now. I knew that would happen," she says lowering her voice. "The nuns aren't professionals even though they're experienced, they were good at this… Now look…"

Finally a female nurse comes in; she's wearing makeup; she's pretty; like a movie actress.

Later *Papá* has something to eat, then I let him sleep. I go into a cafeteria in front, because in the hospital only the sick are allowed food.

I bump into an old friend from San Isidro School, María Luisa. She's accompanying her mother who is about to have an operation.

"You look wonderful," she tells me. "You look so different."

She looks pretty too; we laugh at our new role as working women. She tells me that she and her mother started a childcare center.

"The kids' parents are off to the front. There's no school, so the little ones don't get anything to eat. It's a wonderful center for refugees… You can't imagine… They let us use a convent on Serrano Street; it's got a garden, a library, and toys for children. We've got seventy kids. When will you come to help?"

"I'm taking care of my sisters; they need me, and my father's in the hospital."

"Your sisters are better off in the childcare center. There's plenty of milk there and good food. Also, the garden's beautiful, wonderful for the children who don't have summer vacation; besides, they need fresh air."

She speaks as if she were an adult.

"How old are you?"

"Sixteen."

"I'm fifteen. What a horrible mess we're in, right?"

"Uf, tell me about it. I'm fed up. My brothers and sisters are constantly bickering. And who knows where Jacinto is; he's the oldest. He joined the Falange."

"What's that?"

"I don't know, a political party or an association or something. Luis has gone off to the mountains with a rifle. I'm telling you they're crazy. Poor

Mamá is so worried about them… But tell me about you. Are you still studying? What are you doing?"

From that day on I have a friend to lunch with. María Luisa is beautiful and funny; she doesn't take anything seriously. I remember Madrid, San Isidro School on Molinero Street, Alcalá, after all that time. But no, it's not the same. As we sit together, only for a minute did I think nothing had changed.

I go back to the hospital and show my card to the fat and odious doorman… One day a horrible thing happened at the hospital: I walked in as always, and he yells at me:

"Eh, Blondie, get out of here, you can't come in."

I didn't think he was talking to me, so I paid no attention.

"I'm telling you…, you can't pass beyond here!"

The militiamen and everyone else in the hallway were looking at me.

"I'm here to look after my father, he's injured."

"That's a lie. Let go of all those things you're carrying," he ordered as he led me to a table. "Leave them right there."

"What things?" I had no idea what the brute was talking about.

"The stuff you're carrying. C'mon now. Quick, there's no time."

I was embarrassed, trembling. I could barely speak. I emptied the contents of my sack. My white apron, Dad's shirt, a comb, cologne, the newspaper, rouge, packages of powder…

"Let's see all that," the fat man cried, as if to announce his victory.

He put on his glasses and read: "'Lemon-flavored Magnesium. Exquisite refreshment for only ten cents.'"

"Not this. Show me all your products."

My God, what in the world was this man calling "products?" So I emptied my pockets and showed him the coins in my purse.

"I exchanged a little money before I came here."

"It's not this," said the militiaman.

"Arrest her, comrade Marín."

Another militiaman pushed me toward the door and made me raise my arms, then he touched me all over.

"That's Victoriano. Don't pay any attention to him, comrade."

I went to the hallway again.

"She doesn't have anything, comrade."

"It's not that girl," said the fat doorman. That's not the one who's selling…"

"Oh, not this one?" he asked. "Alright, pick all that up and go in. It's just that a blond lady comes around here trying to sell things to the injured patients. I mean, she tries to sell them the only thing she's got, if you get what I mean."

I have no idea what he was talking about or why the others were looking at me, but I felt ashamed.

I can barely walk as I go into the garden, then up the stairs to my father's room.

"Ay, *Papá*, my *Papaíto!*"

He's alarmed when he sees me.

"Dear girl, what's wrong? What'd they do to you?"

When I tell him about it, he wants to talk to the hospital director, the captain in charge, and the president of the Republic. Who knows who else; I just laugh.

"Daddy, don't worry about it. Nothing happened to me. It was a mistake, that's all."

Later, María Luisa got a big kick out of it.

"Look at the militiaman blocking the door. I've told him I'm a servant from Galicia, and that my mom is my *Señora*. You can't believe what a good little servant I can be. 'C'mon, comrade, don't be so serious,' I tell him. So he tells me that one of the patients is a general who pretends to be sick so they won't kill him. The other day he wanted them to take him out of the hospital in a coffin to save his life, but the others got wind of it."

"Oh my God! Will they kill him?"

"Look, *hija*. I don't think about those things, because if you let your mind dwell on it, you can't be happy… so, don't do that, no… This omelet is delicious, don't you think? I've ordered a steak too. Everything tastes good, even the revolution."

That's the way it is every day. I'm having a pleasant vacation, as María Luisa would say. My smock is clean and my espadrilles are new. I look good in the mirror; the anxiousness of the first days is behind me.

This morning, we go into Dad's room; his bed is empty.

"*Pa… pá.* Where is he?"

I run out into the hallway. I don't see anyone. I ring the alarm relentlessly.

Finally a nurse appears.

"What on earth is the matter?… Oh, your father. They've taken him to the operating room to drain fluid. He'll be alright. They'll bring him back to his room now. You really don't have to make such a fuss!"

At midday he's back; he's pale but calm and in a good mood. They help him get into bed, and when he sees the worried look on my face, he laughs.

"I'm fine, silly. That's just what I needed. The bullet didn't penetrate the lung fortunately; just the pleura. They had to drain the water. The doctor says that in eight days I can go home."

Still, I don't allow him to read, and when Cousin Gerardo comes, I don't let him talk to my father.

"Why did you come?" I ask Gerardo.

"My mom asked about him today, and they told her they operated on him."

Papá hears us even though we're speaking softly.

"Oh, it's you," he says, opening his eyes. "You're one of them."

"Shush," whispers Gerardo as he looks at the half-open door to see if anyone is listening.

Dad says Gerardo is on the other side, and that makes him angry.

"The thing is, I'm not a starry-eyed fool like you. I just know that what you're calling the 'masses' needs a strong hand to show them the way."

Father answers indignantly: "Yes, sure. You're the one calling them 'the masses' because you haven't taught them to read… Years ago, when the budget for education was discussed in congress, one of the delegates said: 'The people…, you want to deprive them of culture, but watch out, when they rule they'll cut your heads off.'"

"He was probably another starry-eyed idealist like you… Just because they know how to read, those 'people' are still the 'masses.' When a real leader emerges among them, a smart one, he no longer is part of the 'masses.'" Ordinary."

The argument about the barbaric "masses," education and barbarism gets heated, and *Papá* loses his wind. Sometimes I agree with *Papá*, and at others, Gerardo.

"Those 'people' who you defend," my cousin reiterated, "are killing scientists, priests, librarians, and gentlemen whose only crime is being gentlemen."

"Nonsense," cries out Father, out of breath. "Lies. All lies! Maybe killing them is right. Fewer traitors..."

Cousin Gerardo storms out the room slamming the door, and *papá* lays his head on the pillow as if he were dizzy. I wipe his brow with water and hand him his scented handkerchief. Finally he gathers enough strength to speak:

"Don't let... don't let that one back in!... He's..."

"Alright, *Papá*, alright. Now you need to rest."

He closes his eyes, and I sit down in front of the open balcony. Who is right? It's horrible to have gotten to this. They're killing everybody. In the mountains and everywhere, it's all filthy, only dust, curses, bad manners.

I must have fallen asleep because when I open my eyes, everything is dark. I raise the shade of the door to the balcony. Dad's eyes are still closed as if he were asleep.

There's a little breeze coming in from the garden, it's pleasant like water from mountain streams. Militiamen are in the patio among the nurses with their white aprons and doctors also in white. More militiamen come in. I've never seen them in the patio until today. The voices in the crowd are getting louder. Suddenly I hear someone cry out:

"Here he comes. They've got him."

I see a group of armed men all huddled together going under the balcony, and among them a bald, fat man dressed in blue stripes.

From everywhere they all follow that group, murmuring as they disappear into a corner.

"What's going on?" asks Father with his eyes open.

"I don't know... lots of people..."

"General López Ochoa is here, he's the one who put down the rebellion in Oviedo. Is it really...?"

The patios are now empty. It's dark. The sky, red a moment ago, gradually turns black.

Suddenly I hear something close by, like a cart unloading rocks.

"It's gunfire," says *Papá.* "They've executed him."

A doctor is crossing the patio and pauses when he hears the noise and goes back, retracing his footsteps.

Father wants me to go back to Madrid immediately. I take the streetcar home before it gets completely dark.

When I leave, the hospital is quiet; no one is in the hallway. As I go out the door, I see a bunch of people on one side of the building following a woman with something in her hand, like a ball.

The group catches up to me, then passes me as I go by the tavern with its lights on.

I hear words coming from the tavern:

"She carried his head in her hands."

"It's because she wants them to see it."

"It's López Ochoa's head."

"That rotten… Look what that criminal did in Oviedo…"

As I pass by these fields, I hear crickets chirping… there's a subtle mountain breeze that brings a nauseating smell with it.

My feet tremble as I get on the streetcar.

TAKEN FOR A *PASEO* IN MADRID

At midnight when I get back home, Valeriana is always waiting for me. She opens the door before I knock.

"How's the *Señor*? How'd he spend the day? He eat anything? What'd he say?"

The girls are already in bed; I go to their room to check on them. Teresina is asleep with her little fist on her cheek as usual, dreaming about God knows what. María Fuencisla's covers are thrown to one side, her tiny mouth is red and soft because she's fallen asleep with her bottle in her mouth.

"Have they behaved?"

Valeriana assures me they've behaved like little angels.

"Like lambs. So good, so obedient, but of course they can't stand this heat." Aunt Julia is reading her missal in the dining room. These last few years have taken a toll on her. She doesn't look herself. As soon as she sees me, she starts complaining about my sisters:

"Two little devils. They haven't given me a moment of rest all day, as if I had nothing to worry about. Did you know they've executed Señor Miranda? Horrible! How can we go on, my God!" Miranda is a neighbor; Aunt Julia talks about him often.

"What? How did it happen?"

She tells me the militiamen confiscate all the cars. "They go to people's homes, call for the owner or his children and invite them for a ride; then they take them to the outskirts and shoot them."

"That can't be."

"Well, it's true. You told me yourself you see dead people at the edge of the river every morning.

"Yes, but I thought…"

"Ay, *cariño*, you and your father, always, pie-in-the-sky; you just don't know what's going on. They executed Maria Orduña's nephew last night, took him for a *paseo*. Later this morning his mother went out to the well and found him dead like a little bird on the ground."

We both kept silent. I wish she wouldn't talk about this because she always ends up insulting *Papá*… and I… I believe in him. Always seems to me he's right about everything, and if he defends the militiamen, it's because justice is on their side.

Maria Orduña is the butt of our jokes, especially mine; they make Auntie laugh. That lady is stone deaf.

"Her son Antonio," Auntie tells me, "ordered her to burn all the monarchist flags."

"Does she have flags?"

"Don't be silly, dear. Just like everyone else, she has flags and all kinds of icons; she brings them out for parades and processions. Well, no more of that; wickedness and godlessness have taken over."

"Yes, Auntie. Go on."

"Well, Antonio told her to burn them all. Turns out María has more than twenty meters of fabric for flags. As you know, her house is on the corner so her balcony looks over two streets. The fabric was good material so she didn't want to burn it. Instead, she soaked it in bleach hoping it would turn white; that way she could use it for bedsheets. But guess what! Turns out the colors were solid and it came out red and yellow, so she hung them to dry in the patio. Imagine! The doorman went up to tell her, for God's sake, take it down unless she wanted to get in trouble."

"So what did she do?"

"She said no because the fabric had to dry… She herself told me that over the   phone."

"Do you talk about such things on the telephone?… Auntie, María Luisa says people listen in on phone conversations."

"I know that, but no one can keep María Orduña from blabbing, especially since she hears more than she lets on despite being deaf."

Auntie imitates her friend's voice:

""She says to me: 'You know, these brutes are killing everyone. They don't even believe in God. They're communists, and they're going to hand off all the women to men. Four of them, not seven like they said before because the others have died… They all want to be skinny so they don't eat, and that's why… I tell my children: You better hide, because if they see you, you'll see what happens…but they don't pay attention!'""

We laugh, and Aunt Julia seems to forget her worries for a minute. Valeriana spreads out the tablecloth and sets the table. We serve the soup. By the second spoonful, Aunt Julia puts down her spoon and starts to cry.

"But Auntie, don't be like that, eat. Is anything wrong with Gerardo?"

"I haven't seen him in three days. I don't even know where he is. May God protect us!"

I found out that Gerardo belongs to that political party or society María Luisa told me about. The militiamen have taken over the house where they had their meetings; they write down names and addresses of everyone, so they can take them for a ride: a *paseo*, which means they're going to kill them. Gerardo is probably hiding. According to Auntie, each night he sleeps at a different place.

Today, when I arrived, Auntie was staring at the door to the study and told me he came back:

"He says he can't take it anymore, that he wants them to find him here… no one has seen him, not even the doorman."

As Aunt Julia brings Gerardo a bowl of soup, I try to talk to María, the servant, about a recipe. She tells me:

"If the *Señora* thinks I don't know her son is here, she's mistaken. It's that I know how to keep my mouth shut… my boyfriend is a policeman, and if I told him…"

"But you won't tell him a thing," Valeriana interjects as she plays with the girls who didn't sleep well last night. "You won't tell them a thing! Don't bite the hand that feeds you."

"If they feed me, it's because I've earned it with the sweat of my brow… those dirty rich people take advantage of me!"

All I can do is let them go on arguing while I go to the dining room to warn Auntie.

"I know, *hija*, I know about her, that woman will be the death of us. I gave her my black silk dress and my winter shoes… For a few days she was reasonable, but now she sees that I don't have anything else she likes, so…"

What has it all come to? Auntie's confession scares me. She gets up to go to her room, and later I hear her arguing in the kitchen.

Valeriana picks up the soup bowl and a plate of asparagus. She's in a serious mood; silent. I ask her what's happening in the kitchen.

"I know nothing and don't want to know. All's I know is everyone's sinning against God."

When she gets back, Auntie seems more relaxed.

"I gave her my brooch."

"But Auntie…"

"What do you want me to do? I have to protect him. All I can do is hope Franco's people will come and save us. May the Lord make it come true."

My cousin has stayed at home hiding in his study the whole day, except at night when everyone is sleeping.

When I tell Dad what's going on with María, he says:

"That, dear child, is inevitable. There will always be bad people who take advantage of the weak. Keep in mind that education and culture shape our minds, give us morals. Those poor people are downtrodden and abused by a society that denies them everything, they respond to the bad treatment with more bad treatment. They'd be saints if they didn't."

"What about Valeriana?"

"Valeriana is all-natural goodness, vocation, dedication… loyal like a pet."

Poor Valeriana, where would we be without her? *Papá* is quiet. Suddenly he says something that makes me laugh heartily:

"In any case, when we win the war, I'll go to Aunt Julia's house and I'll throw that servant off the balcony… along with her silk stockings and her brooch…"

At nighttime I wake up frightened. Aunt Julia seems to be talking to someone in a loud voice; she's praying. The hallway is lighted. I put on my apron. Valeriana appears at the door, covering her lips with one finger:

"They've come for Gerardo. They're with the anarchist militiamen… stay where you are."

"Yes, yes…"

I go out the fire escape door and into a bedroom where three militiamen are looking at me. One of them is wearing a fox skin for a hat with the tail hanging over his back.

Auntie is in the office solemnly consoling Gerardo; her voice is prophetic:

"*Leave this body, Christian soul, and return to your Maker, who from earth created you.*"

One of the militiamen laughs and lets everyone know he thinks she's crazy. Auntie's voice makes me shiver. It's all making me feel distressed and nauseated.

"*Receive, Lord, this poor creature who has always served and believed in you.*"

I hear a voice. It's Gerardo:

"*Amen.*"

"Comrade," groans the militiaman closest to me. He's facing my aunt. "We've waited long enough; you can't say we haven't been patient."

They take him away… Auntie follows. She still prays, now in a softer voice:

"*May the lord save his soul. Deliver his soul to eternal glory.*"

"*Amen.*"

They lead Gerardo down the stairs, the door opens in front of him.

"*Requiem aeternam… May the lord give him eternal rest.*"

"*Amen.*"

We hear Gerardo's voice coming up the stairway. Valeriana and I watch. Auntie stares in the direction of her son as if she were under hypnosis. They slam the door to the street, and Gerardo disappears. Aunt Julia is motionless.

"Auntie… let's go inside. … Auntie!"

She doesn't answer. I think she didn't hear me.

"Auntie."

"Come now, my lady," says Valeriana. "Come inside now… God sees everything, and he'll protect us all."

Auntie's voice sounds broken and hoarse.

"I can't."

Auntie stumbles: Valeriana helps her stand up.

"Help me, Celia."

Between the two of us we hold her steady. Valeriana, who never loses her composure, lays her down on the bed, opens the balcony door, moves a chair close to the bed and sits down next to her for the night.

"Go to bed, Celia, ain't nothing for you to do, and tomorrow you've got to get up early and off to the hospital."

I have no idea what time it is, I must have fallen asleep immediately. Upon opening my eyes, the sun streams in through the balcony.

Valeriana is making breakfast.

"Your aunt left at sunrise. I couldn't keep her here. She said she was off to the well to look for Gerardo so she could bury him. I would have gone with her, but I couldn't leave the girls alone. María took off too. She said she couldn't stay here because I dunno what she said."

"She does not want to be with the Fascists, she probably said."

"Right. That woman has no heart. But don't worry, she'll get hers. Poor Gerardo. And your grandfather too; that man's a saint. Just because he was a… you know, a fascist."

"No, Valeriana, not Granddad. That's Gerardo. Poor soul. I don't know if he was a fascist… Maybe so. Granddad was just the opposite."

"It's all the same. They all get killed for whatever. Mother of God, what have we come to?"

When I arrive at the hospital, I don't dare tell Dad what happened at home. Fortunately, today he's delighted about the news in the papers.

When I come down to eat in the cafeteria, I run into María Luisa. Her father is with her. He's a nice man; he's sad when I tell him what happened last night.

"It's best not to say anything, *hija mía*. They would have executed your cousin either way… who knows? Maybe he was part of a *checa*."

She tells me that the *checas* are prisons established by the communists or anarchists. That's where they take prisoners for questioning and sentencing.

"You mean they have tribunals?"

Either María Luisa's father doesn't know anything or he'd rather not talk about all this. He wittily changes the subject. He's a retired lieutenant colonel; he moved to his grandparents' house in Galicia, where María Luisa will marry a pharmacist.

All this seems to relieve my anxiety about all that happened last night. Poor Aunt Julia, how freighted she must have been! Hoping they didn't kill Gerardo, maybe he's in jail or maybe I'll see him tonight at home.

I get back from the hospital and find Valeriana sitting next to the walkway with the little one sleeping in her arms and Teresina next to her.

"What are you doing sitting here?"

"Don't get scared… It's that… You know any place we can spend the night?"

My God! I can't understand what happened, I want Valeriana to explain it to me in detail. She says Aunt Julia found Gerardo next to the well, she lost control and cursed at them, so they took her away to who knows where. At noon, some militiamen searched the house and took all our identification.

They told Valeriana she had to leave the house because a judge had ordered the premises sealed.

"María helped the militiamen find the identification papers, and she told 'em where Aunt Julia kept her jewels and cash. She told me what happened to the *Señora*. Maybe she's better off if the Lord takes her."

"My God."

The four of us are sitting on the edge of the walkway, it's a sorry picture. Teresina caresses my face when she sees me crying. Bless us all, what'll happen to the girls?

"Did you eat anything today?"

"Yes. I brought down some milk… and all the clothes in the saddlebags we brought from Segovia, and a little bit of bread. The concierge says he don't wanna get involved. That's why we left the house."

As Valeriana speaks, I remember what María Luisa told me about the children's refuge at the end of Serrano Street.

"Let's go, Valeriana. I think tonight we'll have a place to stay, and tomorrow we'll see. It's not far.

Off we go: I'm in front, hand-in-hand with Teresina, and Valeriana is in the back with María Fuencisla in her arms. The streets are barely illuminated.

We cross Diego de León Street down toward Serrano, its section of the street without stores, big hotels, gardens, and trees that cover the walkways making everything pitch dark.

We hear shots close by; Valeriana stops and calls me.

"Celia!"

"Yes, I hear you. Let's go to the middle of the street so we're visible. That way no one will shoot at us. Believe me!"

My own words give me strength.

There's a man over there in the corner. It's a militiaman; I approach him.

"Excuse me, could you please tell me if there is a childcare refuge on this street?"

"Right there," says the militiaman who points to a tall building whose lights shine through the trees. I'm the night watchman for the shelter."

He accompanies us. From the street we go up some stairs until we get to a luxuriant garden. Light shines through a large glass door; we hear children's voices.

They're in the dining room with long tables, maybe a hundred of them, of all ages. Suddenly I see María Luisa approaching me.

"*Chica*, what a time to come!"

I explain what's happened to us. Valeriana, who until now has been very patient, is sobbing, my little sister still in her arms.

"Don't cry, *mujer*," María Luisa tells her. "You can stay here tonight. There's a free room with three beds. This way."

The building is palatial. White marble stairs, huge reception rooms, now makeshift bedrooms for the children. A room with three beds and two chairs and a view of the garden. Valeriana regains her composure. Soon this room turns into our home as María Fuencisla continues sleeping like an angel.

Teresina whispers in my ear:

"Is this our house now?"

"Yes, my love. Now, have some soup and then to bed."

She protests, "are they going to kick us out of here too?"

THE REFUGE

A shrill noise wakes me up. I try to figure out what it is: someone's talking. Then I hear a car go by until there's silence again. It's so hot! From the balcony I gaze at the stars amidst the deep blue of the night sky.

I fall asleep… Again that noise wakes me up. I hear Valeriana say from her bed:

"Did you hear that?"

"Yes, I heard it before."

We both go to the balcony. We hear voices and again the engine of a car. The sound subsides. At a distance rapid gunfire, then single shots.

"Shots!" says Valeriana. "Always shots, all they know how to do is kill."

We fall asleep, but as soon as the sun rises, I get up to wash before the girls wake up.

In the garden I see María Luisa; she's spent the night on the watch. Very pale; her eyes are sleepy.

"At least tonight I'll sleep at home because they're releasing my mom from the hospital. These kids are so restless at night! And such sweet smells, like perfume when they wet their beds, like Laura de los Ríos says. And sometimes it's number two. Ay, ay, ay… I'm telling you."

I tell her about the gunshots that awoke Valeriana and I several times last night.

"Come with me, I want to show you something…"

We go out to the garden; it's pleasantly cool in the morning. She takes me close to a wall that goes up to my knees but gets as tall as three meters further away.

"Look down there."

"Jesus!" I see four fallen men, all in different positions. One looks like he's on his knees as if he'd fallen. Another one is hunched over with a hand over his belly.

"These are the ones they executed last night. Come, I'll show you the other side where the wall meets the street."

There I see just one man with his arms spread in the form of a cross.

"Come along now. Let's let people know so they can take the bodies away before the girls see them. Since you'll probably be on watch some other night, it's good you know what to expect. You need to be vigilant. The other day I wasn't here, and when I came by in the afternoon, the children came up to me and said: 'Señorita, you know? We saw some dead fascists close to the wall, and they were covered by ants, some crawling up their noses. Ha, ha.' Kids are brutal."

We go over to the telephone booth next to the main entrance. María Luisa takes note of the numbers written in chalk on the wall; she calls out:

"Serrano Refuge. No, not many, just five… But around here I'm sure there are more because we heard lots of gunfire last night. Yes, comrade, as soon as you can because the kids get up at seven. It's Serrano Refuge… *Salud*, comrade."

After my bath, I see María Luisa again; she's busy taking towels out of the cabinets.

"Can you help me wash them? Today I'm alone here with Fifina, and there's lots of work."

The bedrooms smell like zoo cages. The little ones are dressed in their blue pajamas. They stretch out to open the windows, and soon they're yelling and throwing pillows at one another… the little devils.

"I don't want to take a bath."

"Me neither."

"Not me."

María Luisa, with Fifina's help, scrubs the children two by two, sometimes three by three, in an enormous tub. Fifina is twenty years old and blond. The water is lukewarm, so the kids cry out yelling they're cold.

I wash the very little ones in a tub big enough for a couple of six-year-olds. After scrubbing their faces, ears, and knees with sponges in thick chocolate-color water coming out of the faucet, we cover them in towels leaving it to them to dry themselves. The entire process yields about seventy clean children.

The older ones are in charge of themselves in another bathroom; they exit the bathroom naked and soaking wet.

A tired woman I don't know climbs up the stairs slowly.

"This is Margarita," says Fifina. "She makes the beds. Later you'll meet Rosario, the official pediatrician."

"*Hija*, we all do what we can and what we know how to do."

Valeriana and the little ones are restless in our room. Teresina loves to look down at the garden from the balcony.

"Can we go down, Celia? Please, please? Will they let me make sandcastles? Are there many kids here? Is this a school, like in Segovia? Why did we come to live here in the school?"

I tell Valeriana:

"That noise we heard last night? It was people being executed. The bodies are close by. Don't let the girls see them. They're coming to take them away."

Valeriana, without saying a word, crosses herself with the rosary beads she keeps in her pocket.

"May God have mercy on them."

"I'm leaving now. Before I go to the hospital, I'm going to talk to María Orduña, Aunt Julia's friend. Maybe she knows something. Her address is probably in the phone book. Take care of the girls, make sure they eat. You, too. Do you need money? Yesterday Dad gave me five hundred *pesetas*."

"Sure, *hija*. We've got all the money in the world; problem is it's worth nothing.'"

I leave as soon as Valeriana and the girls have their breakfast in the dining room with about a hundred kids. Doña Margarita is looking after them without a second's rest tying bibs, slicing bread, wiping noses with her own handkerchief.

María Orduña lives on Ayala Street. As I go down Serrano, I see that the church is open. The streets are filled with debris, and the walkways with pieces of golden frames. At my feet, I see something round and flat. It's the head of an angel surely from the altar of the church. I see a militiaman who is using a confessional as his cabin.

I walk up the street to Señora Orduña's house. A servant dressed in a white apron leads me to a room with red velvet upholstery.

"They've executed Julia and her son!" she tells me disconsolately. "*Hija*, this is the end of the world. I knew it would happen as soon as the bad ones won the elections. Now they're all determined to kill good people. No one believed me, but that's what's happened."

Again I raise my voice to make sure she hears me. I assure her I have no idea where Aunt Julia is. So if she knows anything…

"No use crying, *hija*. Soon Franco's troops will save us and everything'll come out fine. I think they're on their way here. Of course, they'll execute a few. Your crazy dad, for example, and Enrique too, they'll execute them in no time, don't you doubt it."

Her voice is loud; I'm worried people will hear her from the street. So I close the door to the balcony.

"You're like my husband, you always think they can hear us.

Again I try to make her listen, but it's no use. She smiles at me; she pats me on the back like a loving mother and doesn't let up:

"I've always said it… in Barcelona it's the same thing. The bad ones are in charge there too, and all hell is breaking loose… Have you had breakfast? Well, let me serve you…"

I tell her not to bother, that I've had breakfast.

"Justa made some delicious *churros* for us. You're going to love them; wait till you taste them."

On command, Justa quickly brings a tray with a pot of coffee and milk along with bread and a tin of butter.

"Ay, *hija*, you've arrived at the wrong time. There's no fresh butter, no meat either, and you can't find pastry. It's awful to have to live through this; you can't find anything. Everything's out of control. People have no religion or fear of God. People today only mourn for three months. When I was young you had to mourn your dead father for ten years. Ten years dressed in black down to your feet and no leaving the house except to go to mass! Later on it changed, and you could wear a white collar, you know, the ones with pretty lace cuffs… That's the way the rules changed, little by little."

I look at the clock and stand up. It's ten o'clock.

"I'm off to the hospital," I shout so she can hear what I say.

"Ah, yes, the hospital, where your crazy father is. Try to convince him to get rid of his big ideas; he needs to go back to his house on Chamartín. The place looks like a palace now that Julia, poor thing, left the furniture looking as beautiful as can be."

Again I use my loud voice, since it seems to be working:

"What happened to Aunt Julia? Where is she?"

"They probably executed her. Her son was in the *Falange*. Another group of crazy people. They should mind their own business. They think they're the ones to fix the world. Well, I say stay away from political parties and that kind of foolishness. My parents lived in Salamanca, and there was never any reason to organize strikes against them. And when the Republic came…"

She accompanies me to the door telling me about all the strikes and skirmishes in Salamanca fifty years ago. The thought of Aunt Julia's execution puts a lump in my throat… Justa gives me a maternal hug as we reach the door to the stairs.

"Don't be afraid, dear. I know you're like the mom for your sisters, and you have to show them the way. You've got to take care of your father too because he's lost his head. You hear me? He's lost it.'"

I go out into the street. I'm annoyed by this woman who doesn't understand what's happening around her.

It's late when I arrive at the hospital. Dad was waiting for me anxiously; his face lights up when he sees me.

"Finally, you're here," he says. He's worried, wondering what's happened to me. *Papá* is such a good man.

I decide to tell him everything: what happened to Gerardo, Aunt Julia, our move to the refuge.

For a moment he closes his eyes in silence, I sense he's overwhelmed about everything. I kneel down beside him.

"My dear *Papaíto!*"

I caress his cheeks, and he kisses my hand. Two tears stream down his bony face. Today he doesn't want to read the newspaper.

Later that afternoon, we talk.

"I didn't want to tell you anything, *hija*, I wanted it to be a surprise. But we have a house on Chamartín your Aunt Julia exchanged for the one my parents owned in the mountains. That house was so filled with memories of your mom and me. It was our first house after we were married, Julia had all the furniture moved there. It's beautiful… I wanted to surprise you."

He gives me the keys, and we agree that for now we'll live at the refuge, and later we'll move to the new house.

"It's got a garden and a little pond, walkways, and shady trees. It's far from the city; it'll be our own refuge. You'll see, Celia, when the war ends, we'll win, and your brother Cuchifritín will come back from London, and maybe we'll be happy again."

Father cannot allow himself to believe they've killed Aunt Julia; I tell him about my visit with María Orduña.

"That woman doesn't know anything… She's probably under arrest. Who knows?"

"You mean the *checa*."

"Look, *hija*, about the *checa*... that's all right-wing lies, and you shouldn't talk about it. It's a Russian thing."

"That's it… They say they've come from Russia to take charge of the military, and that they're the ones…"

"Don't pay any attention to those rumors, *hija*. Don't believe those lies. What nonsense! I know it's hard for you to see me in bed like this. I'm sure that if I could get over there I'd find poor Aunt Julia… and she'd be frightened to see me."

He talked about Auntie all afternoon. She's his older sister, and she has been like a mother to him and to Uncle Rodrigo after their mom and dad died when they were young.

"She's always been very religious, intolerant, harsh… but honorable nonetheless, loyal, generous, unselfish, with all the virtues and defects of Philip II's Spain. No, I'm sure she's alright. It's enough that she lost her son… I'm truly sorry about that, even though I was never fond of him. Poor Julia, we must invite her to live with us."

Dad gives me an address of a family he'd like me to visit on Ferraz Street. He thinks they'll be able to help us find Auntie."

At nightfall when I get back to the refuge once again, I hear gunshots at the end of Serrano Street amidst the night shade of the trees.

All the kids are in the dining room. Teresina and María Fuencisla cry out with joy; they're happy to see me. They've had a good time on the swings, playing jump rope, running around all day.

"One of our friends is a girl named Nenuca," says Teresina. "She's my friend. She gave me a necklace. I want to give her something too. Will you buy something I can give her, Celia? She takes care of the little ones, making sure they don't hit each other and don't pee their pants. They're very bad sometimes and say naughty things; they pretend to shoot each other like they were in a firing squad. They raise their fists, like this—look!"

She raises her little fists, imitating her new friends.

"And we learned a new song, *The International*. Like this, sing along María Fuencisla: "Long live the poor of the world. Long live the *international*…"

My sister sings out of tune; I don't want her to know the words of this hymn.

"Valeriana, don't leave the girls alone; listen to what they're signing."

"I haven't left them alone. I've had to change them twice because they found a garden hose and got all muddy; I've been washing, ironing clothes, and helping in the kitchen."

Rosario, the distinguished doctor, is in the vestibule. She's very nice. Margarita too, the lady I met this morning, and Fifina with two other girls I haven't seen until now.

Alongside the girls is a fat man with a beard dressed in mechanic's trousers with a couple of guns at his side. He reminds me of someone. Who?

It's Don Julián! I met this man in Santander when we were traveling with Aunt Julia and Gerardo. He knows me too:

"Are you the Gálvez girl? Celia? Isn't your name… Celia? What a coincidence!"

The man is quite a sight with his beard, and guns in his belt. He tells me he's going to shave because beards aren't in style now. I tell him that my father is in the hospital, so he promises to visit him. I talk about Aunt Julia too:

"We don't know where she is. Do you think you can ask around? They executed her son Gerardo the day before yesterday, and then…"

It seems Don Julián is an important person because everyone tells him the refuge needs things like sheets, medicine, and that some children are debilitated.

He answers them saying:

"Tomorrow at eleven come by the office and I'll give out vouchers… But maybe you won't recognize me. I'm about to shave off my beard." And he laughs.

It seems that for now what concerns him the most is his beard. He says goodbye with a handshake and tells me that he is at our disposal for anything we need.

"Cheer up, girl. These are bad times, but soon they'll be over."

Before going to bed I speak to Margarita, who introduces me to the two ladies. One is Carmela and the other is Rosalía. They're going to be on watch tonight.

Carmela is a teacher.

"How do you find this miserable refuge?" She asks pretentiously.

"It's fine, not miserable at all. It's like a palace."

"Of course, but the furniture of that old grandiose building is nothing like the way it was before, so magnificent. We've done what we could by placing our faith in the people, but it's unfinished. The more experience we have, the sooner we'll bring it back to the way it was."

I'm embarrassed by the highfalutin way this young woman speaks.

Rosalía finds her amusing.

"That stupid one," she tells me. "She makes me nervous."

She talks about the children and their schooling.

"We still haven't begun to organize the curriculum, but we need to do it right away so that they forget what they've seen these last few days in their own homes. Margarita and I were talking about this. No raising fists or singing the *International*. What do the children care about all that? Let them play, feed them well, let them sing popular songs… and don't let them think that all human beings do is kill one another. Don't you think?"

The children have gone to bed. We're in the garden chatting. It's a beautiful night, the moonlight shines through the trees.

We hear the telephone ring, and Rosalía runs to answer. I'm alone. Two men are talking to each other at the foot of the stairs. It's the militiamen on watch, protecting us from who-knows-what.

Rosalía calls out:

"Celia, Celia. It's for you."

Oh, lord, what bad news can it be?

I barely recognize the voice. It's María Luisa.

"Celia, Celia, is that you? Something horrible has happened to us. They've been searching the house since five in the afternoon… You hear me?… They want to take Dad and my brother with them. You hear? Speak to someone… surely you know someone… a friend of your father, someone who knows us. Tell them to come, and you come too…"

"Is your father at home?"

"No, I can't talk now. Come…"

We're cut off.

Rosalía is looking at me, but she doesn't ask what's going on.

"That was María Luisa. Today they searched her house, and they want to take her father away."

"So what can you do?"

"I don't know… Poor girl. She relies on me."

I remember don Julián and ask for his phone number.

"Don't trust them," Rosalía says.

I dial the number, but they take a long time to answer.

"What? Who is it?"

"It's me, Celia Gálvez."

"Ah, good evening. What can I do for you, *hija*."

"It's not for me, it's for María Luisa. Do you know her?"

"Yes, dear. I've been a friend of the family for many years. What's the problem?"

"Well... They've been searching their house since five o'clock today and they want to arrest her father."

He doesn't reply, so I continue.

"It's horrible. The poor girl is desperate; she just called me to see if anyone can do something..."

Silence on the other end.

"If possible, could you speak with the men you know and convince them that María Luisa's father is a leftist ?"

The silence on the end of the line is deafening. I ask:

"Can you hear me?... Hello?"

"Yes, I can hear you." But the tone of his voice terrifies me. "What do you want me to do?"

"Since you're in a position of... And you know people..."

"You're mistaken. The people who search property know what they're doing, and... after all, like I said, I can't do anything. I'm very tired and tomorrow I have to get up early. Goodbye, comrade."

I hang up and look over at Rosalía without making a move.

"What? He says he can't do anything? He's a coward, no backbone!"

We go out into the garden again. The light of the moon seems ghostly.

"What to do?"

The voices of the militiamen on watch make me shiver. We go over to them.

They ask me if I'm on watch.

"Not me, it's just that..."

"It's that she won't go to bed because she's worried. Her friend and comrade María Luisa called to tell her they're searching her house."

"Who is María Luisa?"

"She's the dark one," says the other militiaman. "The one with the curly hair, she has an old car she used to transport the children. You know her, don't you?… sometimes she came with her mother."

"Oh, yes, I remember. The other night I was here on watch and she brought me some cherries."

"Well they're searching her house, and they want to arrest her father."

"Alright… but are they on our side? I know the lady is, but I don't know about her parents. You know: some people change colors from day to night."

"I assure you they're leftists, good people, I've known them for a long time."

"What they need to do is to alert the police. If they find nothing in the search, or they think the search is being carried out to unauthorized people, the police won't consent."

"How can I inform the police?"

"They're over there," he points to a magnificent hotel in front of us. You can see the lights coming from the building. "Do you want me to accompany you?"

We cross to the other side of the street. The door to the garden is open. The militiaman explains to me:

"About eight days ago, the police impounded this hotel. Some highfalutin people were living there. I think they were blown away or liquidated, or who knows, and the young lady, a policeman's girlfriend, told him about it, and …"

A pretty girl opens the door.

"Here… This comrade would like to speak to the night watchman."

She takes us to a room illuminated by a chandelier. The only thing I see is a portrait of a beautiful lady.

"What's the matter, comrades?" asks a young, friendly-looking man who has gotten up from his chair as soon as he noticed us.

"Here, the comrade says…"

I plead my case as best I can. As I speak, two men approach with the young lady; they are all listening politely.

"Comrade, you say their last name is Peña? Do they have a son named Tito?"

"Yes, I think so."

"Oh, yes. We were buddies at the Café Comercial. He was a good student like me, although neither one of us studied at all… Yes, that guy was a leftist."

They decide to accompany me. The militiaman goes back to the refuge, and I go down to the garage with the other two young men.

We get in the car, and on our way out, the one I talked to first leans out the window of the ground floor:

"Hey, listen… Be careful with what you do. If the ones searching the house are anarchists, not another word. Just be careful, eh."

"Yes, yes, we know."

As we go down the street, we're silent. Then one of them says:

"After we win the war, we'll need to clean things up… Be careful, because some questionable people have joined the street mobilizations."

The other one says nothing.

The door to my friend's place is open, and the receiving room is filled with books piled up, suitcases, as if someone were getting ready to move. A scruffy-looking militiaman stops to look when he crosses the hallway.

"What do you want here?"

"The police, comrade."

"What's this about, an accusation?"

"They're monarchists," he says shrugging his shoulders.

María Luisa, pale and shaken, sits on a bed in one of the bedrooms close to the entrance. She looks at me and doesn't say a thing.

"Where's your father?"

"I don't know. He hasn't come back. The doorman must have warned him."

"Your mother?"

"They took her one floor down. I didn't want to go down there. I want to see what happens up here."

"Have the police arrived?"" I ask.

"No matter. They won't do anything."

"Your brothers?"

"They took Carlos away…"

I go to the receiving room where two policemen speak to a militiaman with enormous pistols hanging from several belts.

"They're monarchists. I say so because I found a book that says they are."

"What?"

"It's over there," he says, pointing to one of the piles of books on the floor. "Says here … 'The Count-of-Bra-ge-lo-ne…' That says it all."

The policemen nod their heads and smile.

"They've taken Carlos away," I say. "He's the older brother."

"Oh, yes," says the militiaman. "Comrade Arrieta took him. The kid's a fascist!"

"But…?"

"No, no, we don't know yet. They're interrogating him to see if he'll talk. They've taken him to a *checa*."

I go back into María Luisa's room.

"Listen, nothing's happened to your brother. They're holding him, that's all."

"Doesn't matter. They're going to kill him." In an outburst she says, "And if they take away my father, I'll throw myself off that balcony…"

I squeeze her hands; they're ice cold despite the night heat.

The police call.

"There's nothing we can do here, comrade. If you'd like, we'll take you to the refuge."

He's right, there's nothing I can do here either, maybe I can take our case elsewhere.

We leave in the car. There's no one on Castellana Boulevard at this time of night. From out of the shadows of the trees a woman beckons us asking us to stop, but the police don't pay attention to her.

We're on our way up Serrano Street. The moon is shining. I see the blue lights of the refuge. Suddenly the car stops, and the driver says in a hushed voice:

"It's best not to go in now. They're about to take someone out… 'for a *paseo*,' if you know what I mean."

There's a section of the wall in the garden illuminated by headlights coming from the road. Close to the wall, there are several men. There's a woman dressed in black. I can barely see her face in the dim lights. Suddenly, I hear the voice of the woman praying:

"God save you, Mary full of grace…"

Her voice is silenced by a gunshot; the woman falls to the ground unhinged.

"God, God, God!" I cry.

The police gesture me to shush.

We move on. The assassins start the car; as we pass, they say:

"To your health, comrades…"

They leave me at the door, but when I get out, I hear an airplane above, and I raise my head. Almost at the same time there's a frighteningly loud explosion… and then another one, and another…

"They're bombing Madrid!" they say.

"If anything could make things worse, it's this. Crazy! Tonight, those criminals are going to execute half the world…"

I walk into the garden. I see the moon slither by a gray cloud with the airplane in its midst.

CHAMARTÍN DE LA ROSA

Papá is feeling better, and he wants to go home. How do I take him home if there are no taxis? I see a banner on a rundown house close to the hospital. It says, "Carabanchel Anarchist Committee." There are cars parked next to the front door. I decide to go in the house and ask. A horrid-looking man is sitting at a table with a bottle of wine and a glass.

I tell him my father's in the hospital with an injury and I don't have a way of getting him home.

"The comrade president is in charge of transportation of injured people, but he's not here. He's got a cold. If you'd like to go to his house, here is the address."

I go to Argumosa Street, where the 'comrade president' lives.

It's a shack, the stairs are rotting, there's a rotten smell, like a sewer.

A well-dressed girl my age greets me. She's very serious with an air of dignity.

"My father's not here, but he'll be back soon. He's gone downstairs for a haircut. Please come in."

The living room opens to a balcony overlooking the street. Old wooden shutters covering the railing, flowerpots on the floor. White and rose colored carnations in bloom, geraniums and basil. They've all been watered.

"Please sit down, comrade."

The living room is small with a dining room table, a couch, and a cabinet with a mirror. The girl looks me over for a minute, then says:

"Has someone recommended you?"

I tell her what I'm looking for.

"Yes… Well, when Father comes back I'll give him a note to pass on to the committee. All the committee work and presidential responsibility are making him crazy. Since he's well-known in the neighborhood,… and honorable. Everyone loves him."

She tells me her father is an anarchist because he's not happy with any form of government, none of them, all they do is suck the people dry. Nations should only have one administrative body, nothing else. She's an anarchist since she heard comrade Muñoz speak at a meeting but that's made for altercations with her friends. Almost all of them have become communists.

"What about you, comrade? What party are you in?"

I tell her I don't belong to any party. I don't understand politics. "My father," I say, "believes in the Republic, and he always talks about it. Before… at home no one talked about politics, or wars, or revolutions, but now…"

"But it's our responsibility, comrade, a big one."

Now I understand her peculiarity.

Her father arrives, a short, thin man with white hair. His expression is like his daughter's.

As we speak, he takes copious notes.

"You can petition for what you want by making a request to the Committee. And at any time, if I can be of service, just ask… That's what we're here for, to help one another and collaborate in assuring a victory, the victory that's about to come our way."

He goes back to his notes. I'm standing and I look around. On the sofa there's a uniform.

"Are you in the Civil Guard?"

"No, comrade. You ask because of the uniform? That belongs to a man we executed last night… I picked it up just in case my daughter needs the material for winter clothes."

The man's scribbles presented to the Committee were successful. They loaned me a car immediately. My father, my dear father, gets into the car with me and rests his head on my shoulders.

Valeriana is waiting for us in the house at Chamartín, the one I have not seen yet. The cook at the refuge accompanied Valeriana to help open the door. She was excited about the house. She told us about it:

"My God, *mujer*, what a pretty house! Like a candy box, all wrapped up. What a gorgeous lounge chair and what a shiny table and what cabinets and cupboards; it's all beautiful! This is like we died and went to heaven, and look at those pots and pans! At your granddad's place we had what we needed, but everything was all old and used… Here everything's spanking new."

I tell my father that I haven't had time to see the house.

The sun shines on Castellana Boulevard, the racetrack, the press building, and the poplars lining the canal, yellow earth, untended gardens. The car changes direction from Chamartín and enters a roadway. On the horizon, Ciudad Lineal.

"Here, take a right," says Father. "It's the last house on the corner."

Valeriana is waiting outside the door with the girls. Teresina speaks out before we get out of the car,

"… and there's a pond; it's deep and you can barely see where it ends. If María Fuencisla falls in, she'll drown. Valeriana says there are chicks."

"It's like we've come back to life," says Father. There are tears in his eyes.

We can't help thinking of Aunt Julia!

"My God, what a house!... This portrait is of Mom!"

"Yes, *hija*, that's your mother when we were married."

The dining room: the walls are covered in velvet, oak furniture, and mother's oil portrait with an oval frame.

"This here is like a painting of the Holy Mary."

The hallway is spacious with large armchairs; here is the boat that my parents ordered for me when I was a little girl.

On the upper floor are the bedrooms. There is my crib from years ago and the illustrations I traced from a book. Mother's mahogany cabinet. Dad sits in one of the armchairs and looks at me:

"We owe all this to poor Julia. She's taken care of our belongings as if they were all relics. That unhappy woman furnished this house with such love!"

But he immediately adds:

"Well… Gerardo. What happened to him is irreparable. But we'll see your aunt at any moment. Fortunately, they don't execute women…"

I don't dare tell him he's mistaken. The next days are filled with such joy that I forget about the horrible things happening around us.

Dad stays in bed because his fever doesn't subside. Valeriana works from morning to night, cleaning and scrubbing. The girls and I spend our time in the garden.

Every day we discover something. They're delighted to be at the new home. In a corner, under the jasmine, there's a rabbit hutch. The pond has a drain next to a trellis. Behind a little door there are stairs leading to an enormous attic… and a grape vine.

"The grapes are sour, Teresina. Don't eat them!"

"And there's a toad in the ivy on the back wall."

"I wish I were well enough to go down to the garden!" says *Papá*.

The girls bring violets, bundles of rue, and mint, and place it all on *Papá*'s bed.

One afternoon, Valeriana joins me in *Papá*'s room.

"There's a young lady who wants to talk to you. She says she just arrived from Talavera."

"Talavera?" cries *Papá*. "There's a battle going on there."

The lady is tall and strong. She tells me she arrived this morning along with hundreds of others… The fascists have taken Talavera.

"It was horrible, *Señorita*! The whole city was burning. The flames lit up the night sky and turned it red. I got out of there wearing what I have on now, like everyone else. They've given us refuge in that convent by the road, but there's no more room. A militiaman told me to talk to you. I've never been a servant. I was a dressmaker. But if it's alright with you, I could serve you in return for food

I ask *Papá*, and he agrees. Guadalupe stays to help Valeriana with her duties. Soon the girls surround her, tug at her dress, and demand that she tell them a story.

I go back to my duties at the refuge. Twice a week I spend the day there, and another two weeks I'm there for the night. Fifina left, Carmela too, now she's a nurse in the Red Cross. But Laurita de los Ríos, the minister's daughter, is there along with an Andalusian girl, García Lorca's sister. Laurita is ever so patient with the children, like a saint.

When I get to the refuge, I relieve the ones who've spent the night on watch. I leave at six, I walk to the road that goes to Chamartín where the streetcar stops. It scares me to look around. Who knows what I'll see?

I notice a couple of feet on the ground, they're still with their heels in the dirt; they frighten me. Dead people's feet. It's a dead body on the border of a ditch, facing upward, arms spread, greenish eyes. I run off to catch the streetcar as fast as I can.

Sometimes I see women walking along in a hurry. The streetcar conductor leans out to scold them.

"Run, run, dirty women! There's fresh meat over there. Go get it… You're better off washing your feet, you dirty hags!"

A few of the streetcar passengers laugh, but most of them keep their composure, so serious and dignified.

Along the way, several passengers stand up and point to something.

"Look, there's one over there next to the wall."

"There… in the rubble. At the end."

"There's a woman… no, two."

My God! I think of poor Aunt Julia. But *Papá* said…

Some nights I'm on watch with Laurita.

"Tonight is washing night," she tells me with the face cloth and sponge in her hands. "Get ready, Celia."

At nine, all the kids are asleep, and Laurita and I walk around on tiptoes.

"It's best to shut the windows," she tells me. "And at daybreak we'll open them, when the killing stops. The night before last, a desperate man pleaded for help when they were about to kill him. It's horrible. One of the children woke up terrified. Not everyone has the courage to die in silence."

"We talk. Laurita is desperately worried. She thinks they've killed Isabel García Lorca's brother. The fascists killed him in Andalusia. How do I tell his sister?"

"Nowadays anything goes," I say, and I tell her what happened at Aunt Julia's house. Father is recuperating from his operation. He probably knows by now."

Then we talk about María Luisa. She's sick. At the end they didn't take her father away, but her brother had no such luck. He's a prisoner in the San Antón convent. That's where Maeztu is, with Muñoz Seca and some army coronels. Maybe they won't kill them. The other day a truck filled with prisoners left for a castle in La Mancha. But it didn't arrive. They killed them while they were still in the truck.

"I'm going crazy," I say in a moment of desperation.

Laurita squeezes my hand and doesn't say anything… until:

"Let's see if any of the children have woken. That's our job, we can't do anything else."

Some days I don't leave home. It's so pleasant in the mornings amidst the trees in the garden, under the pergola. All that beauty interrupted by horror. I hear an airplane, and far away, sirens sounding their sad warnings.

"Girls, here, come here!"

I grab them by the hands and we throw ourselves on the ground. Laughing, they think it's a game. The plane is monstrous, close to the ground. Boom. Boom. Boom. The bombs fall closer. Dad's upstairs, alone in his room thinking about us. Three explosions more, and finally the bomber plane flies off.

I go up to Father's room to calm him down. Teresina is delighted; she comes up with me, not knowing what's going on.

"… and we threw ourselves on the ground. And the airplane went boom, howling like a wolf, and then… poom, poom poom. Then it left. Will another one come, *Papá*? Say yes… will there be another one?"

"I'm afraid so, *hija*. Many more…"

"I can't wait!"

"It's best she take it that way," says *Papá*. "Imagine what it would be like if these girls were terrified. The other night during the bombing, when I was still in the hospital, I heard children screaming in horror. This was worse for me than the fear of what could happen to me."

Guadalupe comes and goes from the convent where the refugees from Talavera are living. One morning I go along with her.

The convent is an immense brick building within a cluster of other buildings on the road to Chamartín.

We pass through the abandoned garden to the house. A woman is sweeping in a spacious vestibule; she greets Guadalupe and assures her that the children are well.

We go up two flights of stairs to a long hallway with narrow doors on one side. We can hear the voice of a woman singing:

Reverte's sweetheart
has a kerchief,
has a kerchief…

We follow the corridor to the end where we're met with another one, and another one. There's a labyrinth of hallways, all illuminated by torrents of sunlight. Guadalupe tells me that behind each door there's an entire family living in one room.

I catch a glimpse of some of them as I go by the open doors. There are piles of rags, bags, and baskets scattered in the rooms where children sit on the floor and men are huddled together looking at me, and women are anxiously rushing about trying to organize their families' lives as best as possible.

The rooms have white lime walls, typical of convents… but where are the nuns? Guadalupe doesn't know. When she arrived, no one was living in the convent. A few benches remained in some of the rooms along with the straw mattresses. The chapel is now a garage.

We've arrived. At the end of a hallway, some women are sewing in front of an open window while children are playing with an iron hoop that makes a noise when it falls to the floor.

The tallest woman, Guadalupe's cousin, approaches us.

"This is the *Señorita*…"

"No need to call her *Señorita*, that's for rich people. If she's a leftist, better call her comrade."

I laugh. "You can call me whatever you like."

I see immediately that she's been through hard times. She has seven children, and all of them fit in a basket. Her husband was the best watchmaker in all of Talavera de la Reina. Four men worked for him… it's true. Guadalupe knows all about it. They had everything they needed.

"And look what we've come to."

A few hours before she fled, she couldn't have imagined it. Several days before, you could hear the cannon fire, but everyone who fled from the city said the defenders of the Republic had everything under control. That morning she dressed her children like every other day, fed them breakfast and helped the servants with the laundry.

"You know as well as I do that you have to take care of everything in your house."

Suddenly you could hear the loud drone of the airplanes. It was as if the sky was falling… And then the bombs.

People ran through the street terrified. Buildings crumbled, and pieces of glass and wood shattered against the walls, windows broken everywhere. She stood against the dividing wall with her children and husband because that was the safest place in the house.

And when those savages finished their bombing mission, they went back to where they'd come from.

"What a sight, comrade!"

Guadalupe's cousin told us that when they left the house, they could barely move through all the debris… Smoke everywhere, houses on fire, mounds of plaster and bricks piled on top of each other.

"There were a lot of people buried underneath."

Groups of rescuers were organized, no provisions, just aid in moving bodies, both the injured and the dead. Everyone was involved in the rescue: her husband, the watchmakers, even the servants bringing water. And just an hour later, the sound of airplanes again.

"They're loaded to the hilt, that's why they were flying so low."

Many ran for the hills and threw themselves on the ground, but to no avail, not enough time. Again the bombs with the horrendous explosions, splinters, tiles; for a couple of moments, it all looked like an inferno.

"Pure terror, comrade, pure terror!"

The bombers retreated: the people who remained alive didn't dare move. She went on: she said more than an hour passed when the cries of the wounded enticed some people to move. Then came the Red Cross with doctors.

Some said there were trucks in the road, that there are orders to evacuate the city in three hours, that everyone must leave.

"Imagine… how could I do that with seven children? No luggage, just like that."

She refused to leave. She was crying desperately. Her children cried with her.

"But you know, my husband is a real man. When the moment calls for it, he tells people what to do: 'We've got to get out of here, now. Now, I say!'"

The street turned into rivers of people walking toward the road. No one was crying, no. Women with their children in their arms, and men seriously carrying out the task, conscious of the importance of moving on.

Militiamen drove the evacuation trucks, filled to the brim with people who have no idea where they were going; it didn't occur to them to ask.

"Look, I had seven children, now eight because another one just appeared. No one knows where the mother is."

Some trucks dropped people off at San Martín de Valdeiglesias, others went toward Madrid. Who knows where that poor woman is, the one who lost her child. What's more, when the trucks speed up, they become targets for more bombs.

"Why don't they leave us alone if they can see that we're fleeing and that we have children? Well no matter, they bombed us. One of the trucks was hit with everyone inside it."

She said the woman jumped into the road with her children and her husband and headed for the hills; they crawled on the ground looking for shadow under shrubs.

"Scary, comrade. Hair raising!"

The other two women who were sewing by the window ask me:

"Do you think we'll be here for a long time?"

"They say the defenders of the Republic are about to overtake Talavera."

We hear someone, or something, that sounds like a cat from behind a closed door.

"It's Mari Juana," says Guadalupe's cousin as she opens the door.

In the empty cell, there's a straw mattress and a torn blanket covering someone. Under the blanket, there's something small that looks like it might be a child. But no, it's Mari- Juana.

"C'mon, Mari-Juana! Get on with it, you hear? You have to eat… The doctor says that if you don't eat, they'll force-feed you."

I lift the blanket and see a disheveled head on the mattress.

Guadalupe tells me her story as we continue to search for the shadow of the trees that line the road, the sun is in our eyes.

Mari-Juana had gotten married a year ago, and she had a two-month-old baby. Her husband was a field worker. He was plowing the earth at the end of some fields. She brought him his meals every day; she left her child sleeping in his crib at eleven before the bombers arrived. When she got back at one, the trucks were in the road making sure no one could return to the city, especially not the women.

"*Señora*, there's an order to evacuate. You can't go beyond here."

She cried that she had left her child there, she had to go back.

But her cries only served to irritate those in charge of the evacuation. They forced her onto the truck against her will, and the truck went on its way. No one paid attention to her. No one figured out what she was saying since her voice had turned hoarse and unintelligible.

"What happened to the little one?"

"I have no idea! The house was locked, and when the fascist troops arrive, no one will be interested in what's inside such a poor house. The little one will probably have cried to no end…He's probably dead of starvation and neglect."

"Maybe not," I say. I can't bear this story.

At midday, the shadows of the trees are barely discernible among the trunks. Suddenly we feel a mountain breeze, fresh and dry. The leaves are rolling on the ground murmuring as if they were humming a song with a sound of velvet.

"Autumn is around the corner," I say.

I'm feeling that sweet anticipation of the change of seasons… Autumn's coming.

"Hey, *Señorita*. Look out, the bombers… Run, run!"

We run to our house, but there's no time. They're on their way. They're here threatening with the weight of their bombs, flying low to the ground, as if the sky were going to fall on top of us… mercilessly…

EVACUATION!

Evacuation! Madrid must be evacuated. The newspapers say it again and again. My God! Vacate our house!

The girls are playing in the garden with Valeriana; I can see them from the wooden balcony outside of Dad's room, under a radiant autumn sky.

"There's nothing else to do, *hija*. Look, if there's no food, we won't be able to live. We must leave."

"We've got to leave!" In the refuge that's all they say and everyone's getting ready for the departure. María Luisa has gone back to her chores, but she looks so serious; she's sad. Her brother is still in jail and her father is ailing rapidly. Fifina lives with elderly aunts on Ferraz Street. Again bombs begin to fall on the rooftops.

It's been a month now since you could see the fascist troops battling against the Republican soldiers from the tops of buildings on Gran Vía. Every day they get closer to Madrid.

"Daddy… They're right close by. They're coming, I'm telling you. You hear them? Don't you? Hear that faint noise of cannon fire?"

"*Mi hija*, who are you talking to? Only to fascists? All those girls in the refuge are probably right wing. The newspapers say… Yesterday they got a beating!"

I don't want to argue because *Papá* has a fever, but I'm sure about what I said. Fifina has not been to the refuge in two days.

"It's hell outside. You can't go out because the streets are whistling with bullets coming from the Palace. They're already there!"

I'm sitting down next to Father sewing, and suddenly there's a groaning sound coming from over the roof of the house. Then a crash.

"That's a bomb!" he says.

Another one is coming down on us making a whistling sound, like a bird crossing the skies.

"Where are the girls?"

"In the garden."

"Tell them to come up."

The girls are with us; they've climbed up on Father's bed. María Fuencisla imitates the sounds she hears coming from the cannon fire:

"Puuuum! It goes pum, pum. You hear it?"

For an hour the bombs fall close to our house at regular intervals. Father and I do not speak. He only says to the girls:

"You're going on a trip, you know? To Valencia. It's warm there in November."

Close to the house there's a cannon firing back at the enemy's bombs. Today I see another one in the road… and the airplanes pay us a visit two or three times a day.

Valeriana comes up to us.

"Look in front, over there. It's on fire. They say Cuatro Caminos and Tetuán are in shambles. Look."

A hundred airplanes come and go; their job is to terrify us. Workers' houses are burning; they go after the most helpless.

"Wretched!" cries Father. "Miserable!"

"*Papá*… did you know?… The government has opened the doors to thousands of criminals. They're all in the streets?"

Dad is furious with me; I regret having spoken.

"You don't know what you're saying! Who can take the blame for what the people do? Who do you think started this revolution? It was the rich *señoritos*. The 'gentlemen' soldiers, the landowners from rich farms who go out at night for a good time and get drunk. Do you think the people are the only ones who kill? They killed my cousin Ramón from Bilbao, the fascists beat him with clubs, and my nephew Felipe, the one from the farm… they executed him,… and your poor grandfather."

Dad's yelling brings me to tears. "My God. My God. I can't bear it!"

"*Hija*, my love, don't cry. Don't pay attention to me. I'm upset. You're right: they're all the same. Humanity is nothing but swine. The right response for an honorable person should be restraint. Kill yourselves or kill me if you don't know how to do anything else, but in the meantime, just let me do some thinking; that's the only thing left for me, except for you."

I don't want to go through another scene like this again. Dad's fever is getting worse, and he won't let himself tumble into bed.

The children of the refuge will go to Valencia tomorrow; we decide to have Valeriana and the two girls go with them. I have work to do; there's lots of sewing and fixing I must attend to.

The bombings are getting stronger each minute: it looks like they're planning something huge. Night falls, star-filled and cold; the rifle fire seems like it's coming from the road close by.

Father calls me. He's nervous.

"Why don't you go out to see if anything's going on?"

I open the door to the garden. There is no one in the street. Explosions light up the sky. Where to go?… Everyone is locked in their homes. I go uphill along the street. No one. The sounds of the battle get closer and closer. It seems like they're fighting right next to me.

I go back to the house. I place the silverware and my dad's clothes in the suitcase along with mine. I put his typewriter in its leather case. I may have to go to Madrid tonight.

I go to bed. At midnight the phone rings. It's María Luisa:

"Fifina is still in her house on Ferraz Street, unless they've made it impossible for her to stay. Tomorrow we've got to fetch her and her aunts, but I can't go because I have things to do at the refuge".

"Me too. I'm sending my sisters there."

I go to bed without undressing. I'm cold. An explosion close by makes me tremble; I get up.

"What's wrong?"

"I don't know. It was close."

It's Valeriana. She's barefoot and scared. She looks at us without speaking.

"It's nothing, woman," says *Papá*. "Go to bed, tomorrow we have to leave."

We go to bed. When I wake, I've forgotten where I am. Is the window on my right or left? Little by little, rays of dim light appear in front of me through the cracks in the wood… Ah, yes, today is when the girls leave. My little ones!

That's Teresina always chatting. I find them in the kitchen with Valeriana.

"Celia, let's go." says Teresina.

"Yes, *hijitas*. You'll behave, do what Valeriana says, and write to tell me how you're doing."

"I want you to come with us!"

"No! If I go, who will look after *Papá*?"

I go out to the garden. It smells like fresh earth, and the air is fine and cold as though it had passed over snow. It's a glorious sunny day. No sounds of battle on the front, even though it seems so close.

Dad is sad as he bids farewell to the girls. He gives Valeriana a thousand instructions… "Let's go."

Guadalupe accompanies us to the streetcar stop, suitcase in hand. Three women are in the car: they're carrying baskets and suitcases. There's a man who suddenly gets on his feet and says as he points out the window:

"Look out there. Fourteen of them, I counted them this morning."

The three women look out trying to see what the man's pointing to:

"There, next to that corner of the wall. No not there, the tree is covering them. Look over here."

"What is it?" Valeriana asks me.

"I don't know. Best not to look. Probably dead people."

A group of women is running along the road; the streetcar conductor yells at them:

"Run, run! Run to see the dead people, you vultures… Some people've got to put their faces in everything!"

"Last night there was a massacre," says a man sitting in front of me. "What a slaughter! The more bombs and grenades, the more commotion… Seemed like things were dying down, and now here it is again. They're going to let everyone out of jail — the *checas*, or whatever they're calling them — and no one'll be left. They're looking for it. Look, look over there! Another dead fish in the ditch!"

I try to distract Teresina, but she's staring out the window:

"It's not a fish, it's a man. Look, Celia, there's a man on the ground!"

Valeriana crosses herself and prays. The women look at her and look at each other, and then they talk to each other as they look at us.

"Don't be foolish, woman. You can pray if you want, but you don't have to show us…"

"What?… What are you saying?"

She doesn't hear me, the streetcar's engine is too loud because of the noise. When we arrive we don't have anyone to help carry the suitcase, so we each take turns. The refuge is not far from Castellana Boulevard. We go up the hill next to the Women's Center on Serrano Street.

The buses wait as children play in the garden.

"We were waiting for you," says María Luisa. "That's why the bus hasn't left yet."

I say goodbye to my girls.

"My dearest María Fuencisla! You'll behave, won't you. You'll eat your soup every day. And you, Teresina. Be a big girl, you're the older one. Valeriana, take good care of them… I know you will. What can I say? You're everything to them!"

Valeriana's tears run down her face like threads as she keeps an eye on the suitcase and her packages.

"And if you need money, just ask. You know what Dad told you."

Valeriana barks at a militiaman loading the baggage: "Hey, you, look what you're doing! The suitcase'll fall over if you put it down like that!"

The man laughs; he pays no mind.

"Don't worry, he's tying it shut."

We make Valeriana take two seats in the front; María Fuencisla is in her arms, and Teresina is beside her.

Teresina looks at me from the window. She's happy.

"Hey, Celia, is there a Santander in Valencia? Because Valeriana says it's by the sea."

"Yes, it's by the sea, the Valencia sea. Santander is also by a sea."

She can't hear me because the other children are making noise. The center seats are taken.

The first car leaves, and the second starts the motor.

"You're on your way! Farewell, *queridas*, goodbye, goodbye!"

The bus makes a turn and disappears around the corner.

"Now, you'll look after Fifina," María Luisa tells me. "There's a big mess here. We have to order beds and sheets now so they arrive before nightfall. Are you crying? Let's get to work, Celia."

I'm on my way to find Fifina with the address they gave me. The streetcar stops at San Bernardo, so I'm on foot toward Ferraz Street. Because of the grenades, I have to duck in an entranceway along the street. There's an explosion followed by broken glass and falling bricks. Another one... Another one closer, bullets whistle by.

"You can't leave here," an old woman tells me. "Not now. Wait a bit and then go on. Do you live far?"

"I'm going to Ferraz Street."

"You can't get there. They won't let you. I think the militiamen are keeping people from passing. The houses are sunken."

From the entranceway I see a seven-story building, but a piece of it is missing. The rooms only have three walls. They look like dollhouses or a theater stage with the curtain up. On the fifth floor there's a room with a sewing machine, a bed, and a crooked portrait. In another room there's a cage hanging on a nail. I think of the little bird starving or dying of thirst.

The cannon fire has stopped, but bullets continue to whistle by as I take refuge in another entranceway. There I stand next to two women who say nothing. Like me, they wait a few minutes before guns and rifles stop firing.

Coast clear, I run to the next entranceway until I reach Princesa. I make my way through the rubble of a house in ruins, so now I can walk safely on the cement where there are no bullets whistling by. The parallel street serves as a barrier. As I cross the streets descending toward Rosales, I stop to make sure there's no gunfire. But in the middle of the street I feel a bullet whisk by, so I run in no particular direction. If *Papá* knew where I am…!

I don't have any recourse except to try to get to Ferraz by way of one of the crossing streets; I move along, pressing against the buildings and thinking that the bullets are probably flying through the center of the streets. Again I take refuge in the entranceways, I run to the next one under the door's lintel.

I'm on Ferraz Street. Canons fire once again, bombs falling on rooftops causing more destruction. The street is covered by broken glass and bricks, pieces of cement and lime everywhere. Here I don't have to fear the bullets, as long as bricks or an entire balcony doesn't fall on top of me… like that very one that's about to collapse over there. A gigantic hole in the façade of a building behind me is probably the result of a cannonball shot into a room, destroying everything.

Here it is; this is the address. As soon as I go through the entranceway, there's a frightening noise that shakes the whole house. I go out into the street. No one seems to live here. A door opens and a man comes out; he is humming to himself as if nothing were happening.

"Comrade, would you please tell me if the people I'm looking for…"

"Yes, they live here, but last night they moved to their friends' house on Princesa because of the bombs."

"I think the girl is upstairs now," he says. "It's the fourth floor on the left. The elevator isn't working," he says as I go up.

All the doors to the apartments are wide open. I look in and see people moving from side to side.

I hear a frightening explosion on the stairway. I don't know what to do. I'm on the third floor. A bomb probably fell right here!

Fifina's door is open like all the doors on the floor. I go in. There's a small receiving room with chairs tipped over… an enormous hole in the wall and the doors to the balcony are hanging to one side. There's the hallway… The plaster and rubble sink as I step over them. There is Fifina in the bedroom, wrapping a bundle of clothes in a bedspread.

"Fifina!" There's another awful explosion. "What are you doing here? The house is about to cave in!"

"I know," she says smiling. "I know... I've escaped without the aunts noticing, but I have to take these things with me. Last night we went out with what we have on, and while we were gone, they robbed us. They took the silverware, the jewelry, and all the sheets."

"Of course... you left the doors open."

"No, it's that you can't get them to shut. The bombs have thrown everything out of whack."

As she speaks, she continues gathering her things in the bedspread: talcum powder, cologne, a box of relics, a portrait of her father.

"It's good that you came, I can't carry all this by myself..."

Another explosion shakes the building as more rubble and broken glass pile up... cries of desperation coming from other parts of the building.

"Let's go," Fifina says calmly. "Let's go."

"What happened?" I ask trembling.

"Nothing. We've been living like this for eight days. Help me tie this together."

As we start down the stairs dragging the enormous bundle, another explosion makes us stumble. Fifina will not let go of the bedspread and falls one floor down.

"Lord!" I yell. "They're going to kill us!"

The stairway is covered in blood. I'm afraid... I don't know if it's fear or the cold, but my teeth are chattering.

Fifina is still calm as she drags her bundle; her blond hair makes her look like a little golden beetle.

When we get to the door to the street, we find the doorman.

"Are you leaving for good? I'll try to close the door," he says.

"Are any of the neighbors still here? I just heard people yell."

"Yes, that's the woman on the second floor. She lost her hand. It was in shreds when they took her away. I think she'll probably lose her hand, but that's the least of her problems. She was really bleeding. See you later... *Salud.*"

As we leave the building, another bomb falls close by; I cry out. Pieces of iron fly past us. Something hits me on the shoulder; it rips my dress.

The doorman is on the ground; he's not moving.

"Get on, let's go," says Fifina. "We can't stay here."

"And that poor man?"

"Leave him alone. Let's go."

We start to run as best we can, grabbing a corner of the bedspread and dragging it. Now we have to go up one of those cross streets where there's no rifle fire. We have to slow down because of the enormous bundle with Fifina's belongings in it. We proceed little by little, as best we can. The bullets whistle by our ears. There's no one on the street. The sky is gray, damp, cold. I'm trembling.

"C'mom, c'mon," says Fifina. "Keep dragging it."

We've managed to make it to the doorway. There we're met by two old women who make the sign of the cross when they see us.

"God bless us! You're here! Why did you do all that? And you, *Señorita?*"

"It's Celia, the one from the refuge."

We go into one of the interior rooms. It's morning, but the light is on. There is a gathering of people inside. A man, another old woman, a pretty girl, and a young lady who smiles at me without speaking.

"She's deaf," says Fifina.

Two boys in the room. Open trunks on the floor, suitcases, portraits tied together. We hear the clamor of the bombs here too but they're not as loud. I'm told the upper floors are in shambles; the building is seven stories tall so it's likely the lower floors are in ruins too.

"María Luisa has sent me to fetch you, you and your aunts…"

I wasn't able to say so until now.

The two women refuse. They won't leave here for anything in the world. Maybe the bombing will stop and we'll go back home, they say.

"Don't kid yourselves," says Fifina.

Alright, so if they refuse to leave they must be convinced to go back gradually, maybe by short trips, little by little they'll carry over their things: the clothes, the silverware, the Jesus figure…

Fifina looks at me. All their possessions have been stolen.

"What about you, Fifina? Will you come with me?"

"Sure, sure, let her go with you," say the aunts. "It's better that way."

But Fifina is not convinced. Where would she go? There's no one left in the refuge, and her only family is her aunts.

"So come to my house. The Chamartín area is safer. There's space in the house; my sisters aren't there."

But still she resists. It's late, nearly midday, and *Papá* will be worried. We approach the door to the street. The bullets are still flying by; there is no one in the street, and the sound of cannon fire comes in intervals. Everything is gray, all seems wrapped around a tragic sadness. I'll go out after the last cannon fire, calculating that I'll be able to get to Princesa Street.

"But what about the bullets? Can't you hear them?"

But I have no choice; I'll have to take my chances on the upper street.

"I'm going with you," says Fifina heroically.

We run along the sidewalk, clinging to the buildings. We once again hear the bullets and the dry ping sound they make as they hit rooftops and the rocks in the streets.

We're running, running; we cross a street and stop for a moment close to some buildings shielding us from the bullets.

"Should we go on?"

"Let's go."

Again we're off. We cross another street, and another one. We've gotten to Princesa. I lean on a wall and grab my chest in an attempt to slow down my heartbeat. Thank God we've arrived.

"There's still a ways to go before San Bernardo Street," Fifina tells me. "I'm going back."

"But weren't you coming with us?"

"No, I just wanted to accompany you. I had to do it since you've risked so much to come here with us. Goodbye, Celia."

She disappears behind a corner, running alone through a street with bullets flying. I marvel at how brave this girl is. Extraordinary Fifina!

In front of me I see people loading a cart, and another one, and another. They're salvaging what they can among their most valuable and most cherished possessions.

The cart driver comes out of the house carrying a suitcase and a big box; he's complaining:

"If you kill my mule, you'll have to pay me! Damn it! I never should have come, should have looked after myself. Are we off? I'm not loading any more stuff. Git up mule!"

He rolls away.

I move toward the next corner, always clinging to the buildings protecting me. Are there more bullets around here? I have no choice; I must cross this street. Some three jumps later, I'm on the other side. Like that, from street to street and from scare to scare, I get to the boulevard. Now the only direction possible is down this street toward Rosales, so close to the front. There are other people who, like me, don't dare move forward from the corner into the wide-open avenue with bullets and grenades exploding on the street. But there's no choice!

As in a nightmare, I run and run any way I can, my heart pounding so hard I can barely breathe. I see a cart tipped over to one side next to an injured mule.

San Bernardo Street, finally. This is where the carts are unloaded and the contents carried into streetcars. I'm traveling next to a sewing machine and an enormous box filled with mattresses.

María Luisa is still at the refuge arguing with a militiaman.

"They're not letting me take out the mattresses," she cries. "They're going to turn this into military barracks and they say they need all this. What about our poor children? They won't have a place to sleep when they get to Valencia?"

I speak to *Papá* over the phone, but I don't tell him about the beds for the children. He has already eaten. Guadalupe has taken good care of him, but he's worried about me.

I spend the afternoon in María Luisa's house. It's so sad in this house because their son is under arrest. However, they're not in need of anything: meat — there's no meat in my house — butter, desserts. Her mother takes me aside and tells me:

"They're on the outskirts of Madrid. Last night the people next door got a letter from the husband who's a captain in Burgos. They found it underneath the door. It tells them he's right there, just a few paces away."

"Who brought the letter?"

"No one knows. But this means that someone from the other side has moved to Madrid. With all this commotion and killing every night these criminals… They've let them out of the prisons. They're right here living among us."

Last night when I got off the streetcar to get back home, I took the connection to Ciudad Lineal, and I followed a group of men who weren't saying anything. One of them had his hands tied.

They stopped and left the man in front of a door to a garden… I could imagine what was happening!

"No, no, for God's sake, don't kill him!"

Maybe they didn't see me. One of them turned to me and said:

"Run along, comrade. Mind your own business. These women…"

I hurried along desperately and covered my eyes. I ran. I heard the rifle shots!

I went down the street toward those little boarding houses where my house is, always running, always running away from who knows what. There was someone in the door to the garden. She was on crutches. It was Fifina.

"I've decided to go on living," she says. "That's the only way my aunts will decide to leave that inferno."

She sleeps in the room next to mine, in Teresina's bed. My Teresina. I wonder if you'll have a bed to sleep on tonight.

It's still nighttime when I hear knocks on the door. Guadalupe and I, dressed but barefoot, go to see who's there. There are over fifteen people at the door to the garden. It's Fifina's aunts along with all the people who lived in that building. All the people living in the Argüelles neighborhood have been evacuated. And here they are with suitcases and bundles of belongings. They look a little ashamed; they're shaking on this cold and rainy autumn night.

"Come in, come in. We'll find a place for you."

NOVEMBER 1936

Our beautiful house has turned into an encampment. I've covered the sofas and lounge chairs with sheets, I've rolled up the carpets, and with Guadalupe's help, I've taken down the curtains and wall hangings.

The house smells bad! The agglomeration of people who sleep with their clothes on makes everything stink. Also we have to cook with lard because there's hardly any olive oil.

It's raining: the raindrops penetrate the house and dampen our clothes. Evaporation caused by poorly-lit heaters makes everything smell horrible along with all the muddy shoes bringing more grime into the house.

Father, still feverish, stays in bed. He is not aware of all the filth and misery that has invaded us with the arrival of these people.

I pay as little attention as possible to all the pain we've been feeling, the anguish, and bitterness. I don't speak a lot. I sew, read, and eat at a table next to Father's bed. Sometimes we hear arguments coming from the floor beneath us. I've moved the polished oak in the dining room into the vestibule, a room once so comfortable and welcoming. This is where the new people gather to get acquainted. In addition to Fifina's elderly aunts, there's another old woman who covers herself with a black leather overcoat; all you can see of her is her face covered with black blemishes and her dirty hands. A middle-aged married couple argues, constantly exchanging fiery insults.

The deaf girl works all day long without speaking, she cooks and comes in and out, dirtying the whole house with mud from the garden. Her father, a proper and friendly gentleman, swats her for the slightest infraction. He does the same to his son, a tall young man, not very bright. The youngest of the three children is that pretty girl I met at the house on Argüelles Street. She looks like a princess: always smiling with big eyes. Her father always looks at her adoringly.

There's also a woman with the face of a nun, and her brother, a sickly fat man who gestures softly when he speaks, uttering vulgarities as if he were making big pronouncements. Yesterday he called me to his side to tell me he is a Carmelite priest.

"I'm well-known in Spain, *hija mía*, and in the Americas, throughout the Catholic world… and now I've fallen into exile amidst this calamity."

Papá is startled when I tell him about this man.

"As long as this person doesn't cause us any problems."

We decide to separate him from the rest. On the highest floor there's a big room that Father has furnished for Cuchifritín for when he returns from England. This is an appropriate room for the priest. I suggest to him that he make himself scarce, it's best for him not to be seen, that he tell everyone he's no longer living here.

He seems to understand; he settles down in the armchair with his prayer book. His sister will serve him his meals and bring him whatever he needs.

However, in the evenings I find him pontificating in the vestibule surrounded by the others:

"…I had prepared a sermon according to the words of Saint Augustine, and when my brother entered the church, I turned my back on him." He pontificates with his hands together, as if he held the entire globe between them. Then he places one hand on top of the other. "And what was once white I turned to black, those were the words I preached according to Saint Paul, because I knew that my brother had already heard my other sermon on the *Adorati*."

Fifina, who's always running around attending to her aunts, tells me the priest is something of a dimwit.

"*Hija*, I couldn't imagine a priest so stupid; it looks as though he just memorizes what they tell him to say. He says he only gave sermons to the nuns in convents. Of course! Poor dummy!"

Sometimes, Fifina comes up to dine with Father and me, and as we eat we hear the frightful shriek of the sirens, and the bombers swooping over our house. None of us say anything, pretending to hear nothing. But our hands tremble as we bring the spoons to our mouths. Then we hear the terrifying whistle of a falling bomb, then the explosion followed by the sound of walls crumbling.

Fifina makes Father laugh when she tells him about the priest's reactions to the rifle shots and bombers. The poor man folds his ear to hear more clearly and says with astonishment:

"Did you hear that? Shots! I wonder what it's about."

The others try to explain the horrible things happening around us, but he has no idea. Then the sound of another bomb unsettles him again.

"Hear that? What a horrid noise! If this continues, something atrocious will happen. How terrible!"

His is a case of absolute bewilderment. *Papá* laughs and laughs and forgets our woes momentarily. There's no word about Valeriana or my sisters. María Luisa is still distraught about her brother in jail, and no one, not even she, knows anything about the refugee children.

"That Valeriana! I asked her to keep us informed!"

Guadalupe is singed by the wood she uses for cooking since coal is no longer available. She comes to tell us that we're running low on food:

"The only things left are canned asparagus and rice."

"All right… so we'll eat that."

"But what's there to cook it with? There's no oil. Today I bought half a kilo of lard to cook the rice."

We give in and eat the asparagus without condiments… this is our daily meal for this strange month of November.

Father tries to phone his friends, but no one answers.

"There's no one at home! I called Julián, Miranda, and Hernández; I hear the phone ring on the other side but no one answers."

The house is getting dirtier; the grime reaches as far as Father's room next to the bathroom where our guests wash themselves, spit, and throw cigarette butts on the floor along with discarded toothpaste that sticks to the bottoms of shoes, mud, paper…

Fifina is the only one who complains:

"If you don't dare say it, I will," she tells me. "There are orders to evacuate Madrid, so it's time for them to go, since they'll leave eventually anyway…"

The married couple leaves for Valencia, followed by the gentleman with his three children and his mother who've rented a little place on Ciudad Lineal. Fifina's aunts leave as well; they'll be at a farmhouse close to Albacete. I try to convince Fifina to stay:

"Don't go. *Papá* loved you very much. Besides, I'll be lonely without you."

She accompanies her aunts to the station with the promise of returning next month after they've retrieved all their belongings from the house on Ferraz Street. This convinces the old ladies that it's all right to leave their niece.

The priest and his sister are the only ones left among our guests, so Fifina, Guadalupe, and I take the opportunity to cleanse the house of a month's worth of filth. However, we're not convinced we've seen the last invasion.

The Ferraz neighborhood has been thoroughly evacuated, yet the bombs still fall; those who can get away look for refuge on the outskirts of the city. Guadalupe tells me that all the hotels are filled with people who have nowhere to go. Hundreds arriving from surrounding towns; they've got carts, goats, cows, and livestock of all types. The donkeys graze in the gardens.

The mayor accommodates the arrivals according to each family: one room for each family no matter how big it is.

I feel it's sinful to have such a nice home, so neat and clean now with rugs, upholstery, and curtains, all in the middle of such misery.

"May it last a long time, *hija*, good riddance," says Fifina. ""A cyclone has passed through here… let's hope you don't see another one."

Father calls me from his room.

"Hear that, *hija*?"

With all our attention and conversation focused on the upkeep of the house, we don't notice there's a fierce battle going on close by. Father has closed the windows and turned on the lights.

"*Hija*, this is for real! I think they're here now…"

Then I hear him say in a soft voice:

"They'll execute me, but not before I say..."

"My God, *Papá*. What are you talking about? Do you really think they'll shoot you?"

"Of course, *hija*. Prepare yourself for everything. You came to me from Segovia for refuge. But after I'm gone, you must go and find your sisters… you must protect them."

"*Papá*, please!"

I try to make him get rid of that idea, but it's no use. He writes a letter to Uncle Rodrigo in Argentina because he's the only help we have left.

"They're going to confiscate this house."

"But are these people the same ones: killing, taking property, and…?"

"Yes, *hija*."

"So they're all the same?"

Sadness overcomes us for the rest of the day. Fifina and I accompany Father. It's very cold, but Guadalupe has found a way to get coal; fortunately, there's a working heater close to the bed. The gunshots subside before nightfall, so we open the shades to the balcony. The garden is covered in dry leaves withered by the rain. The priest also tries to make the bed more comfortable as Father explains to him that citizens have rights.

"Neither nature nor culture is the property of the few. It all comes from ancestral inheritance since the time the first man stood on his own two feet."

The priest squints, not understanding Father's words although he pretends to. He seems in a daze and says:

"That's just what I said to the Prior. If only other people understood these arduous theological problems. Here we are, day after day, studying these things, and other people with no idea about these mysteries. They eat, they sleep, they live… and they die, unaware of anything. But listen to these words: 'Father, this is not for everyone. Only the ones God has chosen can understand.' That's the way it is."

Papá continues to explain historical matters to him, philosophical things, or whatever. He even talks to him about traditional Spanish dishes… and that the people of Castille have been victims of overexploitation.

"Well, a remedy for that is the Carmelite *tortilla*! I remember a lay sister in the convent who made the most divine *tortilla*: with potatoes, eggs, chorizo, loin…"

His sister calls him to supper, and the priest leaves with a sad goodbye.

"It's time for penitence. This rice cooked in lard is horrid."

When he closes the door, Fifina sits down and mimics:

"Oh, the Carmelite *tortilla*! You beat the eggs, cut the potatoes…"

Someone is at the door. It's eight o'clock, nightfall. Who can it be at this hour? Guadalupe goes to the door and opens it; we hear heavy footsteps climbing the stairs with weapons. Three militiamen.

"Who are these men in our house?"

Papá sits up on the pillows.

"Me, it's just me."

"Comrade, what are you doing in bed? Don't you know there's a battle two hundred meters from here? They want to take Madrid tonight, but they won't do it unless all the men are in the trenches fighting."

"He's sick," I say. "He got out of the hospital two months ago, and he still has a fever."

"No, no," says *Papá*. "I'll get up right now. You're right, comrade. All of us must fight together, especially tonight."

As I hand Father his clothes, they all go into the hallway; he can barely dress himself because his hands are shaking.

"My God… Father, you can't…"

"Leave me alone!"

Finally, he stands up, off he goes wrapped in his overcoat.

"Let's go."

"*Papá*."

"Goodbye, *hija*… Cheer up! We're going to win this war! Goodbye, Fifina."

He kisses me and goes down the stairs, holding on to the banister with the militiamen behind. Fifina and I follow.

Suddenly a thud. Father has collapsed in the vestibule.

"*Papá, Papá!*"

"Don't worry, comrade. He's just fainted… Up you go…"

Now they all help Father up the stairs and put him to bed. They leave, slamming the door.

He looks dead!

The dreadful clamor of the battle is getting horribly close.

FEBRUARY 1937. HUNGER AND BOMBS

I go down to the garden on this cloudy morning. An old gardener digs in what was until now a green meadow where beans are planted. Sitting next to the pond, I enjoy the warmth of the winter sun and breathe in the freshness of the newly-tilled soil.

I've gotten so used to the constant gunfire and bombs of the city that I barely think of them. Only the arrival of airplanes unsettles me.

"A beautiful day, *Señorita*," says the gardener.

I'm not accustomed to people addressing me as *Señorita*; lately it's always been "Comrade."

"Yes, beautiful."

"You can smell the coming spring… If only we didn't have to deal with all this…"

I ask him about Juan, who used to be our gardener.

"They recruited him; I think he's a sergeant. He was a nice boy. I wish him the best."

The old man takes a deep breath and goes back to his gardening.

How sweet the smell coming out of the earth! Guadalupe comes to tell me she's on her way to the store because today they're rationing everything. She has her rationing card and a burlap bag with empty bottles, just in case there's olive oil, or wine, or vinegar. The other day we didn't get our hundred grams of oil.

I observe the old man as he wipes his eyes with the back of his hand. He's crying. Just to get his mind on something else, I say:

"I thought Juan was your son."

The poor man can't help bursting into tears; he wipes his face with a handkerchief he takes out of his pocket.

"No… no, *Señorita*. I had four children, like four pine trees, and I have no idea if any of them are left. Damn this revolution!"

Our conversation is filled with silences as he continues to wipe his face, and in between the strokes of his hoe, I learn that this unfortunate man has lost his three older sons in the battle of Talavera. He knows nothing of the whereabouts of his youngest.

"He was just a child, *Señorita*. So close to his *mamá*, although he was sixteen, he didn't look or act a day over fourteen. A little lamb. But on November seventh they took him to the front. From then on we haven't heard a word about him."

He tells me his wife is getting old, that she cries so much that she's losing her voice. To make her feel better he tells her he heard their little one was alright.

"He's the only thing she has left, *Señorita*."

Guadalupe comes back looking dejected. She shows me a broom and some scrubbing pads.

"That's all they had today."

"What? You mean they didn't give you rice or lentils?"

"No, just this…, and five new brooms. But what are we going to eat? All we have is a little milk and bread."

The gardener tells me he knows where we can buy carob beans. Maybe we can get a bushel. Be careful about the insects. You've got to pick them out before the beans go in the pot; change the water twice as you boil them. Guadalupe is off with her sack to find the place the gardener says we can find beans.

Father sits in his chair on the balcony:

"What do you say… eh? Today I've forgotten everything."

The gardener looks up at him, shielding his eyes from the sun.

"Your father has been sick, eh, *Señorita*? I've heard about it."

"Yes… quite sick. But when he recuperates, he'll have to go back to the front."

"For God's sake! What a life!"

He goes back to work in the garden. Far away you can hear shots coming from the front. A few bees dare to fly over the flowering plants. The sky is light blue, and the earth, still hard from the night's coldness, basks in the warmth of the sun.

"It's almost as if nothing's happening," says the gardener. "And look all around, no one knows who's right, the ones on the left and the ones on the right, both sides convinced they know what'll make us happy, but in the meantime they crush the hell out of people like us who don't know anything. I argued with my sons about it… and they said they weren't fighting for themselves, that each generation has to sacrifice. They were just repeating what they heard in the meetings… that they were fighting for those who would come after us, the next generation. Well, damned if I understand why they've got to take care of people who haven't even been born yet. What about the grandchildren I'm not gonna have?"

In silence he turns his head. He wipes his face with the back of his hand… once again he cries.

Fifina returns from standing in the milk line.

"Today they only gave me a liter, and half of it was water… Look…"

"Leave the milk in the kitchen and come sit next to me. Such a glorious morning!"

Suddenly we hear a long shriek over our heads and a horrifying sound close to us.

"A bomb!"

"A bomb, *hija*," says Father. "Come upstairs."

The gardener is still digging:

"Look, for God's sake!"

Less than a minute later, another shriek, and another explosion so close that the windowpanes shake. Followed by several more. We hear cries in the distance and people running in the fields. Fifina, Father, and I observe from the balcony. The gardener is at the door:

"I'm off. Did you hear me? My wife will be scared. Take care. I'll come back in the afternoon."

He slams the door.

Papá thinks they're taking aim to a military target. We go downstairs; we'll be safer there.

We sit in armchairs; every now and then we hear that whistling sound over the roof… It becomes less and less frequent until it stops.

Father says:

"We should move all the furniture to Madrid. This area looks like it's a strategic target; it's not safe. They could get past the Tetuán neighborhood, and then they'll be right here. Talk to María Luisa. Maybe she's got an attic where we can store our things."

It takes two carts to transport the furniture, books, paintings, rugs. The only things left are the essentials.

María Luisa has taken care of everything, not only the furniture but also acquiring food from an organization that looks after sick people. She's managed to get a hold of luxuries like chocolate, sugar, meat extract, rice, even a can of oil. Surely Father will get better now.

A neighbor promises me an egg every day.... We're almost going back to the way it was. I keep all my treasures in the closet in Father's room. He spends all his time there; they'll be safe.

Father doesn't want to eat all these nice things by himself; we need to make cocoa tomorrow for everyone. Angela, the priest's sister, makes it and serves it. We make it watery so it'll last. We don't mind: cocoa made with more water than milk tastes like a delicacy to us. *Papá* says:

"Every morning, when you go down to the garden, Angela comes in and goes into my closet. Today I saw her put something into her pocket."

I open the closet, and I'm shocked. There's so much missing. Of the three packages of chocolate, there's just one left. I'm upset, but Father just laughs bitterly:

"*Hija*, we're making ourselves miserable. Misery is taking over our souls. Don't say anything to that poor woman, just lock the cabinet."

But I still can't sleep at night. I tell Fifina about my fears; we get out of bed in the middle of the night. There's a light on in the kitchen and a pleasant smell throughout the house. We go downstairs, barefoot.

"Someone is frying something! What is it?"

Through the keyhole we see Angela and her brother. They're frying eggs. And hot cocoa too.

I'm furious. While these two live it up, my poor father has to eat greasy rice! I try to go in the kitchen, but Fifina holds me back:

"No, no. Leave them alone. We'll deal with this later."

In the morning I go down to the kitchen. Guadalupe and Angela have turned on the light and moved the pots and pans.

"Today you're not getting cocoa, Angela. You can make it with the chocolate you took from Father's closet."

"Alright."

She makes cocoa and serves it with no fuss.

I tell Father about my encounter, and as we talk, we realize that the egg our neighbor promised, every day ends up in the priest's mouth. What gall! And what about the olive oil? Where do they get it?

Now I understand what's going on. Angela has made friends among the people living on the street nearby. She takes advantage of Father's injury and generosity by getting them to offer us a little oil, some codfish, even bacon. If they only knew that the offerings go right to the priest!

"Don't say anything," warns *Papá*. The day they find out we're protecting this religious man, they'll force us up against the garden wall and shoot us." And he adds, "I don't blame them; we deserve it for our stupidity."

The house has no furniture, everything looks bigger inside, but it also looks desolate and cold.

A postcard from Valeriana has arrived: "We're safe and happy," it says. "The girls are asking about their father, Celia and grandfather." The return address is Colón 28.

We read it, but we don't say anything. We suspect they're not as happy as they say.

"As long as they're healthy and not hungry," says Father.

At nightfall, it's the same as always. When we're all in bed, there's activity in the kitchen, all so that the priest gets fed.

And since Fifina is sleeping soundly, I go down to the kitchen alone:

"Hello everyone. Well, it's good that at least someone in this house is eating well."

The priest is angry. "Thank God," he says reverently. "You know, *Señorita*, my ailing stomach can't take the greasy rice the others are eating."

Angela turns her back to me and continues to cook God knows what. I'm furious: "The bad thing is that we have to vacate this house."

"What?"

"Yes, Father and I are going to Valencia with the girls."

"Oh," she answers calmly. "But Guadalupe is staying here with us."

"No, sir. We're all leaving, and we're locking up the house."

I don't say anything else; I go upstairs to my room. I'm so nervous that I can't sleep at all.

When I get up, the first thing I see is the priest who is waiting for me on the stairs:

"Good morning," I say to him.

"Thank God," he answers as always, and adds in all solemnity, "We're leaving too. Could you tell me, *Señorita*, how to get to Rome?"

"At this moment, there's no way to get there… Try Valencia or Barcelona, and from there… maybe you can ask…"

"I'd rather go to Burgos."

"That's on the other side."

"Who?"

"Franco and his followers," and under my breath I say, "Lord, this stupid guy is annoying."

"I don't know them… But I wonder, *Señorita*, if my younger sister and I could get to Burgos."

"No, I don't think so, sir…"

"But there's always been a way to get there."

"Not now. We're at war. Didn't you know? The others are over there."

"But maybe we could go by airplane… I'm asking you because you seem to know a lot."

98

This man's ignorance is so unbelievable that I'm stuttering as I speak: "No... no... for God's sake, man. How in the world do you think one of our planes could land there?"

"Well, when I was there, airplanes often flew over the convent. I saw them from my room."

"That was a while ago when there was peace. Now you can't get to Burgos."

"That's just what I say," says the priest thoughtfully. "A while ago when we had to go to Sevilla to say mass, we could take the train. Granada too. Or León, or Zaragoza. I know because I had to go to the convents in those places for novenas. You could go to any place you wanted on the train. So I wonder why you can't go now. Believe me, *Señorita*, all this is upsetting me. This has never happened, you could go to any place you wanted, but not now. The governments are worse every day."

I leave him alone so I can be with *Papá*. He's been dreaming. Soon he'll go down to the garden for a walk or to the fields to get his legs moving. I tell him about my conversation with the priest, but I don't talk about what happened last night.

"I'm happy they're leaving, but not for pilfering food — the scarcity is making us all selfish. Don't be surprised, *hija*. Everyone knows about obstinate priests, the stories about them are true. But they're not all like that; some are cultured and intelligent. It's too bad; it's a reflection of the lack of real spirituality in the small towns."

Father goes on talking about the history of Spain and the Church, but I remain nervous. Again I hear the planes, it's the sound they make when they're loaded with bombs. I look out the window: one, two... three... five... seven. Pum!

"The party's starting again. Since the government headquarters left Madrid it died down, but now here they are again... on top of the cannon fire coming from the front."

In the afternoon I go to the center of the city. People are still fleeing the Argüelles neighborhood and the streets close to the Manzanares River. The residences along Delicias and Santa María de la Cabeza are all in the process of evacuation. The houses along Castellana are filled with refugees. In the doorways there are mattresses and typewriters. My dressmaker, who used to live on Preciados Street, was able to find a luxurious flat on Castellana after her building collapsed. But where she lives now there's a family in each room and they don't get along.

Those palatial buildings on Castellana have been converted into jails or barracks; you can see the chandeliers and tiles through the open balconies. The militiaman on night watch has moved the Louis XV-style armchair to the balcony so he can sit comfortably.

But what is that monster moving down Castellana? People stop and stare — me too. It's a stuffed giraffe! It's on a cart rolling down the middle of the avenue so that its head doesn't touch the trees on the edge. On a truck behind the giraffe there are two bears, also stuffed. Then another truck with pretty birds in glass cages. I hear someone say:

"They're from the Mendinaceli collection."

They continue down Castellana toward the racetrack; I suppose they're taking them to the Museum of Natural Sciences… Yes… There I see a teacher from the San Isidro Institute.

"What are you doing here, *chica*? You're… wait, don't tell me, let's see if I remember… You're Gálvez, right?"

"Yes, sir."

"I haven't seen you for a long time. Didn't you study in the San Isidro School."

"Yes… My mother died… We've been in Segovia, then Santander… They executed Granddad."

I want to tell him everything, but there's no time.

"Come to the museum, young lady. You'll see some strange things. We're trying to save what we can from the ignorance of the people and from the bombs. Did you know that the Bellas Artes Commission has restored *La Tirana*? There are lots of paintings we've managed to save from all this chaos. All those collections inaccessible to common people… Now all of that is available to everyone."

He leaves. For a moment I gaze at the parade of stuffed animals and listen to the comments:

"Lions and beasts of all kinds; they used them as playthings. They didn't have anything better to do. And still they're carrying on with the revolution — the whole army! Lord, what in the world do they want?"

Lots of things that were available in the summer have disappeared from the food stores, things like canned asparagus, packages of tea, and even rice. There's nothing left. Most are half-closed, and if some remain open, it is because they're not allowed to close.

I go toward María Luisa's house; she lives on the fifth floor. The elevator is not working so I go up the stairs. The door is not shut all the way, so I push it open without knocking.

Her father is sitting in an enormous hallway. Is he sleeping? No, he looks at me, but doesn't say anything. His silence and stillness make me uneasy.

"Is María Luisa here?"

"Yes."

I go into María Luisa's room, but I don't see her right away. She's lying in bed with her face to the wall. I call her but she doesn't respond.

"Are you sick?"

"No…"

I don't know what to do. I sit down in a little chair close to the bed, and I, too, remain silent. I remember a story where everyone who entered a palace was bewitched, unable to move or speak… and it makes me laugh. But something must have happened in this house.

"Your brother?"

She takes a while to answer.

"… they executed him this morning."

"My God!... I just saw your poor dad."

"He spent the night with him. He was with him… until…"

She retreats back to her silence. I don't ask her about her mother or about her other brother. This is a house of silence where no one cries, it's all unbearable pain… And I think of Gerardo… and of Aunt Julia.

EVACUATION OF MADRID

Banners have appeared among the lush trees of the Prado Boulevard: "Onward Revolutionaries."

There are fewer airplanes flying above. Some of the buildings of Puerta del Sol are destroyed, but every night on the radio we hear the chimes of the bells of the Government Building; it's a relaxing sound.

Father tells us that as long as you can hear those bells, Madrid remains standing. But one night we didn't hear them, and Father was frightened.

"The bells haven't chimed!"

"I didn't hear them…"

I'm sure my father will not sleep tonight.

However, the morning came and the bells tolled again, and Father's eyes lit up:

"The bells! Did you hear?"

"Yes, *Papá*."

I think a bomb hit the bell tower, but in a matter of hours it was repaired and everything was back in its place.

"A clock like that is like the heart of the city. To aim bullets and bombs at it is an evil crime."

From the time Fifina went to Albacete with her aunts—Fifina, always so discreet, diligent, and quiet like a storybook fairy—and the priest and his sister have to Barcelona, Guadalupe and I are left alone in this empty house to attend to Father. We spend many hours in the food rationing lines.

The sun has not yet risen, and I'm in the milk line. It's a mud-filled street in Chamartín where the streetcar goes. The narrow door to the milk dispensary, with its glass window covered by steam, is closed until five. I get there at three-thirty, and I take my place as the last one in line; there are people lined along the walls, wrapped up like bundles.

It's cool outside, so I cover my chin, mouth, and ears with my scarf.

"Good day," says one of the bundles.

"You don't say, 'good day,' comrade. You say 'salud.'"

"Alright, salud… It's all the same."

"That's all because we've left God behind," says the woman in line in front of me.

Everyone laughs.

"This lady's got us all in stitches."

Behind me there's a woman wearing a shawl. My eyes are accustomed to the darkness, so I can see the tears in her shawl and the enormous milk tin she's carrying.

"Ay," she utters breathlessly. She is eager to speak. "It's early, right?

"Very early… even so, look how many people are in line. Some probably spent the night here."

"Sure, that's the way to make sure you get something. But in our case… who knows? Everything is done badly nowadays No one knows when it's time to wash clothes, or when to turn on the lights, or when to get in line for the meat. Sometimes if you go out toward the roads at eleven, there's horse meat, but mostly nothing. There's no reason to all this."

The sun begins to rise. A man in rags is in line six places down from me. A woman says to him:

"Comrade, eh, comrade. I'm talking to you, the one with the sack. Why don't you go down there, by the pine trees… there's dead bodies over there. Take off their trousers and overcoats the good clothes. And put 'em on instead of those filthy things you're wearing."

"I'm not sure about undressing a dead man, even if he's a fascist," answers the man hesitantly, as if his tongue were jammed.

A car full of militiamen goes by; an old lady waves her hand in a gesture of farewell.

"Goodbye, *hija*, goodbye, goodbye…"

"Who's she saying goodbye to?" asks the woman with a sense of humor. No one answers.

"Well, she's the one always saying goodbye to someone; I think she's Mariana, the money exchanger. What a leech! That old woman, she's always at church." Then she pats herself on the head like she just saw something. "Look at that! Her daughter is in line. That woman is half-blind, she has no clue. I think they were about to take her mother on a *paseo*."

My heart quickens its beat, and my hands are trembling, they hurt so much. The mother was saying goodbye to her daughter because she was about to die, and her daughter had no idea. My God.

"*Señora*… I mean, Comrade. Are you sure it was that young lady's mother…? You think they…?"

A gunshot.

"They gave it to her. Didn't you hear it?… I imagined what was going on when I saw the old woman led away by the militiamen. They got rid of her right there, next to the wall where the priests live."

She's not speaking to me anymore. She turns her attention to the people in line who've gathered around her. The poor daughter, she's the third in line. She probably spent the night here so she could bring milk to her mother. When she finds out… horrible! All I can see is that hand waving: "Goodbye, *hija*, goodbye."

The milk dispensary is open now. The distribution is arranged rigorously, first come, first served according to the people in line.

"If they don't comply with the law now, they never will," says a woman who has nothing to say about the passing car.

They go in one by one, and when they leave, they're triumphant.

"*Salud*… *salud*…" they bid farewell.

The daughter exits as well, and everyone looks at her. She says nothing, she doesn't say goodbye.

"That one's all ready," says the one with a sense of humor. "I always said there was no God and that on earth you suffer the bad things you've done.

All those stories the priests tell us about hell and purgatory, it's all happening right here."

The woman behind me in line says to me in a low voice:

"She's probably gonna get it too."

I look at her again. The woman behind thinks I'm agreeing with her:

"That woman over there, comrade, has eaten with Mariana, the money exchanger, lots of times, and Mariana gave her and her children food Let's be honest about it Don José took her to mass for communion on Sundays and she's the very one who denounced her to the militiamen…and for that they were executed, all of them…I think the cat too… Don't know if they shot the dog… doesn't matter, the bitch was starving…"

Gradually each one in line gets to the opening of the dispensary; the woman with a sense of humor is inside now. When I'm about to enter, the woman dispensing the milk says:

"There's no more."

"What?... No more?"

"Nothing. And tomorrow there won't be any either because it's for the hospitals."

Those still in line leave without complaining. The one behind me sighs:

"I don't know what I'm going to give to my daughter; there's something wrong with her stomach, and she can't eat anything else."

"My father's sick too."

We walk along together until we get to the corner. The poor woman sighs and wraps herself in a tattered shawl.

"Do you live far?"

"No, in a neighborhood off the road."

"I've no other place to live… I used to be close to the university, but that was hell, so I came here. Look, right over there; that's Don José's dog."

I look toward the house and I see a beautiful female wolfhound lying close to the street. She's been abandoned; she's hungry, almost starving. In a paper sack next to her are leftovers of boiled rice.

"I brought it to the dog yesterday," she continues to tell me, "but she doesn't want it. Looks like all she wants is to drop dead. When they were about to execute her owner she followed him and the owner's sons, the whole family. Then she went back to the house but it was closed, so she began to howl and threw herself on the ground like she was about to die."

The story of this beast moves me more than anything else I've seen or heard until now. I say goodbye to the poor woman.

Father is looking out the window, waiting for me; he's frightened because he heard an explosion.

"I didn't hear anything," I tell him. "I've heard so many horrors but not the explosion."

"Don't tell me about it. Don't tell me anything, *hija*. Don't let your compassion change your ideals."

I don't know what Father calls ideals, but he goes on speaking:

"Keep in mind this government doesn't have a disciplined army, it doesn't have an internal police force, it doesn't have anything solid that makes people follow its rules. The 'people,' they say, these ignorant people, undisciplined and foolish…these poor people, we're in their hands, but we're not afraid of them, right, *hija*? We're not afraid. Twice during these months you've crossed the entire city of Madrid to be close to me at the Carabanchel hospital, and I was never afraid for your safety… and now, at night, I hear you leave the house to get in food lines, but I'm not afraid for you… Here I'm sick and alone, my doors are open in this house outside Madrid, and I've never been afraid of anything. No, we won't be afraid of the people because we love them, and they know it. Intelligence might fail us, but not intuition…never."

"Father, I don't want to make you suffer… but I must tell you there's a woman responsible for having an entire family executed, despite the family's generosity to her and her children."

"It's charity, handouts!" *Papá* raises his voice when he's upset. "The people don't want handouts! Naturally, they despise people who humiliate them with that kind of charity. Just like when the kings washed the feet of the poor, but of course they never stopped being royalty, always treating the poor as pariahs. No, it's not that, *hija mía*. The people have the right to work, because everyone has the ability to use their hands, along with their intelligence, for something useful. They want to live in decent houses, they want decent clothing, they want schools for their children. Not those miserable schools; they want schools where the son of a workman sits at the same desk with the son of a

landowner, with no limitations other than those handed to us by nature…
That's what we want, you and I, for the people, and that's what the Republic
would have provided…, and that hope is what this revolution is and it's what
they won't let us have, because it's waged by aristocrats and lackeys."

Father is a good man. But he doesn't stop talking and telling us how
things are and how things could be; he's yelling loud and he's not even tired.

"*Papá*, I think you're better now."

"Yes, I'm better… and it's time for me to leave for the front. I'm going to
ask the doctors to say I'm healthy."

It's decided. *Papá* has made the request to go who knows where on the
front, and in a few days, he'll leave, and I'll go too. Perhaps I'll go to Valencia
early to see the girls and Valeriana. Madrid has to be evacuated; there's little
left to eat.

I'm looking at this lush garden that Guadalupe and I water, the pond
with its clear water, the green grapes hanging from the trellis. How sad to
leave this house!

María Orduña's husband is on the Evacuation Committee; he might be
able to help me get a permission to travel soon. I'm going to talk to him. An
errand boy not wearing a uniform opens the door for me and asks me to wait.

There she is with white and polished hands, playing solitaire next to the
balcony. She's just as plump, just as deaf, and just as happy as always.

The errand boy stays to yell my words to her, since she can't hear.

"You say you want to leave Madrid? Not a good idea. It's much hotter in
Valencia, even though it's winter."

"Father says we must do as the government orders."

"What? What silly things your crazy father says! When the good ones
were in power, sure, you could do what they say—even though I always did as
I pleased. But today the bad ones are in charge."

The errand boy looks at her; he's furious, but he doesn't say anything. She
keeps on talking:

"Yesterday my friend Rosario was here. Riñuelos's wife. You know her?
Well you won't believe what horrible things she told me. Her washer woman's
husband rents chairs and benches for people to watch executions… and the

other day they killed a fourteen-year-old boy, and the poor little one cried and cried, heart-broken."

The errand boy is red-in-the-face and says sarcastically:

"Really?"

María doesn't notice so she continues:

"That lady listens to Salamanca radio every day and says Franco will be here in a month… 'he's a pious man, goes to mass each day, and his wife is a real lady, and they have a darling little girl.'"

The errand boy looks at me; he's disgusted.

"I haven't killed this woman because she's a guest of the house, if it weren't for that…"

Finally, *Señor* Orduña can see me. He compliments me, although he says:

"You'll have problems, *hija*. Ever since they bombed the train tracks, there's no rail transportation. You can travel on a military truck with the soldiers, but you'll have to sit on a makeshift bench, no windows or doors. They're covered with tarps to shelter you from the rain or sun, that's it. But it's good for you to leave."

He says he'll say I'm older than I am so I don't run into problems.

"You look like a serious young woman, so we'll say you're twenty-two instead of sixteen; that way, you won't be underage. That'll help you avoid inconveniences so you can take your sisters out of the refuge and take care of them yourself."

The trip is planned for Friday, eight days to go. It's better that way because there's so much I need to do.

"*Papá*, you know you don't have enough socks. But where can I find new ones?"

I set out to look for fabric stores, but I can't find any socks, gloves, or pajamas either. I need to repair the holes. That way they'll last a little longer. The material stores are open because it's against the law to close them, even though their shelves are almost empty, just a couple of old men in the window looking bored.

Just three days left before I go. Father's already dressed in his uniform—so handsome. He goes out to the yard with me in the sweet September twilight.

When we return to this house we'll have won the war," he says with his hand caressing my back. "The girls will be so happy here, you too. Isn't that right?"

"Yes, *Papá*."

"By then my sister should be back. Surely she's been out there without a word to me, just to make me mad. I've spoken to many people, and some say that she was probably among the first people to move to Alicante or Valencia.

Maybe you'll see her there. So listen, *hija*, send word to me. Write to the address I've given you. I'll be at the refuge until I hear you're with your sisters. You'll find them in Valencia. There's no scarcity of fruit or vegetables there. As soon as you get there, go to the evacuation office to get your rationing card. You'll see, *hija*. There's a field close to the riverbed; there are bridges with dry rivers. The weather is marvelous. I'll be at rest knowing you're alright."

"But you, *Papá*? What about you?

"Me? I've recovered, strong and healthy…it's about time. A year of pleurisy, now I'm fine."

"Yes, but what about the war?"

"We'll win the war. It's about justice! Yes, sir! There's no punishment harsh enough for those who bring on revolutions! To deprive a government of its defenses and to turn us all against the people…that's an unforgivable treason."

Morning has broken. The truck is leaving soon, and I should sleep in Madrid; María Luisa offered me to stay in her house. Father accompanies me, carrying my suitcase.

"Goodbye, pretty house. Adios, Chamartín. Farewell, I'm off to Valencia."

The trees on Castellana are yellowing because they haven't been watered, and the sidewalks are filled with dry leaves. It's cloudy, and there's a crisp autumn breeze.

Father prefers not to go to María Luisa's place, so we bid goodbye in the doorway.

"Goodbye, *hija*. I'll see you soon."

He looks calm, happy even.

"Goodbye, my *Papaito*. Let's hope nothing happens to you!"

He leaves. I see him walking away. He's hunched over. Now that he thinks I can't see him, he walks slowly… carrying a bundle of sorrows on his back.

VALENCIA. SEPTEMBER 1937

I'm in an enormous house whose name I can't remember. The caretakers have turned the building into a boarding house.

They've provided a room split in two by a divider and a mattress on the floor. I sleep badly, and my entire body aches.

No one knows anything about the children's refuge. The cook in the boarding house tells me he saw a truck filled with children on its way to Albacete.

I leave early. The streets are lined by single-story white houses, the sky is clear, the temperature delightful, lots of people coming and going, fruit stores, vegetables, restaurants, cafes… Seems like nothing's happening!

On Calle De la Paz, the window displays are open. There are necklaces, rings, bronze figures, luxurious watches, urns. I see an elegant café and walk in. Maybe I'll have breakfast. Yes! It's goat's milk, but it's delicious.

"Señorita… Comrade."

A militiaman is in front of me, smiling.

"Isn't your name Celia?"

"Yes."

"I'm Jorge Miranda, Adela's brother. Don't you remember? A year ago in Santander."

"Ah…"

I feel my face getting red, and that embarrasses me all the more.

"It's just that…" My eyes are filled with tears.

"Alright, alright… Cheer up. You've probably seen some bad times. That goes for everyone. How's your father?"

"Off to war. I don't even know where he is right now. My granddad was executed. Aunt Julia and Gerardo… executed too. My sisters…in the refuge somewhere around here. I don't know where. I've come for them."

"What do you mean you don't know? I'm free today. I've got time to help. Give me your address. I'll look for the refuge and find your sisters. Tonight you'll be with your little ones."

We talk for over an hour. His mother and sisters are in Cartagena. He's been on active duty. Adela's boyfriend has disappeared and probably won't ever be back.

"She had a boyfriend?"

"Yes, a philosophy student, a good lad, but his father was a scoundrel and…"

He knows nothing about Uncle José and Aunt Carmelina.

"It's better not to know, girl. Because once you find out it's worse."

He's been injured. He was in the hospital.

"I've never had more fun!" he says.

He tells me about his escapades with his friends, conversations, mischief.

"The women in the militia were hurt too; when women join in on the fighting, look out! There's no match! When I was in the hospital with them, they came down for breakfast in their night clothes. '*Chicas*,' I called out to them. 'Night clothes are for sleeping. Get dressed.' And to that they answered, 'What about you? You're in your pajamas.' We couldn't convince them they were doing something wrong, but they were right. As far as I'm concerned, they could have come down for breakfast naked!"

"Don't be silly."

"I suppose you've heard worse things this year."

"Oh, my God. Have I heard worse! On the streetcar from Chamartín, ugly things, atrocious."

"It's the war. It leads to the most beastly and primitive behavior we all have within us. It seems everything that civilization has woven into us gets loose and breaks. Can't you see it everywhere? You see it in people walking down the street. Everything's fallen apart. We've been through a spiritual earthquake; all that's sacred and intimate is shaking and on its way down. Believe me… those who start revolutions are the scumbags."

Jorge talks like *Papá*. We decide to see each other again in the afternoon at this very place.

I'm happy, I don't know why. In the boarding house on Governador Street, I have lunch with other guests, a young married couple, another couple with a little girl, two gentlemen, a woman, and her daughter. We eat fish and rice, a real banquet! We don't speak of the war. They're all surprised I'm alone and so young.

"I'm here to find my sisters and the woman who takes care of them; they're in a refuge. In Madrid there's not much left of anything…"

In these September months I spend naptime in the grand reception room with one of the residents. It's an enormous room, high ceiling, chandeliers, and floor-to-ceiling mirrors. In the middle of the room there's a bronze and marble table with old magazines on the surface. We have visitors; they all ask me about Madrid. Is there any food there? Have they executed many people? What's there for sale? Any material? Are the streetcars running? Are the streets lighted?

No, no electricity. At night Madrid doesn't look like Madrid. On clear nights when the moon and stars are shining you might be able to see the figure approaching you, but on other nights you have to walk with your arms extended like blind people. Also, the streets in the center of the city are under construction like they were before the uprising, still lots of sand, stones, and ditches, and Puerta del Sol is half destroyed, filled with debris between Preciados and Arenal.

At five I'm in the Ideal Room waiting for Jorge.

The café is crowded, not a single table is free, so I wait for him, standing at the door.

"Bad news," he says when he arrives. "The refuge where your sisters were living isn't open anymore; there's no more shelters left. Some have gone to Barcelona, others to France, Albacete, even Russia… Hey, don't look so sad, *mujer*! Hope is not lost! I imagine your little ones went to Albacete because the people who live in the building where they were staying say two cars left for Albacete, and that a woman from Segovia with a little blond girl in her arms was in one of those cars. So off to Albacete. I haven't wasted any time; here's a train ticket to Albacete, it leaves tonight."

"What time?"

"There's no set time. We'll be there at seven… because if you don't go with me, they won't let you on the train."

"Is the ticket expensive? First, second or third class? How much do I owe you?"

"Nothing… What do you mean 'class'? Pullman class, what else? We're not big spenders here. But you.., aren't you coming from Madrid, or Paris… all that luxury? You think we have classes? C'mon, don't be silly. You'll go in third class, first class, the caboose, whatever, the car for pigs on their way to the slaughterhouse… it's all the same. The thing is to get there early to make sure you have a place to sleep for the night, or several nights."

"Don't be stupid. It's just a four-hour trip."

"That was before… before those filthy rich insurrectionists, but not today; now the people are in charge and make the decisions as they see fit. You'll get there whenever. The main thing is to get there."

Just in case I don't find my sisters, I won't bring my suitcase. I'll leave it with a lady at the residence. I arrive at the train station with nothing but my overnight bag.

Jorge was right. The station is like an anthill at four in the afternoon with desperate crowds hovering around the train. I want to get on; I see a mass of people pushed together in second and third-class cars. No first class. A few people climb on top of the cars.

Jorge shoves his way through the crowds and onto the car, and I follow behind.

"Comrades," he yells. Here is a fellow comrade who's sick; she's on her way to Albacete to be with her family. Will anyone offer her a seat, or maybe make room for her, because she's very thin and she'll fit in any seat. What do you say, comrades?"

An old man stands up reluctantly.

"Thanks so much, comrade, *Salud!*" Jorge says to him.

He gives me a box of chocolates and shakes my hand.

"I don't know if I'll be here when you get back, but here's the number of the brigade I'm in. Write to me…"

He leaves… it seems he's upset about leaving me.

It's hot. I'm wearing a sweater under my jacket, the one my dressmaker made, but I don't dare take it off. I'm squeezed in my seat next to a fat woman with a lot of packages and an old man who's sitting on the edge. The noise is infernal, lots of people talking, random words I don't grasp, like:

"These are the only ones left; they're for my sister…"

"They're too big for her…"

"It was at Saler Beach…"

"They took over the land…"

"It's all so deadly…"

Curses, profanity, laughter, children crying… The passageway to the compartments is filled with people. Someone sits down on a suitcase; another sits on the floor. The ones on the platform cram in close to the door, trying to get in. It's like being in a loud and smelly house.

Night has already fallen.

"When are we leaving?" cries a loud voice.

I close my eyes trying not to see or hear. I'm thinking of the suitcase I left in the house on Governador Street. All that's left of the things my Aunt Cecilia bought me in Santander is in that suitcase. I need to take care of it, because for now I won't be able to buy anything. The girls need new shoes because they wear them out. I'll bring them from Albacete to Valencia. They say it's easy to find a furnished place, the ones people have vacated, or the ones available because the occupants were executed. Jorge promised to secure a nice furnished place for me. He's handsome! When we were in Santander, when I went to the movies with friends, the girls called him Gary Cooper, but he didn't pay any attention to them. Me, on the other hand… Ay, no!

An avalanche of people tries to take over the space in the hallway; people are yelling, and it scares me. My God, what a commotion! They're going to kill us. Some try to squeeze together on the floor; I don't know where to move my feet.

"Don't push, comrade, you have a seat…"

"Alright. Do as you please."

What was I thinking? Oh, yes. That they called Jorge Gary Cooper. He's very handsome… and a good man, yes, very good. When I write to Father, I'll say how good he's been to me. If it weren't for him I wouldn't have taken the train and I wouldn't have known what to do. When I get to Albacete I'll go to Fifina's house. I have her address on the letter. Have I lost it? No, no. If I could only move a little.

At once there's a whistle and the train begins to move, first it jerks forward, then back, and then it stops.

The man in front of me cries out: "Damn! Hey, Conductor, it's already nine… and we've been here since six, packed together like sardines."

Again the whistle blows… the train moves forward a short distance and stops.

"It can't handle the load," says the woman with all the packages, the one who smells rancid.

"Maybe we'll have to push."

Finally, the train is moving… so slowly it's barely noticeable… a little faster, rattling on, and we're out of the station. We go past streets, the buildings are lighted, and finally I see the countryside under the moon. If I only had a window next to me! It smells so bad in here that I think I'm about to faint. In my toilet bag I have some cologne. Where is my toilet bag? Maybe under that basket. Jorge put it there and then…

The lull of the constant conversation accompanies the motion of the train as I nod off, confused about my own thoughts: Father, Jorge… they are two separate people but in my thoughts they turn into the same person wearing a uniform. I fall asleep.

The train has stopped again.

"What's going on?"

"We've stopped at a station."

"It's not a station."

"They've got to clean the chimney."

The moon lightens the countryside, but you can't see the houses. The sweet smell of orange trees fills the compartment. The people who were in the hallway have gotten off.

"Is something wrong?" I ask the woman with the packages.

"No, it's that they've got to clean the soot off the chimney because there's no coal, they have to use firewood."

Another woman explains it to me, but she speaks in Valenciano, and I don't understand.

"This girl's Castilian."

"Ah, lots of Castilians are on the train."

An hour goes by. I remember the chocolate bonbons in my pocket, surely they're melted by now. But I give out what's left of them to the women accompanying me, and suddenly two children appear, so I split the last one in two. They each eat their share and stare at me.

"I don't have any more... all gone."

"*Che*, let's get back to your places... this comrade has given you what she has... That's the way we are," she says philosophically, "the more you give us, the more we want."

The train begins to move again. The ones who've gotten off run alongside it so they won't be left behind. People on the train cry out to them:

"C'mon, faster... jump on before it's too late."

Now it's dark inside the train and I'm about to go to sleep. They turned off the lights, and I fall fast asleep... the hours pass.

Suddenly the train stops and I wake up. In the moonlight I can see we're at a station.

Someone coming and going with a lantern in his hand shines light on the passengers. People are getting off the train as others get on. More get off. The woman next to me gathers all her belongings and after wishing us a good trip, she repeats:

"*Salud*, comrades, to your health." And she steps down.

Now I'm sitting next to the window; this allows me to lean my head against the boards and sleep more comfortably. The heavy coat I've had to carry with me throughout the trip now serves as a blanket. There are no more people in the hallway. They probably got off at other stations.

I fall asleep again, not noticing when the train begins to move, nor do I wake up when it stops. Suddenly, the morning cold makes me open my eyes. The sky is clearing. I don't recognize any of the passengers in front of me. They're all sleeping: a man, an old woman, a younger woman who leans her head on my shoulder. A blue-eyed militiaman is sitting in front of me, his eyes opening and shutting as he looks out the window into the countryside, singing. A sweet and sad melody accompanies the rhythmic movement of the train… and the words:

Pour la paix et pour la liberté. (For peace and liberty.)

He's French. I notice his dark face, his broad forehead and clear eyes. He's a Frenchman who's left his homeland to help us! There's something mystical and passionate in his eyes and in his face. He doesn't look at me. He gazes at the morning horizon as it changes color with the sunrise; he's absorbed in his own high thoughts and in the miracle of a new day.

But once again the constant rhythmic rolling overcomes me, and I fall asleep.

When I wake it's daytime and we're in Albacete. Everyone is up gathering their luggage. I don't recognize anyone around me. What happened to the Frenchman?

Here's my toiletries and my coat… I exit into the turmoil of the station; it's all so dusty, filthy… it smells of misery…

ALBACETE

With the return address on Fifina's letter I ask directions of every pedestrian as I walk down the streets and wide tree-lined avenues with kiosks selling pamphlets and newspapers, as if I were in a grand city.

It's a beautifully sunny day with an aroma of thyme all around. The tragic desperation I was feeling on yesterday's train has turned into calmness, a sweet rustic peace evoked by that mystical militiaman. How pleasant the smell of thyme. The aroma goes right to the heart; it widens my thoughts and excites me... makes me happy.

There it is... among those new houses. It only has two stories and a tiled doorway with walls painted green.

I knock on the door; no one answers so I knock again. I move to the middle of the street and call out; the windows are low, not a single one has glass.

Fifina opens the wooden doors:

"Is that you, Celia?"

It's a pretty and comfortable house, and like everywhere in this city, it's filled with the smell of thyme.

"That's because here we light candles with thyme; soon you'll see the donkeys covered with sacks of thyme for sale."

Surprisingly, Fifina's aunts appear at once; they look older than when I last saw them; they chatter incessantly without holding their breath.

"You have no idea how horrible the bombings have been. Fifina'll tell you all about it."

Fifina has to take her place in line for the food rationing so it's the aunts who tell me about the bombs; they shed tears, unable to finish a sentence telling me about what happened that fateful night when they lost their nephew:

"The most honorable man in the world. Such goodness, … wisdom. Twenty years a lawyer in this city. Loved and respected by all… and to die like that!"

They tell me they were safe at home glued to the radio listening to news about the war, and suddenly, a horrid noise, as if the sky were falling again; the balcony doors forced open, the glass breaking, and the whole house rocking as if it were about to fall.

"We escaped onto the street, we ran and ran, there were dead bodies everywhere, the wounded crying out. Among them was my nephew who lived around the corner with his son. But we didn't know, how could we know? Fifina tugged us along and we kept running… I don't know how God gave us the strength to run. The bombing kept up, and the airplanes swooped down so low that we thought they were going to crash on our heads. We ran into a meadow, but it wasn't a meadow, more like a corral with no way out. So we ran out the way we came in, and then kept on running, the roar of the planes and the bombs all around us. It was like the end of the world. Until finally we stumbled out, falling; we arrived at a cultivated plot of land, so we threw ourselves on the furrows… And what do you think those wretched people did? They shined lights on us with their reflectors, and when they saw us running, their bombers came down on us with their machine guns, firing at us from the planes. Scoundrels! I screamed at them. You call yourselves Christians? Did God tell you to do this?"

When Fifina returned we kept on talking about the terror. Their nephew, poor guy, was in his house when they came to tell him he should flee before they destroyed the whole city; so against his will, he left the house with his son.

And when they were on their way out, a bomb exploded in front of them.

They threw themselves on the ground and covered their heads with their hands. And that's where they stayed.

Fifina couldn't stop talking about it:

"You can't imagine what it was like the other day. They stormed into the jails and took the fascist prisoners, beat them, and executed them without pity."

"Bad move," says the aunt who saw no remedy in their behavior. "When their fascist friends get wind of this, they'll come back and… Good God! This is not living! I don't sleep at night!"

We had breakfast. They were able to get condensed milk, even cocoa.

"Not much, *hija*. They sell it to us for the price of gold, we were lucky to find it in all this mess."

Now it's my turn to tell what's happened to me. They haven't even asked me why I'm here. They just keep on talking.

"*Hija*, in these times we're not surprised by anything. Everything is possible. You got here in the middle of all this chaos and destruction… We didn't even ask you how you got here."

So I tell them about my departure from Madrid, how I got on a military truck with the troops, wood panels falling off so there was no place to sit, how the kids tried to fix the canvas covering the truck while some nearly fell out… and the woman who kept yelling…

"*Chico*, you're gonna fall out, and then we'll have to stay here for more than an hour, until they can get rid of your body… like the other guy."

I told them about my arrival at Valencia, that big house on Governador Street, and my interaction with Jorge.

"Stay away from that militiaman, he's just like the others, a scoundrel," says doña Ramona.

But I go on about how I met him in Santander, how he kindly went looking for my sisters, how I was able to get on the train because of him…

"Alright, alright… it's better for you not to see him anymore. You'll never know his intentions, he might even take you to his captain and marry you… because even Mangada's wife is marrying people… and listen, *hija*, any marriage out of the Church doesn't count. I'm telling you this because I know all about it!"

Fifina and I laugh and then Fifina says:

"So is that guy really that interesting?"

"Yes, *hija*, but never mind. We haven't even thought about each other, not him, not me, nothing like that. That's for sure! But imagine what it's like to be in a strange city like Valencia, not knowing where to go and finding help like that."

Here people don't know anything about children's shelters. Some of them were here a while ago, but now they're in Alicante. To make sure, we asked a few people working in shelters, but no one knows where my sisters are.

"They've taken the children away from Valencia."

Some tell me they're in Barcelona, others say they're dropped off at farmhouses in the rural areas where they're safe from the bombs.

I stay in Albacete for two days. Fifina doesn't want me to go to Valencia by train.

"You've seen what it's like to travel like that. It's frightening, and each day it gets worse. We'll find you a car. You'll see."

These autumn days in Albacete are glorious. We walk through the public garden, slowly at the same pace with the old ladies who expose their numb bodies to the sun. At night we listen to the radio as the poor women say the rosary. Doña María, the eldest, the spiritual one, spouts out a child-like prayer:

"Lord, may no one kill anymore, may the airplanes break down so they can't fly, and may the gunpowder get wet, may all be wise, and no longer act like brutes. Amen."

On the third day, they come to tell us that a car is leaving for Valencia from the hospital. I say goodbye to those good women who have shared bread with me, no matter how scarce it is, and I leave with Fifina.

At the hospital she talks to the doctor. The ambulance drives away someone who's been injured; his parents follow behind in a car. They let me go along with them.

Their son is moved by a stretcher onto the Red Cross ambulance. The mother, a white-haired woman who seems to have resigned herself to the situation, is standing next to the ambulance talking to the injured one. The father, a silent man who gestures a hello to me, takes a seat next to the driver.

At last the woman enters the car and sits next to me after her husband calls her several times.

"Good day, señorita."

"Thank you so much, *Señora*, for allowing me to accompany you."

She gestures with her hand indicating there's nothing to thank her for. The ambulance starts and we follow close behind.

"Farewell, Fifina… Farewell… *Salud*…"

For a while we're silent. A radiant sun shines on the stubbles of growth in the countryside, releasing natural perfumes like incense emanating from this dry, burnt, ardent earth… I feel I should talk to this woman.

"Is he hurt badly?"

"Yes, very badly, he took a bullet in the chest… They're taking him to die in our house."

"Shush," utters the father upon hearing her.

We move along in silence. About an hour later the ambulance stops, and we do the same. The mother and father get out of the car and run toward the ambulance.

"They're aristocrats," the driver tells me. "Good people, in spite of it all. No one dares point them out."

They stay close to the ambulance for some time. It seems they are arguing with a person in the Red Cross. Finally the ambulance is ready to continue, and the countess returns to the seat next to me. Her face is contorted.

"Let's go," she says. "My husband will continue the trip in the ambulance."

She speaks no more. Later she covers her face, sobbing. Devastating sobs…

Their son has died along the way.

THE SNAIL

When I arrive at the boarding house I find a letter from Jorge: "Before I left I found a place for you in a dwelling owned by women I know: Colón Street 25. They're expecting you. Jorge."

But if I don't find my sisters I wouldn't have to move, he says…

"*Mujer*, you need to find out what it's about," Angustias says to me; she's the one taking care of my suitcase in the boarding house.

There's a letter from Father at the post office on Constitución Street! "Whatever happens, don't leave Valencia before I get there. Kisses to Teresina and María Fuencisla."

The house on Colón Street is ancient, with a wide terrace and wooden balustrade. I'm greeted by a woman who looks as old as the house, tall, distinguished, reserved.

"There are two rooms on another floor. Come, I'll show you."

She takes me to a dark room filled with closets; we go down the stairs, more closets, a door with stained glass, and a little room with furniture from another century: two chests of drawers, a round table, two straw chairs, an old gas lamp converted into an electric one, and an old picture card.

"Here is where you can tidy up."

A vanity! A table with a mirror and a little drawer. It's a dressing table that looks about two hundred years old.

The room has a balcony, an adjoining bedroom with an enormous bed, and hangers in the closets. It smells like clean linen, apples, and lavender.

"I'll take it ma'am. I'll grab my suitcase, and tonight I'll sleep here."

Here I am, it's as if there's no revolution, no war front, no executions. I've taken refuge in a time of peace in the history of Spain. When? The reign of Fernando VII? Or Carlos IV? No, before that. Maybe something in those historical novels by Galdós.

I go out to the balcony overlooking a quiet, narrow street where no one passes by. The girls can bask in the sun here. Valeriana will accompany them, and I'll watch from the balcony. All three of us will sleep in an immense bed.

My search for the girls has been useless. I talk to the doorman. Yes, he remembers Teresina.

"She was a chatty girl, funny, and the other one had golden blond hair. You know, they're probably in Barcelona," he whispers to me, "I think few of us will survive this. They say the government is moving to Barcelona. Sure… They bomb Sagunto every day, and not a day goes by without troops passing by. It's best to head close to the border just in case…"

I buy roses at the sidewalk flower shop. Heavens, what beautiful roses! I've never seen anything like them. They say they're the prettiest in the world. I haven't seen all the roses in the world, but surely there are no roses more beautiful than these.

I find a modest restaurant for lunch, later for supper I'll just have *café con leche* in the Ideal Room…

I wonder what the women staying in this boarding house think of the war. The mother is very old; she was a pianist, cultured, religious. The eldest daughter has a little girl, I don't know if she's married or a widow. She has another girl too, blond, pretty, modern, who works who knows where; she's out all day. And there's a niece: dark hair, pale, green-eyed, listless, doesn't move much. She's my age, but although she's polite, she never says anything, and she answers me with one-syllable words. It's her house. The doorman greets her reverently. They must be aristocrats. But what's wrong with them? What's happened to the men of this house? They never talk about them. At night they invite me to converse with them, but when the war comes up, they change the subject. They don't have servants. They cook their own food and wash their own clothes with their delicate hands. The blond one accompanies me sometimes to the Ideal Room, and I talk about my sisters and my father. They ask me if I have a boyfriend. No, I say. On my identification card it says I'm twenty-two: they have no idea I'm barely seventeen. There are two married couples. One of these women is young and lovely; she looks like a doll with golden hair. Her fair complexion blends with her hair. The other one is dark, decisive, energetic. They tell me she's an artist and that her paintings are marvelous.

Another letter from Father!

"The girls are in Barcelona. I understand why you worry about them. But now that you know they're safe and content, you must wait patiently for me to arrive. I'm in Extremadura. Send me letters as you always do. I see that you are still judicious, and the family you are with seems agreeable. Please send them my regards."

The autumn days in Valencia are always sweet and pleasant, and the parks are beautifully cultivated. Sometimes I sit under a tree for hours. If it weren't for the troops constantly moving up and down the street and for the constant commotion, all those people rushing around in the middle of the war, you'd think nothing was happening.

One morning the blond one, Isabel, calls me.

"Come up, Celia. A militiaman is looking for you."

It's Jorge.

"How are you? How are your sisters?"

"I didn't find them."

"I'm sorry, *Mujer*, tell me about it! Let's go to the café. I'm on leave for four days. I'll spend two of them here and the other two in Cartagena.

His sudden appearance caused suspicion in the *señora* and her blond daughter who keeps spying on me from the kitchen door. But this didn't keep me from going off with Jorge.

We talk in the café.

"Your father's right. Don't leave here until he arrives. I can't help you because I'm stationed in Barcelona. It's an enormous city, and you, all alone, not knowing where to go, and no clue about where your little ones are…
The people here are a gift either from God or the devil; they'll surely treat

you well… The niece's mother and father are in jail; they executed the eldest daughter's husband. He was caught in a neighborhood in Valencia–Saler."

"How?"

"Saler's the posh beach close to here… They were falling like flies. There've been many crimes! Don't think that on the other side they are any better than us."

"I know, I know…"

"We're a bunch of beasts, just beasts. Everything they call civilization and culture is a façade, like a curtain that falls with the smallest shove. Do you want revolution?"

"Me?"

"No, *mujer*… I'm talking to the ones who started this. So you want revolution? Well there it is… We're all a bunch of assassins."

"Not you."

"No, me too."

"But you wouldn't execute anyone."

"Yes, *hija*, yes… like anyone else. The first days of the war I was in Villaverde with my detachment… they came over to me and said, 'The train from Jaen is about to arrive with the bishop, his brother, and his family, along with pigs and pig farmers traveling with them…" I asked, "you want us to make them get off the train and execute them right here?…""Go to it," they say. The passengers were trembling when they got off. Some of us grab their papers. Yes, it's them, maybe one of them is a Republican… At least that's what some say. 'Alright, get in line.' 'Are you going to kill us?' they ask. The bishop was pale as he blessed them. We lined them up, the forty poor bastards. And bang… The bishop was the only one to fall. They had all aimed at him, covered him with bullets… So again they lined them up and fired. Some ran away, so we hunted them down."

"Lord!"

"*Mujer*, are you crying? *Mujer*! … I assure you that I turned into someone else. Usually, I'm incapable of killing a fly. I catch butterflies in my hand so they can bask in the sun. It's the beast we all have inside us that made me do it… It's contagious, it's about pride, just so they don't think we're soft. *Mujer*! Are you getting mad at me now? After all… I'm mad at myself for being capable of doing such a thing... Actually, I'm more furious at the one who caused it all. That one! I'd execute that one right here and now, and my hand would not tremble!"

"Maybe the one you shot first wasn't a bishop."

"Maybe. Who knows? It's all the same.. he was a poor man... Yes, poor women too, and poor men..."

For the next minute we are silent. Then he changes the subject, but I'm still upset, and I can't stop crying.

"Girl, you're like butter from Soria, it melts as soon as you lay eyes on it. I was thinking of asking if you wanted to go to the theater tonight. Amalia Isaura is performing, and that other one... I forgot his name. Would you like to go?"

"Yes, let's go."

I ask the *Señora* for the key.

"I assume it's alright with your father."

"Of course. My poor father only wants me to be happy and have a good time."

"Yes, I know, that's what fathers want these days."

I don't know what she means by that, but from her tone, I don't think it's anything good.

I wear a clean, white, ironed blouse. I grab a dress and a brooch. My hair is well-brushed; it shines like a golden crown. I like the way I look. My God, is it possible for me to be happy again? It's only been a year since Granddad, Aunt Julia, and Gerardo were killed. I make the sign of the cross and kneel beside the bed to pray. "Our Father who art in heaven..."

The moon lights up the streets. Jorge is waiting for me at the entrance to the theater. Such a happy night! The theater is filled with many militiamen, the balcony too, lots of ladies, young and old, dressed to the nines.

It's true that here in Valencia women dress more formally than in Madrid. There we were all workers and pretended to be so by dressing casually. Here I've even seen a woman wearing a hat.

Jorge's two days off pass by too quickly. We have our midday dinner in a restaurant on Las Barcas Street where they serve two typical dishes: rice and two slices of meat in a sauce. Young waiters serve it to us elegantly on clean tablecloths. In the evening we go to a restaurant below street level on the Plaza de la Constitución, and later on we go to a show or a movie. The night ends with a walk down dimly lit streets toward the boarding house; he opens the door and lights matches so I can find my way up my floor.

No doubt Clara de Monteverde, the *señora*, is scandalized.

A torrential November rain falls for two days. I only go out to eat or to a bookstore. It pains me not to see my little ones; I wonder how they are! I sit in a chair next to the balcony and gaze outside, listening to the rain fall on the quiet, narrow street.

One night, after I go to bed, I hear pounding on the entrance door. Women's voices shouting.

"*Señorita* Celia… Celia…"

I slip on my robe and go down the stairs. It's the blond one, Isabel.

"They're looking for you, Celia."

"At this hour?"

"Three women traveling."

They're in the hallway, illuminated by the lights of a chandelier. It's Fifina and her aunts carrying suitcases and blankets.

"Here we are, *hija*… There was a bombing raid last night so we couldn't wait any longer. We were going to our cousins' house, but Aunt Ramona lost the address. I remembered your address, so we came here."

Sofía listens to the explanation without saying a word. And me? What can I say? This is not my house, so I can't invite them in.

"Is there an inn or a hotel where they can stay the night?" I ask.

In the street the rain continues to fall. We decide that Fifina and I should look for lodging while the aunts wait here. I go back to my room to get dressed: raincoat, umbrella, and galoshes.

"Let's go."

First the Hotel de Inglaterra that's close by, then the Comercio, and then a boarding house, Peña Luisa. When we pound on the doors, they take ages to greet us. Finally, when a doorman or someone who looks like the owner comes to the door, he tells us he doesn't have a single free bed.

"People are sleeping on blankets in the hallways. We're filled. All of Madrid has moved here."

When we go down Calle de la Paz, someone calls me.

"Celia, don't you recognize me? Where are you going at this hour?"

He's a friend of Jorge, a young man I met in the theater. His name is José María; he's from Madrid.

I tell him our story, and he thinks for a moment:

"You're not going to find anything, but…maybe here in the Headquarters of our party, they'll let you stay the night. There's a nice couch, and if you have blankets, you can use it for a bed."

We go with him to a house where there's a light at the top of the stairway. He speaks to someone for a moment and comes back to us.

"It's all arranged. Go fetch the ladies right away because they're about to close."

We run in the rain. Doña Ramona and doña María wrap themselves up in their raincoats, all set to go out. Then doña Clara appears on the stairs.

"No, don't go… You can stay in my house. You can have my bed and I'll sleep somewhere else."

I try to tell her we'll be alright elsewhere, but Fifina and her aunts are so happy they don't have to go out in the rain that they accept the invitation immediately. Here all the beds are enormous, so the two sisters can be in one bed and Fifina in my bed with me…

We talk until dawn.

"You'll see what a good time we'll have, Fifina. We'll go out in the afternoons. There's a beautiful park on the other side of the river. It's the Guadalquivir River; it barely has any water because of all the irrigation."

In a few days they found their cousin's address in the telephone book, so off they go in a streetcar that circles the entire city. Happily it has stopped raining. A radiant sun now illuminates the city, and all the parks are damp from the rain.

Fifina and her aunts move into a small house with children, paper flowers and a clay figure of a black man reading a newspaper… The cousin is a plump lady filled with good intentions.

"I'm offering what I have, and I don't expect anything in return. We'll get along just fine; when there's love and trust…"

Doña Ramona whimpers as Fifina tries to arrange her clothes in a closet filled with the children's toys.

The following autumn days are clear and warm. Fifina and I go out every day. I loan her books, and we try to see if we can get a ration card; I haven't been able to get one.

One night we hear sirens.

"It's coming from Sagunto," says Clara, "as usual."

A screech we hear nearby makes all of us stand up.

"Here it is, *Mamá.*"

Quickly we move toward her room and stop at a corner of the hallway where, as Doña Clara assures us, there's a solid wall that won't crumble. We sit down there and wait. It looks like the noise has stopped, but it comes back. An hour later, the sirens announce the danger has passed. I wonder how Fifina's aunts are doing.

Since the night of their arrival they come back every day at various times. At midnight sometimes I hear them knocking at my door; I hear Isabel's voice.

"Celia, the sirens again. Do you want to come with us? Are you afraid?"

No, I'm not afraid. Sometimes I'm so calm that I go to sleep in the middle of a bombing raid.

"This is a solid house, nothing will happen," I tell myself.

But Fifina can't go out. Her aunts are always scared, and they don't want to be alone. Sometimes in the afternoon I have a chat in the dining room with the paper flowers and old pots and pans.

She doesn't let us in the salon because she says we'll ruin the rug; it's the only room where the sun shines in.

Fifina laughs and doña María sighs. On our way out, Fifina opens the door to the salon to show me the rug that we're not allowed to step on. It's a faded rug in front of a second-hand sofa.

"Our cousin is a nice, orderly woman" Fifina comments. "What can I say?"

I go out at night, and on my way back I hear the sirens, so I take refuge in an entranceway.

"It's coming from Sagunto," I hear someone say.

No, it's not Sagunto this time. When I return I find José María waiting for me. He's talking to doña Clara.

He says he wants to move his parents away from Madrid and that he's looking for a place for them. They're bringing along their servant who's been with the family since he was born.

"Wait a minute. As you can see, the bombers pay us a visit every day…"

"Bah, hunger is worse. In Madrid people are eating grass they find in the outskirts of the city. I can't do anything for them there. And since Celia is doing so well here, and Jorge spoke so well of all of you…"

No, doña Clara says she can't take in any more people… but she has a friend who lives on the other side of the street. So she tells him to come by tomorrow and she'll let him know.

Everything has been arranged: José María's mother and father are living in a house with an old-style façade, fancy railings, and colored tiles. José María has brought her an enormous bouquet of roses, and doña Clara distributes them two-by-two or three-by-three among all the pots and pans that she hangs in the hallways, salon, and dining room.

Hours go by as I sit on the balcony, gazing at the narrow street. The façade in front lets me know when the sun sets, first over the spider webs on the iron railings, and then fading over a corner of the street until it's dark. This morning I heard something or someone whimpering. It was a cat. It looks dead, spread-out on the sidewalk next to the wall… suddenly it lifts its head and meows sorrowfully.

"It's Michi! My poor little one!"

He doesn't hear me; he doesn't move. My God, how sad it is to see a helpless animal suffer! I'm sure doña Clara won't let me bring him in.

I worry about him all morning. When I go back to the balcony after lunch, I don't see him. Someone's taken him away. I don't want to think about it.

I've brought roses; I place them in a vase. Lord, they're marvelous! I prune the excess leaves and clean the ones left. A snail! There's a snail in the leaves! Poor snail! He'll live with me now and I won't be alone anymore. We'll live our lives together.

I place soft leaves on him so he can eat, then I put him on top of the dresser. At night I can't find him… Where could the litter bugger have gone? There he is under the dresser.

From now on every night I'll put him under a dish so he'll stay with me.

NOVEMBER 1937

Jorge tells me I have to join a political party. "You think you can go around in the world without knowing what you want?"

I laughed. What do I know about politics?

"I belong to… whatever party my father and you belong to."

"He's Republican. He's a very good man, you know."

"You've got grand ideas, Celia. You want to belong to the party of the good guys, right? Well, I'm a communist. If you'd like, tomorrow I'll introduce you to members of the party. It's best to be a member of a party these days; that way you have people to protect you when the going gets tough. I had my mom and my sisters join. They don't know much about all that. But they're members of the party, and that's what counts."

"But I don't know what that party is?"

"That's alright, you're not stupid so you'll learn immediately. Tonight I'll show you the party platform and tomorrow I'll introduce you to Ugarte, they'll give you a card… and there you are. Look, I'm leaving on Thursday, no one knows where your father is, the bombs are falling every day, food is scarce, and… by the way, where do you have breakfast these days?"

"Nowhere, I barely eat."

"Christ, so you're just like me."

"There's no more milk, and I've had to stop going to the restaurant because my stomach is really aching."

"Me too, *mujer*. I'm feeling something in my stomach; maybe it's an ulcer. So I can't eat rice or sauce, and no red meat... You?"

"Well with my ration card every two days they give an egg and toothpicks, and scraps. And that's what I eat."

Jorge offers to help me find food. He brings me milk, cocoa, potatoes, eggs; we cook our meals on my electric stove.

From that day on we eat in my room. Boiled potatoes with butter are our first dish, then poached eggs, water, and milk.

Doña Clara probably doesn't approve of this, but her good manners keep her from saying anything; in fact she acts as if she doesn't know what's going on.

Nothing's happening! Jorge comes by around 12:30. I've set the table for him and I'm cooking the potato puree. The room smells really good, like roses and warm melted butter.

"So... did you read the Communist party platform?"

"Yes."

"So right now we'll go see Ugarte... My leave is about to end; before I say goodbye I want to make sure everything's in order."

"But I don't want to belong to this party."

"Really? Now I've heard it all. And why not?"

"Because I don't want to. Because I don't like what the platform says. I don't want to be told what to do, and I don't want to be denounced for this or that, and people meddling in what I do."

"Where did you read that?"

"Right here on this page. I want everybody to do what they want to do, and anyone who wants to live in a palace with gardens to take walks should do it if they can. You know how much I love gardens?"

"Sure, you think you'll be the owner of a palace and all the fields around it."

"No! I'm content with looking at them through iron bars knowing that in the palace there're people who know how to look after them. As for me... No. I'm happy with a little garden."

"Well, many people don't have anything like that little garden."

"You see? I don't like that either. I just want everyone to have what they want, and if they want to have a pretty house, let them have it, and if they want…"

"And if they want a palace…?

"Never. People who have never lived in a palace don't want to. They're like me. Imagine what would happen if poor people lived in those palaces on Castellana and they brought their luxurious armchairs to the sidewalks and sat down to sunbathe. Or if they hung out their clothes to dry on the balcony where you can see the dust on the chandeliers and everything is out of place. They're worse off there than in an encampment in the countryside; when they want to leave, they leave."

"It's because they don't appreciate works of art."

"That's it. The real owners of these things can appreciate art but they don't know there's nothing better than sitting in the sun on an autumn afternoon… and washing your clothes in clean water from the stream and hanging it out to dry in the sun and breathing the delicious aroma of fresh air."

"*Chica,* it's all poetry to you."

"You don't get it! One afternoon Father explained to me that he defended the rights of the common people to go to school along with millionaires and doctors and that there should be no difference between them other than what nature has given them. But he didn't say they were all rich or all poor, or that anyone should tell them what to do. No. The first thing is for people to be free and do what they want."

"*Chica,* with those ideas I don't know which party is best for you."

"None of them. I don't want to belong to a party."

"Well, do you think I agree with everything the Party says? Bah, we'll win the war… or maybe we'll lose."

"Don't say that."

Jorge stays silent for a moment and gazes at the street. His skin is so tan that you'd think he was made of velvet.

"Alright… when the war is over, who knows who will take over the government. I care as much about the government as about the Camino to Santiago. But now, *mujer,*" his voice gets louder, "now for your own good… Remember that I have to leave, and I don't know if I'll get back because I'm going to the front. We don't know when your father's coming back either, and we don't know where your sisters are. The bombings are getting worse. The government is moving to Barcelona, and it's possible you'll have to go there too, alone, just a kid, in the middle of an enormous, unfamiliar city."

"I'll always have God."

"Ah, of course. Now I know what party you belong to, the party of God... Isn't that it?"

"Yes, that's it. If you only knew... I've felt a providential hand guide me through these strange years. For example, right here... when I arrived, what would I have done if you weren't around?"

"Oh, sure. By delegation, that's how you think God makes himself known."

"Don't laugh. That's the way it is. God doesn't show himself like in the icons..."

Jorge is a good man, but he's not convinced of anything, like *Papá*. He doesn't have Father's absolute faith that we'll win the war, it's that faith that sustains him and it's rubbed off on me.

In Valencia there's lots of violence. Every day we see trucks leaving for Barcelona, filled with government office furniture. At night they bomb Sagunto and the outskirts.

But in spite of that, the days remain clear and the bustle in the street makes it look like it's a holiday. There's a candy shop on Blasco Ibáñez Street where they sell sweetcakes, so I get in line to buy one.

There's a blouse too. I've been by the window display, and finally I decide to buy it. It's silk: white with crystal buttons. I try it on in front of the mirror in my room and I see that the shoulders are too big. I spend the afternoon fixing it, and finally it fits.

I need shoes. But since I'm running out of the money Father gave me, I don't dare spend more. I'll just go to a cobbler and have these repaired, and that way I won't have to buy new ones. I've seen a place where they clean and fix shoes. I go there with my shoes wrapped in newspaper. There're lots of people in the shop. Three men are chatting while they're waiting for their shoes to be shined. One is fat with a face that makes him look foolish. The other two are young. They all look like they're well-to-do, even though they're wearing rustic berets.

"The performing company that's come to Teatro Principal is very bad," says someone. "The leading lady is over fifty, and there's an idiot who wears glasses, the other one is horrible, both of them are."

The fat one who has been listening says:

"Today everyone's against you… You walk down the street and you ask someone for directions, and they slap you in the face. There's never been people as bad as that."

The others keep talking, not paying any attention to the fat guy who goes on and on about the evil in the world.

They ask me what I'd like and quote me an outrageous price. "We don't have soles for the shoes, we don't have personnel, and you have to pay the fair price if you want to repair your shoes." So I leave; what can I do?

When I get home I find a letter from Father.

"Go to Barcelona. On Jáuregui Street you'll find a room in the house of some people from the mountains. Wait for me there."

Papá doesn't know my money is running out. I go back to the shoe repair. I tell the cobbler not to fix them. I can't afford it.

Doña Clara is concerned.

"Are you going alone? The trip is dangerous. They're still bombing the trains. Many government workers are moving away with their families.

Later she feels sorry for me.

"It's a shame, Celia. You won't be able to come back here."

"I'll come back to Valencia."

"You won't have this house to come back to. I regret to tell you that since everything is changing… it's just not the same."

I'm not sure what she's trying to tell me, but I do understand that she'll not accept me in the house. I sense my relationship with Jorge is the cause. Poor Jorge! He gave me so much advice Like a brother. José María is now in charge of taking care of me.

"He's got a big crush on you. A big one!"

"Who, Jorge? Nonsense!"

"Hasn't he told you? That guy's capable of not saying a word even when you're alone."

"He's Don Quixote in the revolution..."

I don't know why I can't sleep tonight. Jorge? He's such a good man, so loyal. Could this be love? I think so. He's all I think of. My God, I'm forgetting everything, even my little sisters.

At midnight the sirens wake me up. I'm hearing the airplanes swooping down on us. First the whistle warning and then terrifying thunder. I cover my ears..

"Celia, Celia," someone is pounding on the door. "Celia, do you want to come up with us?" It's Isabel. "Up here?

"No. No, I'm alright... I'm not afraid."

There's another roar; it's so close that the whole house shakes. I listen. Not a sound from anyone. Absolute silence. The space between one bomb and another leaves us all breathless, as if no one lived there in that space. They fly away, further away, then no one can hear them. They've left. The sirens go off. I fall asleep.

In the morning the lady who washes my clothes comments on what we heard last night:

"They've destroyed three houses. Another one on this street. The top floor is ruined and they're carrying out the dead... I think there are others they can't find."

When I go to the market to retrieve the one egg and potatoes they allow me every three days with my ration card, I look around the street.

What if that sunken house belongs to José María's parents. I continue down the sidewalk, and I look straight on. There's José María; his face is dirty, his hair messy. He's carrying a pickaxe on his shoulders.

"José María!"

He doesn't hear me so I call out to him again.

"José María!"

Now he hears me; he looks at me, but his gaze scares me. He doesn't recognize me. He goes back to his task, picking at the debris. He's careful not to stab anyone.

"José María it's me, Celia. Tell me, where are your mom and dad?"

"They're here," he tells me with a hoarse voice. "In the rubble. Here!"

And again he swings the pickaxe digging for his parents.

What horror! Amidst the shining sun! I can't stay here any longer, so I go back to the house. Now I know that the two of them are dead. They found his mother right away, but not his father.

I haven't left the house all day, and I haven't eaten anything. I'm scared to go back there to see José searching in the rubble.

Night has fallen, and they tell me they found his father's body and that the workmen are clearing up the ruins to make way for cars.

I leave the house and I'm on my way to the station. When does the train leave for Barcelona? There's one train every night but it's always so full that there won't be any tickets for eight days, so if I don't get them now, I'll have to wait even longer.

I go up and down talking to people in the station.

"This very night" they all say. "If not, who knows? Looks like all of Valencia is moving to Barcelona."

I buy a ticket. On the ninth I'll get on the eight o'clock train, and I'll be there.

"When or if you get there," says the ticket agent, "it'll be at twelve midnight. There's been a lot of bombings, so we have to clear the tracks of the rubble. Some of the stations are nearly destroyed. In these times, we're all aware of such things… I advise you to be here an hour before to be sure. Don't you have someone who can help you find a seat?"

"No!..."

I think of Jorge, of José María

"No, I don't know anyone who can help."

An old man in the ticket booth waves at me.

"Look, *Señorita*, I'll tell you something, just you. If you can, when you're in Salmerón, go to the office that sells tickets for sleeper cars. Buy a ticket, and you'll be better off. These are cars that belong to the French government, so no one dares assault them. In the other ones you have to struggle to find a seat; the ones who find them are the strongest. Every day there's fistfights. All the windows are broken, and the nights are cold."

"Thank you for the warning," I tell him.

I go in the direction he told me and spend more money on a sleeper leaving Thursday.

Fifina is desolate. Doña Ramona's sick; she doesn't get out of bed, but when she hears the sirens, they have to carry her to the shelter because if not, she starts to scream.

"Imagine this every night."

These nights I spend my time arranging my clothes, sewing socks, and preparing my suitcase. My stomach is feeling better. I stay at home; I spend an hour or two in line to get a slice of sweet cake or something that looks like a pastry. I bring some for Fifina, the little that I've saved; then I send a package to Guadalupe who's still in Madrid, she's probably hungry.

I'd like to say goodbye to José María, but I don't know how to find him. I ask someone in his brigade.

"Comrade Estrada. His parents died in a bombing raid eight days ago; he left for the front at Teruel. He was half crazy... because he made his mom and dad move here from…!"

I'm leaving tomorrow. Tonight is my last night sleeping in this comfortable, wide bed. I say goodbye to the little quiet street, to the parlor, to the old dresser. Where is the snail? He's not there. I've forgotten him and he's left.

The train leaves today. Today at seven I'll be at the station.

"I'll always have fond memories of the three months I've spent with you. Goodbye, Isabel, keep being gay, active, and blond. Goodbye María, kindhearted María, such a workhorse. And you Inés, you've barely said a word to me but you have such divine and mysterious eyes. Goodbye, everyone!"

Fifina is waiting for me at the station.

"Don't go."

"Why do you say that? *Papá* has called for me. My sisters aren't here; there's no reason for me to stay in Valencia."

On the station platform I speak to the one in charge of the sleepers.

"What time do we arrive?"

"*Señorita…* The train that left yesterday was fire-bombed; it's all burned. But the tracks are clear now."

"Did you hear that?" I ask Fifina. She's scared.

"Yes, I knew that; that's why I told you not to go."

"Bah, *hija*. They bomb Valencia every night."

 The man in charge of the sleepers listens to us and says:

"You better get on the train and into your compartment because I'm about to lock the doors before more travelers get here. And don't lean out the window. I'm going to shut them."

"Goodbye, my dear Fifina. I'll write. If you see Jorge, tell him I've had to go. Goodbye."

The sleeper has a soft rug; it's comfortable, it smells of expensive perfume, an aroma I'd forgotten. It's nice to be rich; it's especially good after living in such misery. But Father tells me to always be austere and restrained.

I can hear the travelers through the closed windows, screams… and then a ruckus; they've come to give blows.

I'm alone in a two-person compartment. There's no dining car even though it's a first-class train. I eat two pieces of chocolate and go to bed.

When I wake up it's midnight. We're speeding through a moonlit countryside. The sea appears behind the window. Then it disappears behind trees and houses. At a distance, you can see flames. As the train approaches the fire, I see the skeleton of an entire train on the other side of the tracks. Only the iron remains. I'm awake for a long time before I sleep.

BARCELONA. CHRISTMAS

There is nothing more depressing to me than this cold and cloudy afternoon as I get off the train at the Barcelona train station.

There is just one vehicle for all the passengers needing transportation to the city, so I have to wait my turn. My God, I barely have any money! On the ride from the station I'm thinking that if *Papá* doesn't send me money soon, I'm going to have a hard time.

I arrive at a narrow street with a dark entrance to a boarding house with a filthy stairway. A grumpy old woman opens the door, and when I tell her who I am she cries:

"Herminia… Herminia! Come here. The girl we've been waiting for is here!" And then she says to me, "I hope you don't want to stay for more than a few days, because we've rented your room to a traveler."

She shows me a large room with a balcony whose door is shut because it's nighttime. There's an unmade bed.

"Look, look at the mattress, brand new, and clean. We're poor, but clean."

She shows me how to open the mirrored cabinet.

"Be careful, cause it'll fall flat if you push too hard. That traveler was a strong guy, and when he opened it a nail fell out. But look, if you press here and pull it open you'll be fine."

I place my suitcase and coat on two upholstered chairs with tassels; they're very fragile.

"No, don't put nothing on the chairs, they'll get dirty," she tells me as she places the suitcase on the floor and hangs up the coat. "They're nice chairs; we bought them at an auction, cost us an arm and a leg. If ya don't take care of things, they won't last, isn't that right, *Señorita?*"

"Yes, so true."

I'm tired and sleepy, but it takes me a while to get into bed. Two old ladies help her make the bed. They put a thick cloth between the sheet and the mattress. They smooth out the sheets and ask me one question after another: 'You got a mother? Where's your *Papá?* How come you're traveling alone?'

"So young; it's dangerous out there."

At about ten they finally leave me alone after bringing me a glass of water and advising me to shut off the lights soon.

I'm hungry; I haven't had anything to eat all day. I look for the chocolate that was in my suitcase, but I don't find it. So I give up and go to sleep.

In the morning when I open the balcony, I see something that makes me happy. There's a garden. The sun is shining, birds are singing from a branch: two or three identical notes.

The chocolate appears, and I find an electric burner so I can boil water. I'm almost happy! But I can't let these women know I'm using their electricity...

I wash myself in a sink, the size of a large coffee cup. I arrange my clothes in the cabinet, the one that's so hard to open, and another one fixed to a wall with cobwebs that make it look repugnant. Cobwebs on the upholstered chairs too, and probably some I can't see; I'm sure they haven't been moved in years.

I go out into the street. I've counted the money I've left. It's less than fifty *pesetas!*

I walk by a huge building; it's the post office on a wide street illuminated by a pale sun: there's a plaza with a statue of Columbus. I take a tram to the Plaza de Cataluña. The sun is shining on the plaza where doves hop along the green grass. Statues, fountains Some old folks in cafés sit in the sun, mothers sew and read with their children. A peaceful sensation. I only have forty-eight *pesetas* left. Does *Papá* know there's not much money left? Will I have to pay my rent in advance?

I have lunch in a modest restaurant: soup and a couple of thin slices of meat, eight *pesetas*. I write Father, and after mailing the letter, I go back to the plaza. People look at me. They're used to me because I've been there all day. A lady sits next to me; she speaks with a heavy Catalan accent. She doesn't know where the children's shelters are. She heard that close to the Tibidabo there's a building that used to be a palace where an aristocratic minister lives, and now it's used as a refuge for children. If I want, she'll accompany me there for a visit. No, it's no bother, she says, really, on the contrary. She's happy to help. Tomorrow at ten.

It's chilly; I go to a store to see if I can buy something to eat. Slices of ham and bread. It's not as expensive as eating in a restaurant. My lord, if *Papá* doesn't send me money...

I go back to the boarding house. Under the dim street lanterns, covered with dirt, the house looks filthier and more sordid than it looked in the morning.

"How've you been today, little girl?" one of the women asks. "Don't pay no mind to the room close to yours; we've rented it to a militiaman."

Yes, there he is lying in the dumpy room next to mine. I go into my room and lock the door. What a bad idea! Renting this man a room so close to mine.

I light the burner to warm the milk. I still have cans of food Jorge gave me.

I make the bed. I'm very cold. When I think of the cobwebs, I get even colder. I'll tuck the sheets in tightly between the mattress so that no spider can get in. Suddenly I hear a noise, *chis*, and suddenly I'm in the dark. It's the heater, surely, the heater has blown a fuse.

I hear voices approaching, then knocks on the door.

"*Señorita* Celia, *Señorita*... Unplug that contraption," she saysLook what she's done. See? We've been so good to her and look what she does!"

She goes away grumbling. I unplug it and get into bed in the dark, shivering. I cover my whole body, even my head. I'm about to sleep when the overhead light goes on. I sit in the dining room to eat...

This lady has probably taken the heater that I hid in the closet and hidden the key. Now I won't be able to light it... it's so cold.

What's going on? The light dims and slowly goes out. I'm sure they'll say I lit the space heater. I hear a crash. *Jesús*! What's happening? Ah, the bombing has started again. I don't know why, but this calms me. I prefer the explosions to the shouts of these women. I count the bombs. Two… three… five… seven… two of them together. The bombers seem to be flying away. I can't hear the plane engines anymore. I go to sleep.

Again the ceiling light wakes me up. I get up to shut it off and go back to bed. I don't know what time it is when the bombs interrupt my sleep again. They're close by, so I cover my ears.

In the morning a gray light shines through the balcony; I forgot to shut the doors last night. There's a patter from the garden that sounds like rain. The sky is low, gray, and heavy.

At ten I have to be at the Plaza de Cataluña. I light the burner to make breakfast, hoping maybe nothing will happen. I heat water so I can wash. I warm some milk; it comforts me… and when I unplug the burner, *chis*, again!

I drink the milk, trembling with fear. Why am I afraid? I must be brave. There's no one here to defend me. I come out of my room and hear the two ladies speaking at once when they see me:

"You have lighted that thing again!"

"You know…"

"We can't allow that…"

I wait for them to stop talking… My God, I'm so nervous.

"*Señoras*, I'll pay to fix this in addition to the extra cost of electricity. But understand that I can't stay here without hot water. It's very cold. Also, I need to have warm milk in the morning…"

"Oh, alright, alright… Why didn't you say something? If the *Señorita* pays for it all, she can turn on whatever she wants."

For the younger sister, it's not so easy.

"But every night we'll be in the dark!"

"No," I say, "because all you have to do is pay an electrician to fix the fuse."

The repair will cost me fifteen *pesetas*.

I take the streetcar on the way to Plaza de Cataluña to see the woman who offered to help me. I look to see how much money I have left.

She's waiting for me in the Plaza. It's not raining anymore, but the sky remains gray… a sad and morbid light engulfs everything.

The Catalan woman's name is Concepción Barahona, but everyone calls her Conce. We talk about last night's bombing.

"Do you live in the neighborhood close to the pier? It's dangerous there. Every night bombs fall there… There are entire streets in shambles."

She advises me to move to the center of the city, but I can't. I explain that Father wants me to live here so he can send money to this address.

We arrive at the foot of the Tibidabo. We don't have to take the railway that takes people up the steep incline because the building we're looking for is right here on an enormous avenue with gardens and palaces on either side.

"Here it is."

Are my sisters inside? My heartbeat is driving me crazy... Oh, God, yes, they'll be inside. I can see Doña María in the window. She's the one who takes care of refugee children.

"Doña María! Doña María!"

She doesn't hear me so we go in. It's an immense house, circled by abandoned gardens.

There's a gallery with stained glass windows and a salon that adjoins another gallery with a view of the entire city and the sea… I haven't seen the Mediterranean since I arrived at Barcelona! We hear voices of children. I think I see Teresina!

A woman dressed in a white smock comes out.

"I'd like to know if my sisters are here. They left Madrid last October."

"We don't have any children from Madrid. They're all from Bilbao and Asturias. Not a single child from Madrid. But I'll show you the list of names."

"My sisters are with a nanny who's been with us for a long time; her name is Valeriana."

The lady shakes her head.

"I can assure you they're not here."

"But *Señora*, I just saw Doña María in the window; she worked at the shelter for children in Madrid."

They call doña María; she is happy to see me and kisses me on both cheeks.

"Dearest Celia! ... You thought your sisters...? No, *hija*, no. Your sisters are in France for sure. Good thing they didn't take them to Russia. Last week they... We've been staying at a farm on the road to Sagunto."

"Well I had no idea, and I've been in Valencia for three weeks!"

Doña María tells me about my sisters; she can't say enough about Teresina's grace and goodness."

"I don't know anyone more generous, not a soul! We had to look out for her to make sure she didn't give away her bread and oranges to anyone who asked. Oh, and how she loves you! One day she told us she had two mothers, one in heaven and the other is '*Mamacita Celia*.'

I was touched, she was so endearing. "The other one is a gem. So blond, so fair, with a pair of beautiful blue eyes. And Valeriana is the very picture of loyalty, devotion, and goodness..."

The lady in charge has left. Doña Conce gazes at the garden from the gallery windows while Doña María and I sit on a bench and talk to no end.

We leave at midday. It's raining.

"We can eat around here," says Doña Conce.

"I don't know if there are any modest restaurants close by."

Doña Conce looks surprised. Maybe she thinks I'm rich. I don't want her to know my real situation.

"If you don't mind, I'd prefer eating at my house; they're waiting for me."

"Ah, you eat at the boarding house. You're fortunate. These days there are no boarding houses that include meals."

We say goodbye. On my way back I buy a little dark bread and fried fish. I eat it on the street. It's raining so I duck into an entranceway hoping there's a letter from Father waiting for me.

At four I'm back home in my room. Two weeks waiting for the letter and nothing.

I visit doña Conce from time to time; she lives on Calle del Angel. She's told me about another room for me on Calle Lauria, just off Rambla de Cataluña.

She takes me to see it. It's a large room with a balcony overlooking the street, a huge closet, a beveled mirror, a bed with a wooden frame, and a desk. The room gives the house an air of gentleness, comfort, openness, and dignity with its tapestry, tasteful etchings on the walls, and the nice furniture. Also, they won't charge me any more for this room than for the filthy one I'm living in now. Still, I can't afford it. I only have a few coins left; in a short time I won't even have enough for the streetcar.

"No, I won't give up this room until *Papá* learns how in need I am."

"Look, *hija*, I'm telling you you're such a perfect child, and in these times it's appreciated."

Tomorrow it's Christmas; today I haven't eaten anything. I lie down and try to sleep, but the cold makes me shiver. Someone is knocking at the door. It's Doña Hermina.

"Were you lying down on the bed? Don't do that,''" she says with her Catalan accent. "The mattress will get wrinkled and dirty. I hope you don't lie there with your shoes on."

"No, *Señora*, I covered my feet with my scarf."

"There, just as I thought. We like to rent to males because they don't spend time here; they're always out in the street. Don't you think?"

"Yes… of course…"

"Well I was coming to bring you this. It just arrived. A letter and a piece of paper."

Letter from *Papá*! Doña Hermina keeps talking about-who-knows-what, but I don't listen.

"*Hija, mía*, soon I'll be with you; you must need money. I'm sending you a thousand *pesetas* money-order so you can celebrate Christmas. I assume you found the girls, so you must need a bigger place to stay. Try to find something in the middle of the city and send me the address as soon as possible."

The enclosed piece of paper is a notice telling me where to collect the money.

Doña Hermina has left without my noticing. Immediately, I go to the post office. These cold streets are wet from last night's rain; they're gray and depressing.

I walk up the stairs to the building leading to the entrance of the post office.

"Excuse me, where can I cash a money-order?"

"The office is over there in the corner, but it's closed. It's open from nine to two."

"Nothing I can do but come back tomorrow."

"Tomorrow? Tomorrow is a holiday; it's closed all day. Come on Monday."

I take the streetcar to Plaza de Cataluña. There's barely anyone in the plaza. Everything's cold, dirty, and gloomy. When I sit on a bench, a flock of pigeons descends and encircles me. They're hungry too. I open my hands to them.

"Nothing, I don't have anything for you, my sisters. The day after tomorrow I'll bring you some crumbs."

A strong wind blows at nightfall. The shaking trees cause the rainwater to fall on me, it drags the clouds along with it. It's a north wind, bringing snow and a cruel winter. I'm so cold!

I go back to the boarding house. I only have five *céntimos* left.

The two ladies greet me from the darkness and grime of the dining room.

"Back so soon? It's Christmas Eve!"

"I know, but I'm alone here."

I see two substantial bread loaves in a basket; I have an idea if I can buy a slice.

"Will you do me a favor? I've bought two cuts of ham and since they don't sell bread without a rationing card...""

"Here, here, my little one," one of the ladies says again in her Catalan accent. "Take a piece of bread. Take as much as you want; there's always bread left over. If you want we'll give you ten *céntimos* worth of bread in the morning. But not today, today we'll give it to you. After all, it's Christmas Eve, and God is generous to everyone."

Tonight I'll have dinner in my room next to my bed: a big slice of bread and warm sugar-water. It's Christmas Eve!

No, I don't want to be sad… I don't want to. The day after tomorrow I'll have enough money to move to the other house. Father will be here soon and we'll figure out where the girls are; nothing bad can happen to them if they're with Valeriana… I really don't want to be sad. My mother is with me tonight. I'm not alone! I'm not alone! Jorge is probably thinking of me!

The wind blows, and the trees in the garden are moving. It sounds like the sea.

JANUARY 1938

I just received a telegram from Father. "I'll be there tonight at eight." The landladies have prepared a beautiful room for him next to mine. I make the bed, and… later on: "Celia… your *Papá* is here!"

"My dear *Papaito*! Ay, you're so dark. And thinner! Come, come see your nice room! Will you go to bed right away? Tell me…"

Papá looks sad, pensive.

"Yes, *hija*, yes… I've brought you something to eat. They say there's plenty of food here, but…"

"Oh, don't believe it. Tea and caraway are all you can find in the grocery stores. But the restaurants serve food."

We talk about the girls. *Papá* has received a few notices from the Red Cross without a date or an address. The stamp indicates it's from France, and it's from Valeriana: "We are well. The girls are fat and happy. We are fine. Happy and hoping to see you."

"Surely they're in France, probably the south. If we knew for sure, I'd send you to them. But not like this. All these trips you've taken are too much for you. And you've been alone for seven months!… My poor girl!"

Then he tells me about Aunt Julia.

"I've no doubt they've executed her. It's monstrous; mind you the government is not to blame; it's the ones who tried to negotiate and then fled. It's horrible, *hija*, frightful!"

"Father, tell me. Are we losing the war?"

"If they're as strong as they say they are, yes… The League of Nations is looking for a resolution."

"It'll be like the other times… each side on its own, and nothing resolved. Don't you think?"

"No, I think this time is different, I'm hopeful. The powerful nations cannot allow what's happening to go on. It's a matter of honor. They can't permit the army to make alliances with other nations in order to impose its own government or destroy it. No, *hija*, no. You'll see. I think we're on the verge of a resolution, and we'll be able to go back to our house on Chamartín."

Papá is here with us, but his orders are to start an aviation school. I barely see him. When he leaves so early every morning I don't have anything for breakfast. We haven't had milk or coffee for a long time. For thirty *pesetas* I buy a kilo of a dark powder they say is cocoa. But it looks hideous and tastes like varnish. Father drinks it to please me.

"It's not bad, *hija*, not bad. It warms the belly. I hope it won't make us sick."

They tell me they sell cottage cheese in a dairy store on our street, but if anyone wants it they have to get to the store before daybreak. They only have enough for one person, so *Papá* says he doesn't want so it's for me.

In the dark of the morning I go down the stairs; I open the door to the street and directly to the dairy store. When they open I go in. I bring along a little sugar to blend with the curdled milk so it'll taste better. It's very sweet. I savor it slowly, sitting on a marble table. I sprinkle sugar on it. In front of me there's a girl who looks older than me; her dirty hands are cracked and blistered. She doesn't speak. Close to the corner of the dairy store I see five Australian parakeets in a cage. They're still; their feathers stand upright as if they were cold.

"Yes… they're very cold," says the lady who sold me the milk. "Years ago we had a heater, but not this year. There were twenty of them, and now just these."

A few days later I see a parakeet in the cage with its little legs upright and its claws open like it wanted to hold onto something. Poor thing!

At midday I go to a downtown restaurant with *Papá*. They serve us a small bowl of stew with two slices of meat that look transparent, an orange and a bread roll smaller than the orange. Some days they only give us half a roll.

At night I heat some powdered soup. Usually we don't have anything else, but sometimes Father brings some meat, or condensed milk, or honey. We have to make it last because we don't have this every day.

One day at lunch time we hear sirens, then the bombs. People keep on eating and don't get up until we hear windows breaking. Since then we no longer go to Plaza de Cataluña to eat. We've found a guest house on Gracia Street where they distribute food to hundreds of people.

Some days we go to a café on Cortes Street where they serve malt and small glasses of spirits. It's a pricey café. Before the war it must have been a lovely place. Now its many patrons who talk in frighteningly loud voices; there are fur coats and hats everywhere, and the tobacco smoke combined with the mist from wet tablecloths engulfs the place in darkness and dirt. Some people arrive early to ensure a table.

I like it there because it's warm inside. The streets are wet and slippery because of the rain. The room in the house where we live is always cold, unpleasant, and inhospitable. At night it's dimly lit and depressing; it's hard to read.

Now there are bombs exploding almost every moonlit night. My God, I hope it rains tonight! But nothing doing. It rains in the daytime, and in the night the air makes the clouds disappear. The moon brightens the empty streets. In my white nightgown, I'm at the mercy of falling bombs without aid or protection.

The siren shrieks in an anguished lament. The sound of the street cars subsides, the light dims so that in my room I see only incandescent threads that also disappear. The roar of motorcars is barely perceptible in spite of the weight inside them. Suddenly there's a horribly strident whistle. My God! My God! It's getting closer.

"Celia!" my father calls to me. "Celia, *hija*, are you scared? Come here."

"No, no, I'm not afraid."

Another explosion makes the house shake at the foundation... And then a deathly silence, as though all the world were shutting down, as if it doesn't want to show signs of life.

They're flying away. They're leaving! The sirens sound again, but now it's a happy sound.

On some nights they come two or three times. They tell me it's a good idea to go under the bed. In the ruins of some houses they've found people alive who've protected themselves with a bed.

The sun shines on the city, and now I'm not afraid. I've bought a gray coat with a velvet neck. It fits! *Papá* takes me to the Astoria to have tea.

The Astoria has a small tea salon just above a movie theater. It has pretty curtains, tables with rose-colored tablecloths, and a little lamp on each one. It's heated. They serve tea with lemon and four small pastries.

I've gone to see a friend from the San Isidro Institute.

"This place is the most chic of all Barcelona," she tells me. "And it's so French."

Strange people go there. Girls with blue or green hair, and some even sprinkled with gold; gentlemen with feminine faces and ladies flaunting an air of masculinity.

"They're artists," I say to myself, and I stare at them enviously.

Sometimes, Lydia and I talk about that kind of life, of painter's studios, of unconventional people who live in the middle of flowers and perfume, as if they were beyond human; ugliness never got to them.

"They're rich," I say. "They've never had to make a living, right?"

"I don't know… but look at them! Surely, they never have to think of anything mundane."

"Never!" But then I remember. "What about the war?"

"Yes, the war. Everyone's involved; some go to the front, end up hungry and covered with lice… Others are hungry in their own homes, and others are executed."

"But these are the ones on the margin," says Lydia. "They're like they come from a different world. Look at that blond woman dressed stylishly with an ascot and Scottish gloves. She's divine. Look at her hands. It's like they were made of ivory. You think those hands have done anything other than arrange flowers in glass vases?"

I laugh.

"*Mujer*, there are porcelain and clay vases too."

When we go out onto the moonlit street, I feel a chill on my back. The hours I've spent in the Astoria have driven me into a drunken stupor.

"Right, Lydia?"

"Yes," she says laughing. ""There must be opium in the air because we're giddy...'" But then reality comes back to us: bombs and hunger.

I don't want to accept it.

"But do you really think this is reality? No, this is a horrible nightmare. Reality can be sad, insipid, and vulgar: that was my life before the war with Father and my sisters, working, getting sick occasionally, economic worries... but what we're going through now is not reality. I think we're going to wake up from this nightmare someday."

On the other hand when there are no bombers, life is normal, pleasant, and even enjoyable on sunny days in the winter in Catalonia.

In the mornings I sew and read in my tranquil bourgeois room. Sometimes, after lunch I visit friends working for a magazine, or I go to Salón Rosa, a tea salon on Gracia, with Doña Conce and her daughter Amelita, recently married to a militiaman. They have a little girl.

In the Salón Rosa, with its soft, discreet lights, sometimes there are surprises. The waiter approaches and whispers:

"If you wait until seven, we'll have sweet buns...three per person."

We're served tea, chamomile, or malt, and three buns, not very tasty; it seems they're not made from flour.

And here comes Güeña, Jorge's comrade, a friend of Amelita's husband who's brought me a letter. We join our tables together.

"What's happening in Teruel is disastrous," he tells me. The soldiers have no boots, just sandals, and they have to walk on snow. Their feet freeze and have to be amputated."

One morning, on my way to the metro station, there's something nauseating in the air, like dirty livestock. The metro platforms are crowded with people carrying mattresses, saddlebags, and baskets... They're refugees from the Aragon front. Every metro stop is filled with them. These poor people have been forced to leave their homes carrying whatever they can on their shoulders.

I've written to Jorge and given the letter to Güeña.

"I'm not promising anything," he says. "I don't know if he's still where I left him."

"Is he your boyfriend?" asks doña Conce.

My face is so red I can barely reply.

"No, *Señora*, he's a friend, like a brother. He's been so good to me. I can't repay him."

Everyone laughs, and I can't do anything but cry. I'm not sure if it's from shame or anger. They're all such meddlers.

I'll meet with Güeña tomorrow. I want to send Jorge some warm gloves and a scarf. There's a store on Gracia that sells coats.

I tell Father about this, and he agrees.

"But I'll attach a note to yours, you know; I don't want this guy to think that you're dying of sorrow for him."

"But *Papá*!"

"I know, I know. You're a little one, and you don't think of such things. That's why I'm warning you."

While Father gets ready to leave and attend to his tasks, I also get dressed to go to the store. It's nine. I'm not sure if the stores are open. On my way I stop off at the bakery that might have sweet buns… The sirens again! Oh, God! They're early today.

At the end of the hallway I hear loud voices. It's the landlords. They tell me you can see the airplanes from the gallery window.

"There are at least six of them."

The entire city is silent now, trembling from the roar of the engines. The bombs are coming down on us again. My God, it's terrifying!

"Celia," says *Papá*. "Come here with me, close to the most solid wall. Don't be scared, *hija*."

"I'm not scared."

The bombs are exploding like thunder, closer and closer.

"Scoundrels!" shouts *Papá*. "Even if they think they know what government would be best for us, something we would all love, they have no right to impose it by destroying a defenseless city..."

I can't hear Father as he goes on and on with his indignation and reasoning because the bombs are falling close by and I'm trembling. So many of them! My God! May He have mercy on us!

They're finally flying away. You can still hear the bombs falling, but they're distant. The sirens sound three times, indicating there's no more danger.

Papá puts on his fur coat and goes out.

"Are you leaving too?"

"Yes, Father, didn't I tell you...?"

"Yes, yes...I know."

I go outside. It's a nice sunny day. The sky is clear and blue as usual here in Barcelona. There are chickens around the trees, pecking at the earth. They belong to the neighbors who leave them out in the sun. Today you can buy large cages for three or four chickens and put them on the balcony. This way you can feed them leftovers, and every now and then they'll lay an egg —a miraculous gift these days.

The bakery on the corner is still closed. A boy is about to open it.

"Will there be any sweet buns around eleven?"

"I don't know, come by at ten-thirty because we'll run out in fifteen minutes."

The small elegant shops on Gracia and nearby streets are open now. Lovely shops where they sell expensive gloves, velvet slippers, scarfs, and silk flowers. It's all French and in short supply. I go in a store, but they only have one pair of leather gloves.

"Very elegant, *Señorita*. Smell the insides of them. It's a delicious aroma that comes from I-don't-know-where."

"But they're for a militiaman on the front."

"No matter *Señorita*. That leather perfume is like a gift that'll make him think of you. They're in a standard size, perhaps a little large but no matter."

They're very expensive, but since she assures me I won't find anything like them in all of Barcelona, I take them. They don't have men's scarfs, so I go down to Cortes Street on the corner of Ramblas, where I see a store that sells posh shirts.

When I cross the street I see Güeña.

"Eh, Güeña."

He's so distracted that he doesn't see me.

"Hey... didn't you see me?"

"Is it you...? You're right, I didn't see you, I'm thinking of something that happened this morning."

"What is it?"

"You don't know? ... You don't know what happened to Conce and Amelita?"

"No!"

"Well... I don't... You heard the bombs, no? It was horrific. Well, Doña Conce's house was blown to bits. On Calle del Ángel, three houses were buried."

"What about her?"

"I don't know, probably buried under the debris. Not much hope for her, but maybe Amelita..."

"But doesn't Amelita live somewhere else?"

"Yes, but the plaza where she lives was bombed too. They found her and took her to the Red Cross, but she died."

"Oh, my Lord!"

"Poor thing! Apparently her little girl was sleeping in another room; she heard her crying for more than an hour; the two of them are under the ruins. They dug them out."

"Dead..."

"Yes... Imagine what it's like for him. Losing your family. He's still there... at the Red Cross. If you want to see them... I'm going over there this afternoon. Believe me, it's better to be on the warfront. I haven't seen anything like this on the front... I think it was someone named Ludendorff who invented totalitarian war."

"What?"

"In this war, innocent civilians living in cities minding their own business are the targets. I'm telling you, there's no hell big enough for the ones who've committed such crimes."

TOTALITARIAN WAR

I like Barcelona. It's spacious, light, and stately. I even like the things that *Papá* dislikes: those strange buildings on Gracia that look like rocks on the tops of mountains, or the ones that have statues in balconies with planters. And how about those little bronze fountains with pretty figures of children adorning the gardens!

I'm almost happy. I got a letter from Jorge thanking me for the gloves and scarf. He tells me he's fine and that soon he's going to come here. We even received word from the girls. In addition to that, no bombs for eight days.

In the afternoon I go to the movies with Lydia. There are underground movie theaters where you can't hear the sirens. But everyone knows that when the lights go out the planes are on their way.

Sometimes I see airplanes on the movie screen… I can't stand the sound of the motors. Please, not that! I don't want to be reminded.

It's snowing. The Plaza de Cataluña is unrecognizable in the snow. A few of the pigeons die in the cold. They stretch out a wing and fall to one side with their little legs apart. They're hungry, and the freezing temperature is too much for them.

I found a little dog shivering next to a wall. He's so thin that you can see his ribs… I'm sure he has no one to take care of him.

Lydia pets him and looks into his watery eyes.

"How can we leave him here? I can't take him home because they'll scold me."

So I lift him and carry him under my coat; he lets me pet him without resistance, but there's no joy in him either. In my room I feed him bread and heat a cup of soup. He devours it in a minute.

His paws make a pattering noise on the bricks. He's a poor little dog, abandoned who-knows-when.

"You don't have anyone to take care of you? Who looked after you? Were your owners executed? Did they run away from the city?"

When he hears my voice his head rises but he doesn't look at me… he looks at the street from the balcony windows. Someone knocks at my door; | it frightens the dog. It's the landlady.

"So you've brought a dog to the house?"

"Yes, I found him trembling and…"

"And you think you can keep him here?"

Since I don't answer, she says:

"No, not that. We don't allow dogs or cats in the house. They're a lot of trouble, they're dirty and break everything… You understand, don't you?"

"Yes."

She leaves. It's cloudy and cold. The poor little dog gets out from under the bed and gazes at the street… He hasn't looked at me at all; he seems to ignore me.

I don't know what to do with this animal. If Father comes he'll object to the dog's expulsion and there'll be a conflict… We'll have to move to another house.

The dog's whimpers and his fixation on the door makes me think he wants to leave. I go outside with him. As we approach the stairway rapidly and open the door to the street, he disappears. Alright. At least he has eaten; maybe he'll find a warm spot where he can sleep.

Sunny days return, pleasant mornings on the Paseo de Gracia, the afternoons in the Astoria are interrupted only by an occasional bombing raid.

Lydia has some friends who go to the Salón Rosa. They always talk about the war and the shelters for children.

"They have to learn to hate the bourgeoisie, to have contempt for rich children, to…"

"No, no," I counter. "I don't want my little sisters to hate anyone. All children are the same."

There's a heated argument, and I don't have a clue what to say. I don't know anything about politics or sociology. They yell words I don't understand directed at me, so I can't answer them. They're all against me.

When I get up from the table, I hear one of them say:

"The girl's a fascist."

"They're talking about you," Lydia tells me.

"What's a fascist? I know what it is to be a communist because I learned about it in Valencia, and I don't like it. But I don't know about being a fascist."

Lydia says we shouldn't go back to the Salón Rosa. That accusation can cost me dearly, she says. But I laugh; after all, what can they do to me?

"I don't know how you could have lived in Madrid in the middle of all those political executions without knowing about these things."

"So you think they're going to execute me? *Papá* explained that those things can't happen to us, not to me and not to him.'"

Nonetheless, I don't go back to the Salón Rosa. That incident, still incomprehensible to me, is only a bitter memory.

Sunny days. The air is getting warmer and the trees on Ramblas and Gracia are budding. Spring is almost here. Sometimes I surprise myself humming a song.

Father is surprised too and asks, "Are you happy, *hija?*"

"Yes… I know I shouldn't be… right?"

"Of course you should, *hija*. Yes. You're happy and that's natural."

"But not always, I remember granddad, that night when…, and I remember what happened to Aunt Julia and Gerardo, and… now doña Conce, and…"

"Yes, *hija*, but it's better to put all those memories behind you. Especially now in the horrid times we're living, you have to turn your back on the past. The ones who've been left behind don't suffer anymore. We, the living, have that to console us. Spring is here, and everything is new, and the larks sing every morning. You hear them? From the balcony every morning I see flocks of birds pass by. Furthermore, *hija*, even though you insist on feeling sad, you can't be. You're only seventeen."

It's true. I can't be sad for very long, much less on this sunny day when Lydia and I go shopping. I love the beautiful starched collars they sell at Royalty!

"I don't know what to do. Don't you think a white and violet collar like that will make my black dress look new?"

"Yes... It's probably expensive."

"Should we ask?"

Yes, it's expensive, but so pretty. So I buy it, and another one too; it's all white. Lydia buys a Scottish style blouse to go with her blue dress. We notice a scarf with a Persian design; it's beautiful.

"This will go with my coat. It'll look beautiful, don't you think?"

"Sure, but it's one hundred *pesetas*."

"If you ask your *Papá*, he'll say yes."

"But I'm in mourning."

"*Hija*, so what? No one goes into mourning these days. If everyone who's lost a loved one went into mourning, all the streets would look like a funeral procession. No! Don't do it! Wear what you want and..."

We gaze into a bookstore display. So many books!

"Have you read anything by Valle-Inclán? Not me."

We buy two books and ask for a catalogue.

"I have to ask *Papá*. He wants to read *The Magic Mountain*, so I'm going to buy it for him for his saint's day."

Compared to January, there are hardly any people sheltered in the metro anymore. Lydia tells me they've found housing for them in barracks. As we go down Ausías March Street, we hear singing coming from a school.

"Everything's coming back to normal," I say.

"Yes, *hija*... Everything comes back to the way it was regardless of all the commotion. Look, when we got here from Madrid with two loads of furniture, they allowed us to leave them in the hallways and stairways... My mother, my aunts and uncles didn't have the strength to move it all, and much less me... No one has moved our furniture... at least as far as I know. Can you believe that it's no longer in the stairways or the halls? It's all moved against the walls on their own, or maybe we've moved it all with our steps as we go up and down. I have a closet and a bed in my room, and the table and chairs are in the dining room. So everything's as it was… See? Soldiers rise up in revolt, prisoners break out of jail, schools are closed, people are executed, there's nothing to eat… So a year and a half later children go back to school, people eat their lunch at one o'clock, and they buy gloves and starched collars…"

I laugh but Lydia goes on:

"There was an anthill on the door of my house and Aunt Dolores threw a bucket of water on it. We saw the ants swimming away; it was a catastrophe for them. Imagine how the water flowed through their dwelling, through the bedrooms, the salons, carports, and bathroom… Well, the next morning, the anthill was just like it was before, as if nothing had happened. The ants went out shopping, they took their offspring for a ride in their carts, they gossiped with the other ants in the neighborhood, whispered messages to one another… like nothing had ever happened. So Aunt Dolores, who is stubborn like you wouldn't believe, this time threw insecticide and three buckets of water on them. The poor ants fled their smelly residence, so Aunt Dolores cried out triumphantly, 'I've gotten rid of them!' Sure, sure, she believed that. Next summer, the incorrigible ants came back, singing along with the children in school who bought themselves starched white collars… just like us. It's impossible! You can't change people's habits: getting up at eight, at nine, and off to school, returning at five, at six a snack, at…

"Ay, *hija*, it's dreadful!"

We laugh, it's so funny… The children are coming back home from school. Lydia and I say goodbye at my doorway, and Lydia goes back to her house on Aragón.

I'll have time to write María Luisa a letter before *Papá* gets back. I run up the stairs two at a time.

It's such a nice day that I open the door to the balcony to feel the sun and air. I look in the mirror. This gray coat fits well. The material is ordinary, but it's elegant. I look older than I am. When the girls are back with me, people will think they're my children. Teresina's so sweet; she says I'm their mother.

Oh, no, the sirens! How horrible on this glorious day. I was beginning to think I was far away from the war.

"Celia," someone is pounding at my door. "Come here right now. At least ten bomber squadrons are on their way. None of us will be spared!"

Lord! I go out to the hallway with the landlady who is tall and refined. We go to a dark room with a maid; they say it's safer there. The sirens continue to whistle, and the explosions follow the whistling… They're getting closer.

"That one's fallen on the wharf. And that one on the plaza. Good God! Lord!"

Then she cries out, covering her ears; this one explodes very close to us… The bombers are flying right over the house, making a terrifying noise.

"Ay…" Now I'm the one screaming.

It's fallen next door. Maybe on our house… Then they begin to fly away… They've gone.

"No, another one is coming. They're getting closer again. And they're loaded."

In the darkness of the room, I feel a hand groping for mine. It's the maid, poor thing. She says nothing… she's terrified.

"Don't be frightened, María. Nothing will happen to us. The bombs we hear can't do us any harm… And we won't hear the ones that kill us."

"*Santa de Covadonga*," I hear her sigh, clasping my hand. Her hand is deformed and wrinkled.

Again a bomb falls close to us. Another one! And another! It's as if several of them were exploding at the same time. And the bombers don't fly away. Perhaps they're encircling the city like eagles hovering over their prey.

"They're leaving! They're going away."

"Thanks be to God. Blessed God!" says the landlady.

The sirens sound three times, and we go into the gallery close to a grove of palm trees… But what's this? Again?

They're coming back, they leave, and they come back again. The sirens begin to set off the signal for the end of the danger but they don't get to the third whistle. They sound off again like the sound of a funeral hymn.

"They're coming back… again!" says the landlady. "Get back to the safe room, they're on the way here!"

Again the sound of the explosions, ferocious, cruel, relentless… back and forth, back and forth… The bombs fall rhythmically… approaching, approaching closer; it sounds like this one will fall on us. But no, it just missed. Maybe it hit the house next door.

"They're Italian!" says *Señorita* Subiría. "They're Italian. They have to find foreigners to kill us. Ours don't dare do this… They're Italian or German. God help us! My sister-in-law is going to have a baby, poor thing will be born having fits. These days all newborns come into the world with nervous fits, Dear Jesus!"

Finally they go away for the time being. We hear the sirens followed by Red Cross ambulances honking their horns.

The Red Cross hospital is close to our house; we hear a big commotion. Injured people are arriving. *Señorita* Subiría and her servant lean over the balcony of my room, but I prefer not to look.

The street noise is getting louder. More ambulances and people yelling.

"Come, Celia. Come see… Two injured boys along with a young woman. Here come the fire engines; there's probably a fire around somewhere close. Don't you hear it?"

"Celia, come, come see this!"

She's insistent, so I go over to the balcony. There are people gathering around and ambulances carting off the injured. Some have blood on their clothes, and their faces are so pale they look dead.

"There! There! Look over there!"

Two Red Cross medics open a path to the hospital among all the people gathered. In their hands they carry a blue rubber container of human organs: arms, legs, pieces of flesh that have no form, all covered in blood. Horrific!

I back away from the balcony because I'm faint and nauseated; I feel sick to my stomach and throat. The ones remaining on the balcony don't notice me; they seem hypnotized by all the horror.

I sit down on a little chair in the salon and wait for *Papá*, who should've arrived by now. Has something happened to him?… No, nothing. Nothing has happened to him. I'm sure of it!

I begin to pray mechanically. I hear *Papa's* footsteps in the hallway. He's startled when he opens the door.

"What's wrong with you, *hija?*"

"Nothing, *Papá*. What about you?

"Nothing… The bombing was in the center of town. Just as the children were getting out of school… Dozens of dead little children. Worse yet, some of the survivors have no legs or arms, faces smashed. There is no forgiveness for this kind of crime. And your friend Lydia's house has been cut in the middle like a piece of cheese… and since they don't have stairs to bring down the ones still alive, the firefighters are doing what they can to rescue them… I've just seen it."

"But Lydia?"

"She's alright. Her family too. They managed to get out of the house."

MARCH 1938

I'm getting so thin. I'm looking at my emaciated arms and hands; they look transparent when I hold them up to the sun.

"Girl, why are you scared of everything," asks Lydia laughing. "Are you afraid of death?"

"No, not death, it's not that. What scares me is losing my arms or legs… or my eyes, or a gash in my face… or…"

"Oh, be quiet! Let's not think of such things, or else we wouldn't be able to live."

Papá wants me to go to the movies every afternoon. There's a movie theater close by. It's below ground level… But why do they have to show airplanes on the screen? When I see the planes I can't help screaming."

And just like that, the image seems to darken… The only lights are kerosene ones, and they leave them on just in case…

"They're here."

Although we don't hear the sirens or the engines, we know they're close by, flying over our heads and dropping bombs that bury houses. Will we get stuck here under the debris?

"Let's go outside."

"No! Are you crazy?" shouts Lydia.

My teeth begin to chatter; I can't control my jaws even though my hands are holding them, and I feel cold on the top of my head; it makes my hair rise.

"*Mujer*! Don't be that way. We've had it worse. What would you do if you had to go through what happened to us?"

"Be quiet! It's what I saw… that rubber container filled with limbs. My God!"

When the danger is over, I laugh at my own fear. How silly I am! And I'm the one who tells everyone not to fret.

One afternoon when we're in the movie theater, they interrupt the film. But there's still an image; it's a young woman who cries out:

"Comrades, one and all. The government speaks of peace. But we don't want peace! Onward until victory! All of you in the theater, show you're against cowardice!"

Many get out of their seats. But not Lydia and me. No one can force us to leave. But the woman next to me stands up.

"Aren't you Celia? C'mon, stand up! You can't sit there with your arms crossed like that and let the bourgeois government have its way!"

So we go out into the street. It's nighttime. The opaque blue lights coming from the lampposts make everything look even darker. We find ourselves mixing in with the crowd marching up Paseo de Gracia. I grab Lydia's hand, and she whispers in my ear:

"Let's go to your house… No one will see us."

We duck into a crossing street. Lydia laughs as we go up the stairs.

"You're the last one I should talk to about being scared! Or about ending the war."

But I'm not the only one who's scared. The other day when I went out into the street after a bombing raid, I saw the fear in people's eyes. A woman was shaking, there was terror in her eyes, and her hands grabbed her jaws like mine do when I'm afraid.

They've announced the opera schedule at the Teatro Principal, the performers are French.

"Yes, they say it's worth seeing," says *Papá*.

Jorge arrives at midday.

"Jorge, how did you find me?"

"You're not looking good," he says laughing.

"That's not what I asked… I'm asking how you figured out where I am."

"Oh, that's not the point. You've gotten really thin. What does your father say?"

"He's lost weight too… so have you."

"But not as much as you."

"It's that I'm afraid… I've lost strength and…"

"We've got to turn that around. Come with me tonight. I have two tickets to the Teatro Principal; I bought them when I went by the theater."

Papá appears; he's happy to see him; we have lunch in a restaurant close to the Tibidabo.

"I can't tell you how grateful I am to you for helping Celia. She told me about…"

Jorge says it's not important and changes the conversation to talk about the war. I don't know why it seems to me that the soldiers coming from the front don't know anything. They think the war is won when they advance just a few kilometers and take a couple of towns.

Father also acts as if he's on the front. All day in the barracks, or maybe because of his military training, he's convinced everything is fine. But I say to them:

"Don't kid yourselves… The war might go on for a little longer, but we've lost."

Papá is indignant.

"Don't pay any attention to her. She's just scared. Child, what do you know?"

"I know. Italians and Germans are bombing us. How can you fight against two nations?"

"Bah," says Jorge. "The Italians ran away from us. They're probably back in Rome by now…"

"Also," says *Papá*, "if we had no allies you'd be right. But the League of Nations…"

"*Papá*, you told me many times that we were winning, that this will all be solved in a few days, but then sometimes you change your mind and say that negotiations failed, and later you say that in about three months or six, they'll resume talks."

I've lost faith in *Papá*, in Jorge too. They're wrong. Not that I know so much, but I listen to people talk, but there's no solution. What's going to happen to us? What's going to happen here?

Papá and Jorge keep on talking about politics: the ministers, what Azaña said, or Negrín, or Álvarez del Vayo

Jorge interrupts:

"Listen, I'd like to take Cecilia to the theater. It's the debut of the opera season and…"

Papá shakes his head.

"I'd be too nervous. Tonight there'll be another bombing raid on the border. You'll see. They've given the impression that we're all safe and that we're living with the threat of bombs as if nothing was happening… That's all fine and good, but this will cost us dearly… You'll see… You'll see what happens tonight."

Jorge is silent. I think he's disappointed that we're not going together. I feel so torn up that I'm beginning to realize how I feel about him.

We have tea at the Astoria, in a corner dimly lit by a rose-colored light from a lamp on the table shining on us and on other couples nearby. I'm wearing the gray dress and starched white collar I bought along with the new coat.

It's a beautiful afternoon. Jorge continues to talk about the war, about his comrades, about how much he admires them, and about the generosity of the people.

"I think war gives rise to hidden virtues that we're not aware of. We've all become too serious, girl… Tomorrow I'm going back to the front."

"No!"

"Yes, yes, they've only allowed me forty-eight hours and the train takes twenty-four to get to the front… When we see each other again, the war will have ended, and then I'll tell you lots of things, Celia…"

I'm stunned and embarrassed. I can't look at him straight on, and I feel my blood rising to my eyes and face.

He squeezes my hand on the table, and the pressure moves me. We're silent a few seconds… it seems like a century. At last, he turns to his watch and says,

"It's seven; it's time to go back."

On the way back, it seems I've been flying over the clouds because I don't remember how I got here… I didn't notice any open storefronts or if it was dark. I only know that when we said goodbye, Jorge squeezed my hand tightly, then he raised it to his mouth and kissed it! I thought I saw tears in his eyes, but suddenly he turned around and left without saying goodbye.

I cry too as I go up the stairs. What a feeling! I can barely speak and I'm glad that *Papá* is not back yet. Jorge loves me. And I love him more than my own life!

I can't sleep at night. The curtain has probably gone up at the Teatro Principal by now… the first act must have started. I close my eyes and it's like I hear the orchestra. Then suddenly the sirens…!

The street noise has subsided and the dim light that was coming in through the balcony disappears, making everything absolutely dark. The sound of distant planes is getting louder as they approach. I can hear Father's voice.

"Celia, you hear it? Didn't I tell you?"

"Yes, *Papá*."

"Alright. Go to sleep. The bombs will drop on Rambla de las Flores, the same street as the Teatro Principal."

My God! Jorge is on that street.

The bombs fall… that horrifying noise again and the antiaircraft cannons fire over our heads… Some bombs fall close by… maybe on this street. But then there's silence… they're leaving. Yes, they're flying away… No! They're coming back again. Ay, no!

The glass in the balcony windows is shaking like it's about to break, and suddenly the doors open as if someone was pushing on them from the street.

"Don't be afraid, *hija*." It's my father's voice. "Don't be afraid!" he says again.

I can't talk; I'm too scared. I'm freezing, I'm trembling… I feel my skin getting wet as if I were sweating.

Finally they fly away, but they come back twice. The next day the newspapers don't mention casualties or injuries, only the reaction of the spectators in the theater when they turned off the lights and sang the Hymn of the Republic. What has happened to Jorge?

Ever since the inauguration of the theater, the bombing raids have been constant day and night. The opera season is over because the performers have gone back to France.

Lydia has moved far away. The street cars are slow because the drivers are looking for cigarette butts, and when they see one in the sidewalk, they stop the car and pick it up. Men gather cigarette butts dropped on the streets by the people who can afford to smoke. One of *Papá's* friends who comes looking for him says:

"I'm happy! I've got a treasure here."

"What?"

And he shows him a pillbox where he keeps his cigarette butts.

I'm saying all this because, since Lydia moved I have no one to talk to, I'm almost always alone; fear has taken over me in every way. I look for the women of the house for company; they're scared too and they're preparing for a trip to Gerona. They leave so I'm home alone all day. When the bombs drop, I go over to the staircase to try to find someone, anyone… But I don't find a single person because I don't want to knock on any doors.

"This is not life! Barcelona doesn't even have shelters. The metro doesn't go deep enough into the ground for safety. You have to protect yourself from the bombs because there's no help… they're constant. I count how many times the bombers swoop down: eighteen. They say there's a body part of a woman hanging from a tree on Diagonal Street. I've seen a sticky mess of a brain on the wall of a building. Yesterday there was a man running with his hand separated from his arm. It's horrible what's happening!

The moon, white and defenseless, shines over the city; it offers itself silently to death. My God, what a nightmare! Sometimes I crawl for cover between the two mattresses of my bed. But what good is this if the building falls on me? I'm on the third floor, and there are two on top.

It's daybreak after a sleepless night when I hear someone at the door. Who can it be at this time?

I throw a robe over my nightshirt and look through the peephole.

"Who is it?"

"Does Mr. Gálvez live here with his daughter?"

"Yes ma'am."

"Tell them that Jorge's mother and sister would like to talk to them."

"Hello… I haven't met you. How are you?"

Lord, how dirty they are! Their clothes are torn, their faces disjointed.

"How do you think we are, *hija*? We had to come here almost the whole way from Tarragona on foot."

I would not have recognized them. Adela is taller than me. Pilaruca is plump and blond. Wasn't she dark the last time I saw her? Doña Paulina, whom I don't remember fondly, is speaking to me, so I open the door. She goes on and on.

"*Hija*, what a disaster this war has been! This is the end! The end I tell you… We left Santander at a bad time because Jorge enlisted. We left all our belongings, then off to Valencia, then Cartagena, and later to Tarragona because Jorge assured us…. What was he thinking?"

"*Mamá*," Adela interrupts as her mother continues to speak.

"If you ask me, what good are wars? At the end everybody just goes home, but the dead are left underground… until it starts again. Lord, Holy Mother of God, help us! They're dropping bombs on us again. So where do we go for safety?"

When she finds out that Barcelona has no shelters, she cries out at the sky.

"What a place we've come to! We're all going to die here! Our children too… what sorrow, these poor children!"

We go to a moderately sized bathroom for shelter. When the sirens sound announcing the cessation of the bombing, Doña Paulina is persistent in telling me about their trip from Tarragona.

"It was hell, worse than hell… With the bombs falling like hail and people running along the road…and others on a burro or a goat galloping through the fields… Lots of towns have been taken… and you can believe what people are saying about what happens when the other side takes over."

Pilaruca comes in, then she goes around the house peeking into the rooms. Doña Paulina keeps on talking on and on tirelessly while Adela asks me:

"Is there anyone else in this house?"

"Yes, but the owners have gone to a town in Gerona. You can stay here if you don't have another place to go. We have our meals in a restaurant close by; a cleaning lady who lives next to us comes by every morning."

"What are you saying, Celia?" Doña Paulina looks at me perplexed, and without waiting for my response, continues her rant. "As I was saying, we've been on this God-awful road for three days… By car and then in a truck carrying bombs…then walking, and when the bombs came down we'd duck in the furrows… I'm telling you those devils from hell come after you from everywhere… Imagine what would happen if one of their bombs hit a truck carrying bombs. All we could do is run and run… and falling here and there… and what luck, the carriage didn't wait for us, off it went, so there we were in the middle of a field thousands of kilometers away from the world…"

"*Mamá!*"

"…Then a car passed by, and another one and another one… No one would stop for us… so I went into the middle of the road and I shouted they can either kill me or…"

"Have you had anything to eat in those three days?"

"Someone stopped and told us he could only take us to a town…I don't remember the name of it… Ah, you asked me if we've eaten? No, *hija*, not a bite in three days… sure… we've been fasting so we can receive the Holy Eucharist… I'm not feeling sorry for myself, I just feel for Pilaruca. They left us in that town, so off we went again in the night, on foot. That was the second night we've been traveling. I didn't tell you we spent the first night in an abandoned castle off the road… it was deathly cold… no one around… because a bomb had fallen on the castle, no roof over our heads. Ask my kids how scared they were. Rats everywhere!…"

"I have a little bread and almonds. I'll go fetch them."

Doña Paulina gets up and follows me to my room still talking about how they got together with other travelers and how a truck picked them up all huddled together "like God and the Virgin Mary wanted,"… and after another twenty-four hours, they arrived at Barcelona at daybreak.

"At daybreak?"

"Yes, *hija*, it must have been two or three in the morning when we saw the city. And the bombing! There was a silvery moon, so the driver told us he wouldn't drive into the city like that, exposed by the moon, and told us to get out… Oh, this house is so nice! Where does your father sleep? Right here in the room next to yours? Ah, I didn't know. Surely I've woken him up."

"*Mamá*, don't speak so loud!"

"It's my habit. I've always been a loudmouth." Then she said in a softer voice, "You're comfortable here! Is this a boarding house?"

I tell her we've rented two rooms, but that the landladies have left so they can stay in their room.

"What luck for us! I told the girls. We don't know anyone here in Barcelona, but the Gálvez family is here, and they're very good people, Jorge said. He talks a lot about you in all his letters; he sent us your address, just in case. Such a stroke of good luck! The bad thing is the bombs… We've spent the night just outside a door. Freezing cold! The beast of a driver told us there's shelter in the metro, and we could be there until morning. But we didn't know where the metro was, how should we know? I've never set foot in Barcelona, *hija*… I never should have left my house…!"

Pilaruca gobbles up the bread and almonds before the next bombing raid.

"Here they are again as always!" says Doña Paulina, frightened. "We're gonna kick the bucket in this place. God have mercy!"

I take them to their rooms with a view of the garden as Father comes out of his room to greet them.

"The sirens again! My God!"

"This is not life," says Doña Paulina.

"There've been eighteen bombings in the last twenty-four hours," says Father. "The planes take off from the Balearic Islands, which are right next to us; after takeoff, they get here in a matter of minutes."

Papá is pleased that he doesn't have to leave me alone when he goes to the barracks. But I can't think of anything except the continuous bombings, the constant drone of the engines, and the explosions.

That morning we're terrified as we take shelter next to the walls of the house. Pilaruca is still hungry, but I don't have anything else to give her. Adela is so pale that I fear she might faint. Poor girl! She hasn't eaten in three days. Doña Paulina gets into bed with Pilaruca, and the two go to sleep. At twelve-thirty, I wake them up to have lunch at the restaurant.

"Will they give us anything? Do they let everyone in? What do they have? Is it expensive?"

All these questions and more of them are from doña Paulina as soon as she wakes up, but she doesn't wait for a reply; she just combs her hair.

As we walk to the restaurant, she wants to know if it's far, if there's any danger, if they'll allow us to take refuge at their door if the planes come back, if my father will be there waiting for us…

Papá waits for us in the vestibule of the third floor where the restaurant is; he tells us we have a table but we have to wait until it's free.

"Something smells so good!" says Pilaruca. "It smells like something is frying, real food."

The smell coming from the kitchen seeps into the rest of the building, even mesh armchairs and pillows in the vestibule. People are coming and going from the dining area to the stairs. At times they leave the door open allowing the cold March air into the restaurant, the wall hangings shivering against the wall.

At last we can sit down to have lunch. Adela, Pilaruca, and their mother smile beatifically, as if they were looking at God. These poor souls will eat at last!

They serve each of us a potato stew with a pair of eggs and tomato. *Papá* and I share our food with Adela and Pilaruca; doña Paulina eats half of it.

"*Hija*, you're so well-off here," she says after a few moments of silence. "Do you eat like this every day?"

Papá replies that some days they serve meat, roasted or fried, with lentils or green beans.

Suddenly an awful explosion shakes open the balcony doors, causing a table to fall to one side. In all the chaos, we flee to the vestibule as people cry and push.

"I didn't hear the sirens!"

"I didn't either."

"I thought I heard them but with all the talking…"

"How awful, it's horrifying!"

"We're not going to survive this one!"

Everyone is speaking at once. Doña Paulina says:

"I left my orange on the table; you did too."

Papá says it's best to wait. A waiter approaches and says the balconies are no longer intact.

"That's our last meal," someone yells.

Papá goes to pay for the meal. Doña Paulina insists that the oranges are still on the table:

"It's not right to pay for this if we haven't eaten them… tell your dad to grab them."

Papá pays for the meal, unaware of Doña Paulina's protest until I tell him.

"What? What are you saying? We're in the middle of a bombing raid. Don't fret about oranges. When it's safe, we'll go back home."

When we go out into the street, there's no more sidewalk, it's buried under debris and glass. The street is almost deserted. It's cloudy, and the milk-colored light makes this tormented city look tragically sad.

They say an entire block of Cortes Street is destroyed and that in the Plaza de Cataluña there are several sunken buildings, also on Ramblas all the way down there… From here you can see…

Looking at all the destruction, all the rubble piling up everywhere including the middle of the street, no more trees, it's terrifying.

"*Papá! Papá!* How dreadful!... Look… Don't you see?

"Yes, *hija*, yes… I think maybe you should go back to Madrid. There's nothing for you here. Guadalupe is there in our house on Chamartín; you'll be fine there. They won't bomb there anymore because the munitions dump is no longer in the city. I'll try to get food to you from here."

RETURN

From the bus I can see the Mediterranean, its blue waters illuminated by a shiny sun. There can't be a war on such a nice day! The fields are spotted with yellow and white flowers. The air brings on the sweet aromas of March. The bombs have buried almost all the houses along the road, but every now and then, on this pleasant spring morning, I see women sewing in the sun outside their doors.

Occasionally, trucks filled with soldiers pass by on their way to Barcelona, and when they see us, they shout:

"*Salud*! *Salud*! Comrades!" with an air of solidarity, affirming their alliance with the people living and suffering for the same cause.

"There's nothing that unites people more than hatred," says Father.

At midday we arrive at a town filled with greenery, although it's muddy due to the recent rain. The bus avoids the summer heat of the sun by moving under the shade of an awning.

Some of the drivers get off the bus to ask:

"Is there anything to eat here?"

"They're serving roasted potatoes and onions."

"Roasted?"

"They don't have olive oil."

I'd rather not get off. A fat woman whom *Papá* has asked to look out for me tells me several times to stay in my seat, that she'll find some water for both of us.

I eat some pieces of chocolate and quince preserves he got from his military rations. Doña Paulina and her daughters take advantage of Father's rations, but he promises me that he'll send me a good portion when I get to Madrid.

In the afternoon we arrive at Valencia, the streets are illuminated by the milky white light of the Mediterranean, there's a sweet smell coming from the flowers in the parks.

Fifina is waiting for me; I'd told her we'd be arriving.

"Listen, I've found you a boarding house on the Plaza Castelar… It's very nice, and it includes board and everything!"

"But aren't there places for us close by?"

"Sure… they've always been here, but when you government people took up all the rooms…"

I laugh at her for calling us "government people." But I'm happy. I'm going to be alone in a hotel like an actress.

"Well, aren't you the lovely one."

"It'll only be for a short time; tomorrow I'm leaving for Madrid."

"Tomorrow? That's impossible, *hija*. There're people who've been waiting for a long time. You'll probably be here for six months."

I'm worried about this, so before we go to the hotel, we stop at an office that organizes trips out of the city.

"Why are you going to Madrid, Ma'me?" asks an office employee.

I try to answer him, but I'm flustered.

"My father is asking me to go so that…"

"Your father? What is he?"

"He's a military man. Head of aviation…"

"Oh, alright, alright… Official business, no? You can go to Madrid tomorrow in an official car."

He hands me a ticket with the seat number and jots down the time of departure.

"Girl, what luck!" says Fifina as we leave. "You're clever. Why did you say you had official business?"

"I didn't say that, it was him. I was going to say that I've household responsibilities in Madrid…"

The boarding house is cold and partly ruined, but I'm so pleased with myself for my independence and for daring to be in the boarding house unaccompanied. I sleep well, but in the morning I'm freezing. I use my clothes and coat for covers.

At the door I find a note that says, "Due to the present difficulties, we are unable to serve breakfast."

I go out into the balcony; I'm surrounded by pleasantly warm air. People are bustling along the streets; the city looks normal. So many times I've thought the war turns the streets into anthills! Like when people venture out into danger, they flee and hide, running madly, and like ants, they go back to their tasks as if nothing had happened.

Fifina and I go to the market, and I can't resist buying a bouquet of beautiful budding flowers.

In the hotel they serve a lunch of rice with tomato sauce, but the rice is hard, it tastes like pebbles.

"I can't eat this," I say to the waiter.

"Do as you want," he answers curtly. "The cook says that if they want it, they'll eat it, if not, they'll leave it."

I'm very hungry, but I can't bring myself to swallow this. I notice that the other patrons get up and leave with an orange and bread in their hands; they're the only edible things they've served. I do the same and eat them in my room.

Suddenly sirens! Again I'm terrified, my hair is standing on end, so I go downstairs to the dining room.

"It's nothing," a man says.

"They're on their way to Sagunto as always."

"But the other day…"

I learn that they've destroyed the sidewalk to the Hotel Inglés, next to the Count Dos Aguas Plaza that gets its name from the day the count and countess died while having dinner. But this time the roar of the engines subsides in the distance. I've got to sit down because my legs are trembling.

"Why are you so scared?" the waiter asks me.

"I'm coming from Barcelona, where…"

"Barcelona isn't Madrid. Since the government left, the bombers come by."

I take a walk with Fifina to Colón. This is a happy city! I prefer to live in Valencia, but…

Fifina, who knows her way around, takes me to Obispo Street. Too bad it's buried in debris. We go by the market to visit a friend of hers who lives in an ancient palace. The entrance is under a dark-stoned dome. I've never seen anything like it.

"It was probably a dream, or it's your imagination," says Fifina. It's just like you: that wild imagination of yours."

She's right. I read a story once titled "Fruela's cross"… It didn't have pictures, but I figured the palace of the king of the Visigoths was like the one her friend lived in.

I wanted to tell Fifina about it, but she only wants me to talk about Jorge. She's sure he's my boyfriend.

"No he's not. If that were true, I'd tell you. Why would I lie?"

"That's just what I say."

Fifina's friend is sixteen years old; she just got married two months ago.

"It's the easiest thing in the world to get married these days. You present yourself to a judge and that's it, if not a judge, then an army colonel, and if not an army colonel…"

After we go through two patios and up stone stairs, we get to a door with big fat nails in it, like the ones in ancient buildings. We knock.

"Girl, this palace must be ages old!"

A young servant opens the door; she's wiping her hands on her smock as she takes us to an enormous salon with straw chairs. There's Amparito, sewing in front of a gigantic window.

Amparito is all smiles and pretty, like a rosebud. When Fifina asks about her husband, she turns ten shades of red. She talks about the danger she's been in. Her husband is a doctor. In the first days of the revolution, they wanted to execute him because his father is the administrator of the duke's palace.

"Typical property administrators, the ones who increase peasant farmer's rent, and if they can't pay, they evict them."

In the nighttime they took Amparo's husband to Saler—at that time he was her boyfriend. They forced him into a car and brought him close to the beach. They made him get out, and two militiamen who were in the area approached the drivers.

"Who's this?"

All they knew was that he was the son of a man who managed the landowner's property.

"His father is a dirty lackey, a leech sucking the blood of the poor."

One of the militiamen said as he put his hand on her boyfriend's shoulders:

"Aren't you Martínez, the pediatrician?"

"Yes, that's me."

"Then don't kill him," he said. "He saved my boy's life last winter… when everyone was suffering from diphtheria."

But they didn't want to let him go. They had lost so much time that night, so much work for nothing. But the other guy insisted so much that they went back to Valencia in the car and left Amparo's boyfriend behind.

"When they got back, they took the duke's wine from his wine cellar, right here in this salon. They drank it and ate sweets that my mother-in-law made. Now they all come around when they need Antonio's medical care. He's everyone's doctor; he even says they're good people. But I don't want to have anything to do with them considering what they did to him that night."

Amparito is now my friend.

"Why don't you get married? Don't be a fool, you have a boyfriend. It's so easy these days. When the war ends, everything will be back to normal: talking about what you'll need for the house, invitations, dealing with parents who say they don't have any money."

When we leave the house, it's almost nighttime. Tomorrow I'm leaving, so I have to get up early. I say goodbye to Fifina; I'm not going to see her for a while, and her aunts are getting older and more tired every day.

"You don't know what it's like to live in this house; we can't even move for fear of bothering everyone," Fifina says teary-eyed.

The bus appears, coming up a narrow street off the plaza. I'm the only woman among the passengers. The conductor, a state official, looks astonished when he sees me. When he looks at his list of passengers, he says:

"Official mission."

The other passengers are no longer interested in me. They offer me the best seat on the bus and ask me if I'm carrying anything to eat.

"No, sir."

"My goodness! There won't be any place to eat on the way."

At once they bring food to me from their seats: a can of sardines, another of meat, slices of salami, even a piece of tortilla between two slices of bread.

I've bought a book by Myriam Harry for the trip. I read it voraciously. At noon I look up to see where I am.

The bus has stopped at the entrance of a town with brown adobe houses and a few white ones here and there with balconies on the upper floors.

"Do you want to get off the bus for a while?" the conductor asks me. "If you wish, you can have coffee over there in the plaza… It's malt, really, not coffee, but it warms you up."

I get off the bus with him. I tell him about Father, and he says he's heard of him.

"So you're his daughter. Of course, that's why you're on an official mission."

I tell him what happened, and he laughs. We go down the narrow cobblestone streets. They're so narrow that two people walking can barely get by without touching each other. But on one side there's a building with a portico; it's probably the town hall. The café is next door.

On the bus again with the Myriam Harry book. Every now and then I look out the window to watch the scenery go by. The plains have turned green… Birds frolic, dampening their wings in puddles. It's getting dark, but on the horizon you can see flashes of light far away.

"There's a battle going on over there," I hear someone saying. "It's probably the Thirty-Fourth Brigade."

The lights of the bus are on; I see we're getting closer to Madrid because I recognize the names of some of the towns: Vicálvaro, Pueblo Nuevo, and finally the road to Alcalá leading to the street with the same name. It's a very dark night. An occasional streetlamp here and there allows me to see people on the streets. The bus comes to a stop. A youngster approaches me.

"Will you carry my suitcase?"

"Yes, ma'am."

How strange! Madrid has changed in this short time, people go back to addressing me as *Señorita* and not comrade, like they did two months ago.

I get on the streetcar going toward Ciudad Lineal with the youngster carrying my suitcase, and after an hour's ride, we get off at Chamartín. We cross the street, and I'm delighted to see light coming from my house.

"Guadalupe! Guadalupe!"

Guadalupe comes to the window; she cries out when she sees me.

"*Señorita, Señorita*, it's you!"

The house is cold and gloomy. But the portrait of my mother is still on the dining room wall, my sister's bedroom on the first floor and there's the rosewood closet that's always been in my house.

"I'll be here until the war ends when *Papá* comes home with the girls."

"You must tidy up the house for their arrival."

Guadalupe wants to serve me some lentils cooked without oil, but I'm the one who has decent food: meat, sardines, salami. When she sees such delicacies, she's speechless.

"All I want is to sleep in my bed, lie down under the blankets and sheets my mother embroidered. Please don't shut the window, Guadalupe. Each time I wake up I want to see the Madrid sky, so deep, like velvet… and so many stars. The air smells like Madrid…!"

SPRING IN MADRID

Poor Kinotín. There, there, there! Michito... He's so thin!

"I feed him what I can," says Guadalupe. But what can I do? All he wants is meat, and I don't have any."

Kinotín follows me around like any dog. The yard is getting greener, and the ground is hard and frozen, except for loose soil where Guadalupe has planted beans.

"My arms are still sore from all the digging."

It's a rough, cold spring, not like the joy of previous springs. But the pleasant air of the plains surrounding Madrid, smooth, clear, subtle, transparent, and cold, like a bubbling stream, engulfs and refreshes me as it breezes through my fingers.

Springtime!... Springtime in Madrid; it's the coldest of all springs… I know it, and *Papá* assures me it's true. The cold mountain air waters my eyes.

"Come to the phone, *Señorita*, it's *Señorita* María Luisa."

I run to the phone.

"Is it really you, María Luisa? How did you know I was here?"

"Yes, it's me. You thankless girl. I've been calling every morning to cheer Guadalupe up and to ask where you are… and today…"

"That's so kind of you! Tell me how you're all doing."

She seems reluctant to tell me about her family, but we agree to get together in the afternoon:

"Be here promptly, like three or three-thirty."

Guadalupe laments that they're not distributing rations today, that they only have garbanzos, and it's taking a long time to soften them.

"Do we have coal?"

"No, *Señorita*. I use crumpled-up paper I dried in the sun. That's how we cook. The problem is the whole kitchen gets so dirty... Yesterday the gardener came by when I asked him to help me get rid of the soot."

Fortunately, I still have the provisions the bus passengers gave me, so we eat well. By two-thirty I'm waiting for the streetcar on the Chamartín road to go to Madrid. It's the first day of April. Airplanes are flying over us.

"They're Russian," I hear a woman who's waiting for the streetcar say. "They're coming to defend us."

Defend us! Bah!... While I'm on the streetcar I notice the countryside is getting greener here and there, green grass of Castilla, more sweet-smelling than anyplace else... The air is subtle and transparent as if we were submerged in a crystal lake, cold and clear, impalpable. Again my eyes are moistening. Every day I'm getting more and more teary-eyed!

I get off the tram at the racetrack. There are lots of people waiting for the tram at Puerta del Sol; I'm waiting too. Madrid has changed so much! I'm looking at Castellana, a wide boulevard; it's sunny, with trees not yet blooming on both sides, there's no one on the sidewalks. No cars, no streetcars. The gardens in front of the Natural History Museum have been bombed. I used to know the names of all the plants. The stony pond is dry. I see a man sweeping the streets and another one raking the grass. I thought they wouldn't take care of the greeneries, but I was wrong.

That streetcar, where could it be? People are complaining. I see a man who works on the tram line. I ask him:

"I don't know," he answers. "A while ago the tracks were shelled... They'll be fixed soon."

"Shells?"

"Yes, coming from the university. Yesterday they bombed this whole area. Look at that mailbox!"

I see a red post on the ground next to a ditch. So here too? And *Papá* said that…

It's already three, so I decide to walk. Others give up too, but there are those who stay, leaving a few hopeful people on the sidewalk.

I walk slowly, distancing myself from everyone; soon I'm alone. Madrid looks like such a small town. As I walk on the streets in the center of the city, La Castellana looks like a road on the outskirts. There are clotheslines tied to the trees where some old women sitting in chairs sew and hang their clothes. The palaces along Castellana are open. There's a beautiful old chair that's been left in the yard of one of the palaces, it's a gem, a museum piece. How could it have withstood the rain and the harsh winter? Some shabby little kids play hide and seek as they run in and out.

Everything's peaceful nonetheless. It's not an everyday type of peace, like the tranquility of women sewing, but the peace of a Sunday afternoon. Next to the tall buildings and the railings around the yard, I see men and boys smoking cigarette butts like they used to do on Segovia Street and Ribera de Curtidores. These are the people like those who used to live close to the Manzanares River or the ones living in shanties in the Tetuán neighborhood. Everything around here is strange, disagreeable, not what they're used to; the sun is an exception, the sweet sun that shines tenderly over the palaces as well as the shanties.

A man and woman go by with a goat on a leash… Everyone looks at them.

One of the women yells at them as she sews:

"Look at that. Some people showing off what they've got. Hey, you ain't so lucky?"

The couple with the goat turns around abruptly as if they'd been stung by a bee.

"Hey, lady, we're taking care of this creature!... and…"

I can't make out what they're saying because the woman is on her feet gesticulating and the rest of them are all yelling at the same time. It's a funny scene; I'm going to tell María Luisa about it.

Beyond the Castelar statue, there's more people on the street; it's like a small town on a Sunday afternoon. People stroll by, not in a hurry as they converse peaceably. No one is well-dressed. But at the same time, there's something palpable in their faces and gestures. As I gaze at them they become refined gentlemen and ladies.

I'm on Ayala Street. Close to the corner I see María Luisa. The doorman recognizes me.

"You're very thin."

I don't dare answer him by saying he looks like a skeleton.

"The elevator ain't been working for a long time. Now that everybody's weaker and hungrier, they have to climb the stairs. See? Today everything's the other way around. It's like that."

When I get to the seventh floor, I'm exhausted. María Luisa opens the door.

"Girl, look at you!"

"Well, look at the both of us!"

She's skinny too. Her mother has been sick for a long time; María points to a closed door. Her brother's a soldier on the front, trying to forget the people who've been executed... Her father...

"Look, girl... it's best not to talk about the family... How's your Jorge?"

"He's not *my* Jorge. You say such things!"

"Well, you know, everyone thinks of him as *your* Jorge. Look at the way you blush! You write him letters and you're always talking about him... that he's so nice, so distinguished, that he's..."

"Well, all that is true! You'll say the same when you meet him. Right now he's on the front in Aragón. But I'm telling you, there's nothing between us. Sure... he talks about how we'll be after the war... You can't imagine how delicate he is, how refined, such a good person...!"

"There, you see? You're crazy about him!"

"You say such crazy things!"

I try to change the topic: Barcelona, Valencia, Fifina, Barcelona again, the bombing raids...

"Is there anything to eat?"

"Sure, but not much, and it's not very good, but at least it's something."

"When it all started, we ate the cows and the oxen the refugees brought from Talavera... Then we started on the mules and old horses... There's no more dogs or cats, so we've begun to eat donkeys. They'll last until the end of the war since there're lots of them."

She laughs and I laugh with her.

"Hey, be quiet," she tells me; suddenly she's serious. "It's been years since anyone has laughed in this house."

Then she tells me about a family of lice-ridden beggars living in the flat next door.

"At least they have furniture. It's probably got lice on it… Well, at least they have something."

"Who knows? A band of thieves probably robbed them of everything including the furniture; they didn't even leave the nails. So all they have is a pan and some burlap bags filled with straw, and that's where those poor people sleep. Mom helps them as much as she can. But look at us: we don't have anything either! It's just two families that lived here before with whimpering children. I'm telling you…"

"Poor people!"

"Yes, that's what I say. Poor them. And poor me and you!"

We go for a walk on Serrano Street. The stores are open, but the shelves are empty, just two or three strips of fabric on the counter so I can make a dress.

"I can make it myself. I have lots of free time."

I ask the clerk:

"Do you have…?"

"No, *Señorita*," she curtly interrupts.

Her immediate response surprises me.

"But I haven't even told you what I want!"

"We don't have anything, nothing at all!"

When we go out, we laugh at her. What a joke, I guess she doesn't want to sell anything.

"No, they don't want to," María Luisa says. "They're sure we'll lose the war, and today's currency won't be worth anything. That's why they want to keep their merchandise, hoping it'll always be worth something."

"So why do they open?"

"Because it's the law. Don't you see the open grocery stores? But all you can buy is cumin and pepper, other stores have paprika, maybe even chamomile. In the mornings they distribute rations to each store, and since there's so little to sell, they just sweep and read the paper."

"What did they do before?"

María Luisa, with her Madrilenian humor that she never lost in spite of all the grief in her family, tells me about how the grocery stores were filled before the revolution with all kinds of products.

"You can't believe all the asparagus," she says. Yes, I remember it too.

"Where did they get so much asparagus?"

"From their basements, *hija*. Where do you think? When we finished the asparagus, they brought out the tea. Tea from China, tea from Ceylon, Lipton tea… *Mamá*, who never has tea except when she's sick, says all her stomach aches are gone. Then came the bags of beans with insects in them. Imagine: some people had bags of beans stored since San Isidro day. We still have some. They're delicious; you'll see. When we get back, I'll give you a handful for tomorrow, Sunday…"

I say no, laughing. But she's serious, she wraps them up and gives me instructions on how to cook them.

"But not at night. We haven't had electricity in this town for over a year; you won't be able to see what you're doing. They said we had to turn off the lights because of the bombing raids; we were so cautious and obedient that we haven't turned them on… When it's a cloudy night you've got to be careful not to hit your head on the wall… Ok, move along, get out of here before it's too late."

Guadalupe is very pleased to see the beans, and she puts them in water at once and assures me we'll get rid of the insects.

I go to bed at once. The lights are so dim that I can't read or sew. And, worse than that, the dimness depresses me, it makes me uneasy, as if the darkness were falling on top of me.

Kinotín lies down at my feet.

"What has he had to eat?"

"Nothing. I don't have anything for him. He ate some garbanzos at noon."

"It's not enough."

Guadalupe shrugs her shoulders and leaves. She comes back with the empty can of sardines we ate at noon; just the oil is left.

"I kept it for cooking oil since we don't have any. Let the cat have it."

After his feast, Kinotín licks his lips and purrs as he jumps on my bed.

"Kinotín, don't you dirty the bedspread... my little Kinotín."

"Poor thing! He's going to lick his lips all night. I haven't given him a banquet like this in a long time."

Guadalupe doesn't leave, so I imagine she wants to tell me something.

"What's the matter? Tell me…"

"Well, I'm thinking, *Señorita*, that maybe tomorrow we can dig up the garden and plant tomatoes and lettuce, maybe even potatoes… Next winter's going to be very hard. Listen… Do you hear it?"

I try, but I can't hear anything.

"Yes," says Guadalupe. "Shells are falling in the center of the city."

"Are they falling here?"

"No, not here, *Señorita*. If we had food, we'd be so well-off in Chamartín. No bombs fall here. It's been a while since they bombed us. Just shells in Madrid."

The telephone rings, and Guadalupe answers. I'm right behind her tying my robe.

It's María Luisa.

"She says shells have destroyed the attic where we store the furniture. The water pipes are broken, so it's possible the whole house is flooded."

"My God!"

"I'm calling to tell you to come right away. It's probably best to move the furniture to your house. Don't you think?"

"Yes, of course. Thank you, María Luisa."

"We know a driver who can take us there if we give him some food. He doesn't want money."

"But…"

"Don't worry, we'll give you something."

"Thank you again, María Luisa."

She's always been my salvation.

I've moved my furniture back home. Fortunately, the water that came in through the attic did little damage.

I'm happy arranging the paintings, unrolling the carpets, washing the Bohemian crystal cups and the porcelain plates, as fine as eggshells. I remember *Mamá* doing the same so many times!

Guadalupe and I iron the curtains and dust the velvet drapery and hang them on the stair railings.

These are busy days; I don't have time to go outside. María Luisa comes over to help, and sometimes she stays to eat with us. We're fortunate to have meat and potatoes, and sometimes a boiled egg we sliced into three pieces.

She's brought lettuce seeds, tomatoes, carrots, beets, and we plant them in the garden even though there are lots of pebbles. Have we tilled enough soil?

I can't help going into the house at all times to make sure everything is alright in the vestibule: the thick red carpet, the upholstered armchairs, the oak bookshelves, and the miniature figure of Columbus's Santa María that my parents bought me when I was a girl And in the dining room, there's an oil portrait of *Mamá* in an oval frame... and a silver crystal lamp, and oak furniture...

Papá's room on the upstairs floor is the one that's taken me the most time to arrange. All his books are there in wall-to-wall shelves, the huge map of seventeenth-century Madrid covers an entire wall that goes from the balcony to the door, his sofa bed, his ample desk.

Then I enter my room. There's the sweet-smelling cedar closet that used to be *Mamá's*, and her little bed, and next to my room, my sisters' room with little white beds and a children's closet.

"Celia!" María Luisa calls from the garden. "What are you doing inside, *mujer*? It's such a marvelous day."

I go out to the balcony.

"I'm contemplating the house. It's so beautiful, don't you think? I'm going to plant geraniums out here in the balcony so that you can see them from inside.

At night I write *Papá*: «The house is waiting for you and the girls. It's so beautiful, I think you'll love it. When we're all together'»

I can barely see in the dim light, so I have to continue the letter tomorrow. Far away I can hear rifle shots and explosions.

I had forgotten about the war.

HUNGER!

Summer has arrived. The beans Guadalupe planted are sprouting, and the buds are tender and juicy, so we eat them immediately. They're tasty, and they nourish us for a few days.

We wait until the carrots are fully grown under the earth; we check on them dozens of times a day, weeding and watering them.

""They're too close together," says María Luisa. "You have to get rid of the weaker plants to give room for the healthy ones."

The tomatoes are small and warped; they only last two or three days before they're all gone.

It's too bad we don't have oil or lard. Guadalupe says to me in a hushed voice:

"They're selling a dozen eggs for fifty pesetas."

"Well, buy them as soon as you can!"

"There's a newborn rabbit too… for fifty pesetas."

We buy him and bring him into the doghouse, and I put up a mesh fence around him. His name is Blas.

Kinoto approaches him, curiously sniffing the fence wires.

One afternoon walking with María Luisa on Serrano Street, we see a group of people gathered around a man in front of a door. He has two sacks filled with huge carrots, the kind that we fed to the pigs before the war.

"How much?"

"Ten pesetas a kilo."

We take off our scarves, and María Luisa considers taking off her jacket too, using her clothes as a sack for the carrots. María Luisa's mother sits in her armchair next to my bed and tells me how to cook them; I notice how pale and thin she is.

"First you cut the carrots and onions into pieces and boil them in a well-fastened stewpot; then add oil and bay leaves."

When Guadalupe sees me come in with all this bounty, she shouts with glee.

"*Señorita, Señorita!* We've got enough to eat for a week."

There's no more coal left, so we move the pot to a little electric stove that barely gives off heat and leave it there for the night, hoping that by daybreak it'll be done.

I can't sleep thinking I've burnt the carrots. The entire house smells like seasoning.

"Guadalupe! Guadalupe!"

The clock says it's two. Guadalupe sleeps soundly; not even a cannon's going to wake her. I go downstairs barefoot.

My worries were for nothing. The stew is still boiling; there's still a little water in the pot. But María Luisa warns me that you have to let it boil in its own juices, if not it'll taste insipid. What to do?

I decide to bring the little stove up to the bathroom with the pot in it. That way I'll be able to keep an eye on it all night. A sleepless night!

In the morning the carrots are still hard, so I leave them in the pot all day. The house smells good now, the stew promises to taste yummy and makes our mouths water.

The stew will last three days for sure; Guadalupe and I look at each other and smile from ear to ear.

"What a banquet!"

But the carrot stew is soon gone, so every day María Luisa and I go up to that door on Serrano hoping to find the man selling carrots. But he's not there.

"The carrots we've planted should be ready now."

Say no more: a minute later we yank the carrots from the ground. They're small and tender. What a delight it is to pull them out of the moist dark earth! Guadalupe quietly gathers them in a basket. Suddenly she says:

"What a miracle, *Señorita*, don't you think? While we go about doing our daily chores making noise, the earth doesn't make a sound, just goes along nourishing us… Look how tender, how rosy, how good they smell!"

But these carrots, the ones we share with María Luisa's family, also run out, so again we're stuck with the forty grams of lentils they ration every three days.

One morning Guadalupe wakes me up to give me horrible news.

"There's no more salt. I went to the store and they told me that it ran out a long time ago. And the gypsy woman who lives in the nearby hotel doesn't want to give us any, same with the gardener who used to work here. And…"

"Alright, so we'll have to eat the lentils without salt. What else can we do? We don't have oil either."

Without any fat to cook with, I'm getting terribly thinner every day. My eyes are dry, and my facial skin is getting tighter.

Papá sent us two boxes of food for the month of April, but Franco's troops have blocked the roads so nothing arrives for ten or twelve days.

María Luisa calls me:

"Mother wants you to come for lunch today. She managed to get a long horse's tongue, a tongue so long it went from the mouth to the tail," she says.

"What?" I say astounded.

"You'll see. We've got gullets too, and more and more meat like that. Scraps, *hija*, that's all we have. A while ago this would be disgusting to us, but today it's mouth-watering. I can't wait!"

At night I bring Guadalupe some meat in a sauce. It's a real gift!

But later come days and days with nothing to eat.

"Don't get out of bed today, *Senorita*, Guadalupe tells me. I'll bring you a hot water bottle for your feet… we don't have anything to eat…"

"But aren't they rationing today?"

"Yes… but look what they're giving out."

She shows me a pair of enormous espadrilles.

"They say the rations haven't arrived, there's nothing. So they had to give us something… anything, and here you are."

I'm in bed all day. At noon I eat a little bread: I divide it into two slices.

"How's Blas?" I ask.

"He's so cute, *Señorita*. He likes rose leaves but not geraniums; too bad there're no more leaves on the rose bushes.

"What about Kinoto?"

"He's out and about meowing at everything."

"Bring him up here so I can give him some bread."

I share my bread with the cat but both of us are still hungry. Kinoto carefully smells my bare arms; I cover them. Who knows what he thinks about my arms!

Two days later María Luisa calls.

"Come over before lunch."

Someone has told her that in a tavern on Belén Street they're selling small dishes of meat and potatoes.

It's true. We go in, and in a narrow dining room with dirty wine-stained tablecloths they serve us small plates. There are a couple of pieces of who knows what kind of meat in a sauce even more questionable with bits of turnip.

"They're turnips, not potatoes!" I say sadly.

"No, that's dog meat, probably from their dog."

"It's good!"

"Yes, so what?"

María Luisa wants to bring her mom and dad a dish of this, and I think of Guadalupe too.

A man reading the newspaper is sitting in a corner; he looks like he's the owner, the man in charge of the tavern. He disappoints us.

"There's no more, comrades. Not a bit of meat, not even turnips. I'd really like to give you some more, but we've served you all we have. We only gave it to you because I thought you were nurses living next door. I promised it to someone else; when they come they'll be upset."

When we leave we look at each other.

"It was Juliana who told me about this tavern. Imagine that!"

"Who is Juliana?"

"That girl who went to the same school as us. Juliana Ocampo, the plump one. Now she's a nurse in the Red Cross."

"Well, we've eaten her ration."

"So what do we do now?"

And like this it goes on from day to day; lentils distributed when they have them, which is seldom.

Guadalupe and I decide to eat only three days a week; that way the little portion of lentils is larger. But Kinoto is disgruntled about the new arrangement, he's meowing all the time. He's so weak that he has to drag his hind legs. I can't look at him because it breaks my heart.

"What about Blas?" asks María Luisa. "When are you going to eat him?"

"If you could see him! He knows me, and when I get home I find him standing upright with his ears pricked."

"Come on! You're telling me he's a member of your family?"

"That's right!"

Guadalupe says the same thing sometimes.

"Are you capable of killing him?"

"No, *Señorita*, the workman's son will do it; he lives…"

"Alright, let's not talk about it. Blas is waiting for the end of the war just like us. *Papá* will probably say…"

I don't tell *Papá* how hungry we are when I reply to his long letters in tiny handwriting convincing me that the war is about to end because the League of Nations is negotiating a peace agreement.

At times Fifina sends me green beans and garbanzos. But just two kilos in one month; it's not enough.

María Luisa phones me.

"Anything to eat today?"

"Not today. Just a little bread."

"It's the same here, but they say that in the Torrijos market they're selling greens."

"Greens? What kind of greens?"

"Ay, *hija*, I don't know. Maybe roadside weeds. The kind the militiamen 'water.'"

"Militiamen water the weeds?"

"You're so innocent, Celia, you've been like that all your life."

Now I understand what she meant by "watering." I laugh.

"You're so naughty!"

"So what do you say? Do you want me to buy weeds? They say they taste like spinach. But I'm not sure they're not poisonous and we'll all get sick."

"No, please. We have enough grass right around here. All we have to do is go out to the countryside. I know something you might be interested in. But I'm not sure. In the Argüelles neighborhood they're selling rats, really big ones."

"I'll tell my mom."

In the afternoon, María Luisa and I go over to Argüelles. I hadn't been there since I went to find Fifina when the bullets were flying everywhere.

The reflection of broken glass makes the ruins shine as if they were covered with diamonds in the sunny and scathingly hot afternoon.

When we cross a street, two policemen stop us.

"Where are you going? You can't go over there because the buildings are still falling."

But María Luisa is determined to buy rats even though she can't find anyone selling them; she takes me by the arm and escorts me down San Bernardo until we get to Reyes Street.

Then we wander around in the debris, trying not to be seen. There are people digging with sticks, looking for things in the debris.

"Imagine digging around for two years, but by now they've probably taken everything."

A woman dressed in black with a little girl by the hand asks us:

"I lived right there, you know? And now I can't even find the door."

She points to a pile of rubble covering all the sidewalks and streets.

"Maybe that door lying in the middle of the street was part of the entrance. But no… that can't be. My street was somewhere else."

María Luisa tells her it's no use to look for your house because the rubble has covered everything, and that all those poor souls digging around won't find anything.

"If they're no rats, there's nothing of value," she says, still determined to find what we're looking for.

"Rats!" the woman yells. "No, not rats! Right over there, my three-month-old baby is somewhere under all the wreckage…. Not rats!"

I grab María Luisa's sleeve and lead her to a little street that's in a little better condition, only a balcony attached to a building about to fall.

"Run!" I say to her when I see it.

"Yes… let's go down San Bernardo," she says. "I don't care about finding rats anymore… Of course that's why they're so fat, they've probably eaten the dead bodies."

We climb up and down a pile of debris where grass has begun to grow. Then a few young boys approach us.

"I'll sell you a pet rabbit for a hundred pesetas."

He shows the skinned headless animal.

"It's a cat!" I say. "A little one…"

"It's not a cat or a rabbit… it's a rat."

In spite of what María Luisa said, we buy it and wrap it in the bloody paper the kids brought with them. Then we put the dead animal in the burlap bag.

"You know? Maybe it's not a rat, and if it is, it hasn't eaten human flesh, or if it has, no one at home will know. You won't say anything, will you?"

Two days later Juliana, the nurse, invites us to her flat for lunch.

"Am I included?" I ask María Luisa.

"Yes, you too. I'm always talking to her about you. They've given her five kilos of donkey meat, and if we don't eat it right away with this heat it'll go bad."

I eat lunch in Juliana's flat on Fortuny Street. She has six brothers, and a father and mother… They're nice people, generous. The mother's name is Rosario, a tender woman, blond with blue eyes. I'm fond of her.

"Eat, love," she tells me. "Eat to rid yourself of hunger."

When she finds out I'm alone in Madrid, she gives me a little jar of honey.

The father is a tall man. He was probably fat at one time because his jacket doesn't fit; it looks like a robe. He's kind, energetic, manly, and ingenuous, like a boy or like a giant. I'd have to write a whole book to describe all his goodness.

From that day on, I have another home. And when I don't have enough to eat, it's because there's nothing in María Luisa's or Julianita's house; there seldom is.

So we don't see each other anymore. I lock myself up in my little dwelling. It's so pretty, I've fixed it up elegantly. And I read… mainly cookbooks. At no time in my life have I wanted to learn more about cooking. When the war ends, I'm going to surprise *Papá* with succulent dishes. Not the inexpensive ones I used to cook when we were in Santander.

On one of those days when we're down to a miserable ration of bread, Guadalupe says:

"The woman who lived in the hotel nearby died this morning. She hadn't eaten in three days."

I find out she lived with her daughter and grandchildren and that they ate everything.

All the old people are dying little by little. It might be because they have less endurance than the young and because they're tired of being in this world, but it might also be that they give all their rations to their grandchildren… It's all possible.

Now the ones who used to be generous and altruistic have turned into miserable misers. María Luisa tells me her father's old friend died.

"Now we've got a problem. There's no wood for a coffin, so the family has given us a wardrobe but we have no way of covering it. He'll have to lie in an open coffin, just like everyone else these days."

"An open coffin?"

"Of course, girl. Don't you know? Dead people today look up out of their open caskets face to the sky with their bellies hanging over the sides."

"Be quiet! How horrible!"

Since I've been living on the outskirts of Madrid for several months, I don't know anything about burials or funerals. At first, there was no more black fabric to wrap the unvarnished coffins, so they were covered in blue and purple cloth, sometimes with flower designs. But even these fabrics ran out, or they got so expensive that they're only used for more necessary things, more urgent than covering the dead, so the coffins are made of naked and knotted pine with no fabric cover… But wood for furniture has run out too, so now families have to pay a carpenter to turn a closet or chest of drawers into a coffin, and that's almost never enough wood to include a cover.

"So the carpenter sells the little remaining wood so he can buy something to eat. But that's not the worst of it, it's that the ones in charge of the burial refuse to do their job for money, only food."

"So what are you going to do?

"I don't know, *Mamá*'s offering half a kilo of garbanzos and the dead one's nephew a pack of cigarettes. We can only hope this will be enough for them to start digging… and if not, the father and his family will have to do it."

When I learned of all this, every time I saw a funeral I was curious about what they carried in the coffin. It's true what María Luisa says, sometimes you can see the dead one's nose and belly, sometimes even his crossed hands. He's probably very disgruntled about all this display.

"You've never seen anything like it," says María Luisa. "My little niece, the one who lives on Alcalá, spends all her time on the balcony yelling, 'Look Mami, it's a really fat man. Look, look, come see what a paunch…!' Since we can't go to the theater anymore, we can enjoy this one with the open caskets, so inspirational and instructive!"

I'm getting obsessed finding enough to eat; today I go out to find some grass for Blas. He's no longer a kitten; he's getting as big as a lamb and he needs to eat every day.

I climb over fences looking for something green, but everything is dry and shorn. In the fields some families keep a goat for milk, but the goat's eaten all the grass, and fields close by are filled with refugees from towns nearby, they've brought their oxen carts carrying sheep and rabbits. The animals eat everything in sight, all the weeds, even leaves on the trees… Of course there are no more oxen, sheep, or rabbits. All that remains in these barren fields is trash where children roll around, and their mothers comb their hair and look at their combs to see if they have lice.

As I walk in these fields I hear braying; seems like it's coming from the sky. A donkey has poked his head out of a turret window with his mouth wide open, showing his teeth as he brays loudly and pitifully

"How has that burro climbed up the turret?"

A man basks in the sun smoking a cheap, ill-smelling cigar; he turns his head and looks at me:

"I led him up there."

I look surprised, so he tells me about how tiring it was to get that donkey up the narrow stairs.

Meanwhile, the donkey continues with his head out the window looking upwards and continues his heart-rending lamentations as if he were calling out to the heavens.

Two families living in a boarding house have squabbled. The family living below has prohibited the family living above to keep their donkey in their corral. Not having any other place for him, they've had to carry him upstairs to the turret.

"God knows if I'll be able to get him down. He'll probably break his legs cause he's really clumsy!"

Soon we'll probably eat him. We've already eaten most of the donkeys around here, and every time they put up a sign in the butcher shop: "Tomorrow at ten, donkey meat with your rationing card." Guadalupe is beside herself; she comes to tell me:

"*Señorita*!… Tomorrow we'll have a nice stew. Too bad there's no oil."

The meat is tough despite having been boiling over the electric stove all night; the entire house emits a smell that reaches every corner. The broth is disgusting.

At other times, we leave the meat outside because some say that's the way to make it less tough, but the smell seems to upset Kinoto to no end. His meows are heart-breaking; they don't let me sleep. One night when he was at the foot of my bed, he jumped up in my arms, and I saw a bit of madness in his eyes like he was going to attack me.

"Shoo, shoo, Kinoto! The animal's going crazy!"

IN MY HOUSE WE DON'T EAT, BUT...

Summer has passed, and an inclement autumn follows, dragging the fallen leaves along the ground and darkening the sky. The yellow leaves are rolling on the ground like silk paper, and they sound like frying potatoes; they're good for fuel when we burn them in the winter. Guadalupe and I box the fallen leaves and pack them in the coach house. So many piles getting bigger and bigger up to the ceiling. When we squeeze them in our hands they look as if they're in pain, they're rough to the touch. It's grueling work for Guadalupe and me, and since we haven't eaten much…

"What have you done with the espadrilles they rationed you?" asks María Luisa.

They're repairing the sidewalks on the left side of a section of Alcalá Street, down from Torrijos. They call that area "Bolsa de Contratación."

María Luisa has a treasure she can sell: a pack of Virginia tobacco cigarettes. And I'm carrying a pair of espadrilles that are too big for me.

"You see?" María Luisa points to a group of people shouting to advertise what they've got for sale.

The closer we get the louder they shout:

"Two cigs for a half kilo of sugar!"

"A ball of wool for a half dozen eggs!"

"A shirt for a kilo of salt!"

"Who will buy two kilos of potatoes for a coat? Comrades, winter's coming!"

María Luisa advises that I can get two cans of condensed milk for my sandals.

"But you've got to shout loud so they can hear you. I'm going to try for two dozen eggs and a kilo of sugar for the pack of cigarettes."

I cry out:

"A pair of espadrilles for two bottles of milk." I hold the espadrilles over my head.

At first no one pays any attention to me, but later a man says:

"Let's see, comrade. Let me try them on."

"Just one," says María Luisa.

We separate from the crowd, and the man sits on a doorstep to try on a sandal.

As he tries it on, I can see his foot covered by a dirty sock that was once white. It fits.

"It fits like a glove."

"Better," says the man who accompanies him. "Much better. Just put rags in the toe and it'll fit perfect."

"Let's see the other one."

"What about the two cans of milk? Do you have them?"

No, he doesn't have them here. He says they're at home.

"Well then, comrade, when you bring them to us, you'll get your sandals. And if you don't show up soon, we'll sell them to someone else."

Finally, it's all settled. His companion offers to bring the cans of milk. Soon they're in my possession, and María Luisa has her eggs, potatoes, and even the sugar.

"Now let's get out of here, because if someone sees what we have…"

As we run along Hermosilla Street, we see a couple of kids jumping off the balcony from a flat on one of the lower floors.

"These kids are having so much fun."

There they are, right in front of us, laughing and crawling around, happy to be free.

We pass by a garage door with a sign on it saying, "Attention: News of Brigade 34 Needed."

"Comrade, do you know anything about the 34th Brigade?" asks one of the kids.

A man walking by says, "Nothing… we have no idea."

"We don't either," yell the kids as they run away laughing.

"Naughty boys!"

We leave our things in María Luisa's house and go to the Café Roma, on the corner of Serrano, to have a glass of vermouth.

"It's delicious… even though it's half turpentine, half gasoline, and the rest rot-gut alcohol."

"Sounds horrible! I don't want any!" I say.

But María Luisa laughs and shoves me inside. It's crowded, noisy, and stuffy. We sit at a table behind a column, and we're served two glasses of a gold-colored liquid.

"No, don't smell it," says María Luisa. "Putting your nose in a glass is disgusting. Didn't you learn that in school?'

We laugh as I take a sip of the strange looking liquid. Yes, it does taste dreadful, but it's sweet, and I end up liking it.

"It's good, no?"

The war has taught us new things. Who would have thought that before today we could drink this, or the fried potato skins with onions, how could we have figured out that leaves could turn into an exquisite vegetable.

The vermouth makes us tipsy, especially since we hadn't eaten. María Luisa turns red and all smiley as she pats my face, and I assure her I'm the happiest girl in Madrid.

"Of course you are. Everyone knows about you and all those stories you write! "

"Imagine, when I go out, people point at me and say, 'That's Celia. It's her, the great writer.'"

I know what I say isn't true, but an unfettered impulse makes me say it.

"They'll put up a statue of you!"

"I know. But I won't be nude like Goya's Naked Maja, I want to be cloaked with a Roman toga, with a book in my hand."

"Yes, and I'd be at your side because I'm your best friend!"

"Sure, but they won't allow it… unless…"

"Maybe you'd prefer Fifina."

"No… although she's been very good to me, and…"

"But not your best friend…"

"My best friend! That's silly! They're all my best friends."

I don't like her to go on like that; it seems she's insulting Fifina, and she shouldn't… No. Fifina is lovely and intelligent, the smartest one in the San Isidro School!

"More than me?"

"More than you and more than anyone."

"In other words, more than you are."

I can't admit that. I disagree. Because if they're going to put up a statue of me, there must be a reason!

"You're unbearable!"

When I stand up, I feel dizzy; everything's going round and round. María Luisa is crying inconsolably.

Tears are streaming relentlessly down her face to the floor. But I don't say anything to her. I'm really worried about my dizziness; besides, I'm feeling sick.

"I think I'm going to die," I whisper. María Luisa hears me and keeps on sobbing.

"María Luisa "

She doesn't answer, so I say to her:

"María Luisa, forgive me. I didn't want to offend you. I swear."

I can't go on because I'm crying too, and I hide my face in my kerchief.

Suddenly, I feel someone's heavy hand on my shoulders, and a man's voice says enthusiastically:

"Hell, look at these girls… You've been here all the time?"

It's María Luisa's father, surprised to see us both weeping.

"For crying out loud, what's the matter with you?"

María Luisa tries to explain, and I fill in the blanks, but an inconsolable sadness overtakes us, and we keep crying and crying.

"What the hell? Looks to me like you're drunk! What have you been drinking?... Barman! What were these girls drinking?... Give us the check?"

As we leave, we're hanging on to his arm, walking on Ayala toward Castellana Boulevard. Autumn's cold air and the smell of dry leaves sober me up. When we reach my house, I hesitate. María Luisa does not look me in the eye. We're both ashamed.

I stay in my home in Chamartín for a few days without going to Madrid even though we have nothing to eat. Yesterday we finished the garbanzos— war time garbanzos, the miraculous ones, the ones you can't find when there's peace. Guadalupe stares at them and says:

"These aren't garbanzos, they can't be."

Sometimes when we had lentils, we soaked them at night, we didn't recognize them. They were so small. But now we don't even have that.

It's cold. The lettuce I planted begins to sprout in the cold, naked earth. Guadalupe and I, all bundled up, go out to the garden and begin to loosen the dirt so we can transplant small shrubs and dig ditches for irrigation. A dozen heads of lettuce must be our only food for a while.

In the afternoon, Guadalupe goes to the post office and brings back a letter. It's from America! … Argentina! I remember *Mamá's* friend, a woman with a little girl. I can't believe it when I read the letter. They know about our situation. They found the address of our house, and two months ago, they sent a box of food.

I call Guadalupe, and together we read the list of things they've sent.

Sugar… cocoa… condensed milk… coffee… oil… codfish… sardines… dried fruit.

Both of us start to cry. The only thing we've had today is water.

"Do you think it'll get here?"

"Of course!"

"It's just that they say…"

"Don't pay any attention. It'll get here!"

I call María Luisa to tell her about it and hear her yell out gleefully:

"Girl, what luck! You've hit the lottery! How wonderful!"

Days and weeks go by; it's December and there's no news of a package.

Every day, we gather lettuce from the garden. There are no more grapes because Fifina doesn't send any.

"I look everywhere for something to send you, and I can't find anything," she writes.

There's a heavy sadness over me; it makes me shiver for hours in *Papá's* library. The thermometer says it's three degrees Celsius. I've covered myself in blankets, and I hear Guadalupe in the kitchen. What's she doing? There's nothing to eat.

"I'm cleaning," she tells me.

"With what?" I say. For a long time we don't have soap, how can we wash our clothes?

"I've boiled ashes in water, then I've strained it through a fine cloth, and then I soak the clothes in the water... There's a lady who lives in the house behind ours on Padilla Street. She told me how to do it."

She goes back to her wash.

I'm sad. It isn't just because of hunger, what saddens me is looking into the mirror, my straight hair, not wavy and golden like it used to be. I don't go to my hairdresser anymore because they took away her tools. So she went to work for a cooperative. But she left Later I went to a hair salon on Gran Vía, but I think it's closed now.

I try to get in touch with my former hairdresser by phone.

"Who? Celia Gálvez? Yes, I remember you. But it's just that... Do you have food?"

"No. We're having a hard time..."

"But don't you have a garden? Haven't you planted anything?"

"Yes, I have lettuce..."

"Fine! If you bring me a few heads, I'll fix your hair. But no money, please. It's not worth anything."

When I go to the hair stylist, she doesn't only wave my hair, she gives me a manicure. I feel better about myself now. Mr. Aguilar, her husband, invites me to lunch. He lives on Recoletos; his house is warm and cozy. His wife and mother regale me so attentively that I let out a few tears. The meal is like a banquet.

But then again there's the hunger. My house is freezing. The hair stylist waves my hair in return for a cake I made from a recipe María Luisa's mother gave me.

Christmas is near. It's raining and it's cold. The rain makes the streets sparkle. I walk on the right side of Serrano Street, looking for a lace that sells buttons for a worn-out coat.

I pass by a store with a metal shutter halfway down. The shelves are empty, and the owners are bored, walking around with their hands in their pockets.

As I come across a street that adjoins Castellana, I see a glorious color that makes me stop dead in my tracks. Oranges! A truck transporting oranges. Its color is warm, bright… it's as if the sun had turned into a piece of fruit, it illuminates the street. Everyone who passes by stops and stares… me too.

"Oranges!"

"They're oranges!"

"Are they for sale?" I hear someone ask.

The truck continues its route toward Castellana and turns the corner and disappears. Some people run after it, as if they were in a trance.

When I get back home, María Luisa calls me.

"You were in my neighborhood and you didn't stop by? Well I've got good news for you. I think a package of food has arrived at the train station. Maybe it's yours."

"No one has gotten in touch with me."

"*Ay, hija.* Don't wait around. Go to the station and ask. Bring your identification card and the letter… and something to tie it so you can drag it home."

The sun has come out in the sprinkling rain, and the air tastes like mountain snow. I get to the station at two in the afternoon.

A man walks over to me.

"Are you waiting for merchandise?"

"Yes…"

"You'll need help taking it home."

"Yes, my house is far away."

"I'll carry it for you… for half the cost."

"What?"

"I mean half of the contents of the box you're waiting for, or whatever you've got…"

"No! I'll pay you the money I owe."

"Money? Bah, you can't eat money, comrade. I don't want money."

I search from one office to another, from one storeroom to another. Finally, I locate the blessed box. It has my name on it, and it weighs fifteen kilos.

"You're in luck," says the man who hands me the box. "It's the only one that's not been broken into. All the others are open and ripped apart."

I'm on an incline leading to the street from the station. How can I carry it home? No one wants to help me, not even for money.

Luckily I've brought a rope to drag it along. I tie it to the box and pull it. I'm like a kid wheeling a wagon. I keep an eye on the box as I drag it along; I make sure it's still tied to the rope and that it doesn't go off to the side.

No one is looking at me. Three years of revolution and war have made people oblivious to all the bad things they see… blood, ruins, or strange people. No more curiosity about such things.

I manage to get to Atocha Street where I wait for a streetcar.

"What are you carrying there?" asks the conductor.

"Old books."

"Funny books?"

"Yes, a couple of them."

"In my house we don't eat much, but we do laugh."

"Help this girl," he says. "Don't fret, just help her."

Someone helps me raise the box to the platform. I'd like to stand next to him, but I have to sit down.

"Go on in, it's cold here. Go ahead, I'll keep an eye on your box. It's not going anywhere."

It's getting dark; night comes at five now as I drag the box along the road. Sometimes there's a rock in the way, so I have to push until I get to a flatter part of the road. If Guadalupe only knew what I've got! If she knew, she'd be waiting for me anxiously. But she doesn't know. I haven't told her anything just so she doesn't get her hopes up.

I go down the street lined with boarding houses. I'm making so much noise that a dog barks at me. It's one of those hungry squalid dogs with protruding ribs; it's the only dog left in this area. Suddenly he stops barking, ears pricked. He smells the box and his tail begins to wag wildly.

No windows are open. No one complains about the noise on the streets in this neighborhood just outside the city. There're so many tanks, soldiers, cannons, people passing by without speaking; the only sound you hear is feet walking along the road looking for a place to lay a man down, loud people, women and children running toward a butcher shop that sells horse meat or donkey meat. People's curiosity about these strange things has died. No one cares about anything anymore! The noise or all the people on the streets doesn't matter; everything will be the same.

"Guadalupe! Guadalupe!"

"*Señorita!*" She unlocks the door, making a loud noise, and crosses the yard hurriedly toward the gate.

"Here's the box of food. It's from America!"

She's so pale and disconcerted that she can't manage to open the gate.

"It's huge!" she says.

The two of us carry the box inside and close the door… In this house hunger is everywhere.

We manage to open the box using a hammer and pliers. Nuts and almonds spill out.

"*Señorita!* Look, *Señorita!*"

A glass jar full of goodies has fallen out…and a package of something that smells like chocolate…and a little white box wrapped in decorative paper with golden letters. It all looks like Christmas presents.

I feel Guadalupe's hand tapping my shoulder:

"Listen, *Señorita!*"

I raise my head. I hear the rhythmic breathing of a man at the door.

"They want to come in," she tells me. "Maybe they saw what you were dragging."

We both approach the door. I look through the peephole. In the late afternoon light I see a figure moving and breathing heavily on the last step to the doorway.

"It's the dog…! That poor thing is all skin and bones."

As he comes in the door I see he's frightened, dragging himself along the floor determined to put up with the blows he expects as long as he gets a bone.

WINTER. PAPÁ!

María Luisa calls me on the phone me and says this afternoon she'll come quickly because she has to see me.

Not only does she arrive promptly but she brings an afternoon snack: twelve raisins for each of us, a little slice of bread, and an empty cologne bottle half-filled with wine.

"A glass for each of us, including Guadalupe."

We go up to the study since it's the room that's least cold, and we talk about dress designs.

"I've found a seamstress in the house next door; she's a refugee. Ten families in one flat. She used to live in a building on Preciado but it collapsed, and three stories fell on her.

"How did she survive?"

"That's what I ask myself. But she got out; she even managed to save a closet of material and a sewing machine. I think she's an able seamstress; she says she'll fix my blue dress by sewing it together with the one with blue squares. I think it'll look good on me. I thought maybe she could do the same with your gray dress."

"So that's all you came to tell me?"

"No, *mujer*, it's about something else."

"Well what is it?" Then a horrible thought came over me. "Is something wrong with *Papá?*"

"No, *mujer!* No. Nothing's the matter with him. It's that… Do you listen to the radio at night?"

"Yes, every night."

"Do you listen to the news about the war?"

"Of course, *hija.* It's the same thing every night. "Our troops have taken over two-hundred-and-three towns. We have had to retreat according to the orders our leaders have given, but the bases are being fortified."

"Doesn't that tell you anything?"

"What could it tell me? I don't know anything about war."

"Me neither…, but when troops retreat, it's that the enemy is bigger and stronger. They've just taken the small towns. I bet your father's side hasn't taken any cities. On the other hand, Franco's troops…"

"Seems to me that you don't know anything about war either."

"It's true… But look, your father is worried about you. He thinks you're happy, that you hope to get the house ready for your him and your sisters… But the war is lost… That's the truth."

"No…!"

"Yes, it's the truth. Everyone knows that… everybody but you. Little by little Franco's troops are taking more and more territory."

"You mean his allies."

"Yes, all of them."

"Well, then *Papá* is doomed. They'll probably execute him!"

"Maybe he'll escape."

"But *Papá* says in the last letter…"

I look for his letter among the papers on the table. Here it is; it's filled with hope and promises. "Soon we'll be together. The girls are fine, and I'm looking forward to sending them to school."

"Don't forget it's January."

"He's talking about autumn when schools are open".

María Luisa says no more as she gazes at the garden. I'm silent too. I don't want to say what I think; I, too, am silent. María Luisa's father is happy about our impending defeat. After all, it's our troops that killed his son! And, of course it's natural to believe what we want to believe. María Luisa seems to know what I'm thinking and says:

"My father is a civilized man; wishes you no ill feelings, but he knows that…"

"Do you really think your father knows more about what's happening than mine; my father is in the army."

"Yes, I know… and you know it too… You told me that when you were in Barcelona with your father and Jorge, you were astonished at his ignorance of anything having to do with the war."

Again, silence between us. We go down to the garden. The sun is out, but it's so cold it waters your eyes. I barely notice the tears running down my face.

We go in the house. The dining room's freezing. Guadalupe brings us blankets to warm us up and two tubs of hot water for our feet.

"One day our noses will fall off," says María Luisa. Mine has turned into an icicle.

We laugh; we don't bring up the war anymore. For the next days we say nothing about it.

January of 1939 is passing us by, cold, blue, sunny crystal skies, transparent in the cold. What's happening? María Luisa comes every day, and she always brings some food no matter how small the amount. Twice I've startled her on the ground floor whispering something to Guadalupe.

"It's been eight days since the last bombing raid," I say to her.

"Of course… why would they keep bombing? They've almost won."

Everyone is waiting for something coming soon. I look at the faces of people in the streetcar, and I think they know something that I don't know.

No one says anything. The first days there was chaos, and now it's silent… The first days people were moving around like bees around a hive working happily and defying the danger, and now silence, sadness, and fear of what's to come.

One morning I go looking for one of my teachers from my old school close to the racetrack.

They've turned a palace close by into a building with large and cheerful classrooms, the morning winter sun shining through the windows.

"We've worked faithfully for a better future," *Señorita* Amelia says to me.

The School for All project has given me hope. That boy over there is the caretaker's son, the one who lives on the nineteenth floor, and the little one next to him grew up in the shanties of Tetuán. He could barely speak his first day of school, and the one who's sitting next to him is the son of Elorrieta, a conservative lawyer. And the blond boy is from an aristocratic family... Listen to the class presentation by the boy from Tetuán; he's talking about bees. Each day all the students speak for five or ten minutes about a certain topic. This gives them an incentive to study, confidence in themselves, eloquence. I'm a little embarrassed because *Señorita* Amelia makes me sit close to her, and all the kids are gazing at me.

I can barely hear what the boy from Tetuán is saying. From carton boxes he's made a beehive all by himself and explains how bees bring nectar to the hive.

When he concludes, he goes out into the playground and Amelia and I go out too.

"Did you see that? What we've been able to achieve in a few months is miraculous. It's a pity that all this is going to end."

"Do you think so?"

"Yes, all this is lost! It's the fault of a few people here and a few people there." She sighs, and her sadness goes right to my heart.

"Do you really think so?" I ask again.

"Yes," she gives me an odd look. "But... You will go to France, no?"

"France?"

"Your father will cross the Pyrenees and... I'll stay here... Whatever happens." She says this as if she were talking to herself. "I'll stay here... I don't know what they'll do to me for the crime of loyalty to democracy."

"But surely..."

She's not sure why I'm so anxious and says:

"Well I'm sure they'll take me to jail... That's for certain... I'd throw them in jail too just so I wouldn't have to worry about them rising up again."

I'm on my way home, and I'm sad. It's also because of Jorge. He only sent me two letters in three months and none for the next four; he's forgotten about me. *Papá* is the one who sends news. In last month's letter he says: "Jorge is on the Ebro Riverfront. He is a hero."

They're all heroes: *Papá*, Jorge, *Señorita* Amelia and Maria Luisa's dad for staying in good spirits in spite of all his suffering… I'm just a lost child amidst all the people, alone, without a family, not knowing what to do.

At night both my head and stomach hurt. My hunger has been nauseating me for days. Today *Señora* Aguilar called to take me to the doctor.

We're in the clinic at three. It's on Alcalá. The doctor sees us in his office. Then he takes us to an X-ray and diagnostic room.

"You need to expose your torso," he says. "It's cold but there's no other way. I need to examine you carefully."

With Rebeca's help, I get undressed; I see that my arms are covered with goosebumps. She places a metal disc on my back and listens with a stethoscope. In the room the only thing you can hear is the tic-toc of a clock.

"Bah, it's nothing. Just weakness. Your stomach's tired of all that crazy garbage you've put in it. Get dressed."

As I put on my clothes, I hear him talking to Rebeca.

"Today's a good day! Have you heard? They've taken Barcelona!"

I turn my head to listen to him. I'm terrified.

"Who? Who's taken Barcelona?"

"Franco… his troops. They entered the city at three, it was on the radio."

My hands are trembling so much I can't even put my coat on.

"My father is in Barcelona! My father's a colonel…"

"They're not there anymore," says the doctor. "Two-hundred-thousand people have fled Barcelona for the border."

When I leave the clinic, everything looks different to me. The street, the sun, the blue sky. Rebeca says to me:

"Don't worry, little one. Your father will be fine… And you'll come to live with us.

I start to sob; I can barely breathe. My God! My God! What's happened to *Papá*?… And deep within me, another question: What about Jorge?"

I'm devastated when I get to Chamartín. The cold engulfs me like an immense cloak of grief. They're all disappearing: *Mami*, Granddad, Aunt Julia, Gerardo… my girls, Valeriana, and now… My God! My God!"

Guadalupe is crying too…

"Kinoto is very sick… He can't even walk," she tells me.

My little darling cat! He opens his eyes when he sees me, I take him out of his basket and put him in bed with me. All three of us go to bed without eating.

We shared the food that arrived from America with everyone who helped us, and in a week there was nothing left.

"And we're thankful and very sad."

"Why thankful?"

"Well, because we don't have anything to eat, but since we're sad, it doesn't matter."

Poor Guadalupe, she says such strange things, like María Luisa always says about her.

At midnight I hear soft meows of pain that wake me up. I turn on the light… It's Kinoto, he's dying. It's the hunger. Poor little kitty! Poor Kinoto!

The cat responds with his soft voice, his sad eyes fixed on me.

"What to do?"

I have a can of condensed milk, it's a treasure hidden away for when the hunger is too much for us. I puncture two holes in the can and spoon a couple of drops of milk that Kinoto laps up eagerly.

"Poor, poor Kinoto! My darling cat, don't die!"

I give him a few more drops, but suddenly he drops his head; I think he's dead.

"No! No! My little cat!"

But he's still barely alive, he opens his eyes and answers me with a human groan… then he drops his head and breathes pitifully.

"Poor thing! My poor cat!"

The color of his head is turning ashen, his snout is pale as he shows his sharp feline teeth… You can see his protruding ribs under his skin; he gestures ferociously… He's dead!

I wrap him in a towel and lay him down on the rug.

THE WAR IS LOST!

February passes by; you can tell spring is on the way from the buds on the rose bushes.

Every morning I go to the central military offices where they tell me how I can find the whereabouts of *Papá* and Jorge. An officer in the Aviation Office tells me:

"We've had no news of your father for over a week. The last we heard was that he was in a farmhouse in Gerona where our headquarters were… But they've been taken over… By this time he's probably crossed the border. If you're all alone here, the best thing you can do is go to Valencia. Once you get there, it shouldn't be difficult to find a merchant ship that can take you to Marseilles."

There's no way of knowing anything about Jorge.

"What?" María Luisa says, "The War Ministry should know where his brigade is, so possibly they'll know where he is too."

We go up and down the stairs of the ministry asking in various offices, but we get no useful information.

"Brigade Thirty-Two?" asks an official. "Ah, come here. I think that… Do you have a family member in that brigade?"

"No, sir," answers María Luisa. "He's a friend, but we're interested in his whereabouts.

"He's one of the soldiers on the Ebro front," he says. "The Ebro battle is totally lost. Look on the list of disappeared or dead."

The very thought horrifies me. "I won't look on that list. I just want to know where he is."

María Luisa pays no attention to me; she carefully looks at the list and points at a name:

"Look «Jorge Medina dead».

I read it, but I don't understand.

"It can't be…"

María Luisa grabs my arm. "Thank you , sir, thank you very much." She leads me past the offices and down the stone stairway.

"It can't be true. There must be a mistake. How can they know?"

The sun is shining; it warms me, but everything looks dark, misty, and dirty.

"I hate Alcalá Boulevard!"

"Let's go. On Negresco they're selling chestnuts," says María Luisa. "… if they still have any."

María Luisa is so kind. She doesn't look at me, as if she were trying to forget everything. This allows me to act as if I were alone. Besides, why should I rush anywhere? What they said about Jorge isn't true. It's just not true. The ones who die were predestined… They… I don't know. Like Aunt Julia and Gerardo… but not Jorge. I remember that dark night in Barcelona with him. He kissed my hand! He was so strong, so tall, so full of life. Was he? If it's not true, how could he have disappeared?

We're sitting at a table in a salon on Negresco, and María Luisa says to the waiter, "The lady will have the same as me… white wine. Yes, please! We'll have white wine to go with our *escargots*."

Something suddenly seems to have melted in my chest and moves up to my throat… It's a river of pain, and my eyes and mouth can't make such pain go away.

I sob disconsolately with my head on the marble tabletop… I feel a hand stroking my hair… I cry even more. I cry until I'm empty, unconscious, without memory… I lift my head.

"Go ahead and eat," says María Luisa. "This is good for you. Eat. Aren't you hungry?"

"Yes…"

So I eat voraciously, like I was starving. And I drink this horrid wine that tastes like vinegar… But it makes me feel better. The salon is crowded. All the tables are occupied. It's all dark, smokey, grey, as if we were in a basement with a bunch of drunkards.

"I've seen a painting like this somewhere… in an exhibit," I say.

"Or in a nightmare," answers Maria Luisa.

February 20

I have lunch at Juliana's house; they're pampering and caressing me, as if I were sick, without asking me what's the matter. Maybe they know.

The mother of the family says to me:

"What are you going to do, Celia?"

"I'll go to France."

Suddenly it occurs to me that my response was instinctual, like it had been inside my head unconsciously.

"France?"

"To be with my father and sisters."

"France is a big country! How will you know where they are? If you just stay at home here, eventually you'll get news of them. Besides, how will they know where you are if you're not here?"

I think about it.

"María Luisa will open the letters that arrive, and she'll tell me the news… And I'll write to all of you so you'll know where I am."

"That's very complicated. Believe me, it's best you don't leave."

After the meal, I talk to Julianita's father in his study.

"What are you going to do in France, *hija mía?*"

"It's no use to stay here. Will *Papá* be allowed to come back?"

"Here? No… He won't be able to come back for many years."

"So if he can't come back with my sisters, why should I stay here?"

"You're right. But I don't know how you'll travel since you're a minor."

That doesn't matter to me. *Papá* gave me a false ID that says I'm twenty-two, but I won't tell this kind man anything.

February 21

I get up early to go to the center Madrid. The offices that take care of passports are on Serrano Street. I've seen people crowding around the entrance. It's on the top floor. The marble staircase is dirty and the colored windows are covered with dust. People are hustling up and down the stairs trying to find the appropriate public office.

I'm told that for a passport I need an identification card, a certificate of good conduct, a certificate of verification of residence, an employment card… I go back down the stairs. I'm not leaving, I'm sure I won't be able to leave the country, but I have to try. It's my duty… I need to be with my father and sisters. I'll do what I have to do to get a passport and…

I'm back on the street. There's a pale sun trying to illuminate Castellana Boulevard, but it's cloudy and hazy, like a cobweb that forms on naked, frozen trees.

Poor Jorge! I'm alone! Terribly alone, more alone than at any other time of my life. Jorge is no longer on his feet… but his soul surely is…

The tears streaming out of my eyes are cold. As I wait for the streetcar, I'm crying, but no one notices. I've seen lots of people crying these days, and no one is surprised. I dry my eyes and get on the streetcar. Everyone is silent, every face is in a daze… Are we home yet? This is how wars end.

This afternoon they're dropping bread from an airplane, hundreds of small loaves wrapped in paper with a Spanish flag on it. No one eats them. I see a woman who gives the bread to dogs on the street.

Every morning I get up early to go to the office in charge of dispensing identification cards. It's in a palace on Lista Street, and later on back to City Hall…

I've managed to gather all the necessary documents.

"I'm leaving, Guadalupe… I'm going to Valencia, and then a boat to Marseilles to find my father and sisters…" I say this to her without really believing it.

"But *Señorita*, what will I do?"

"You'll stay here taking care of the house. *Señorita* María Luisa will give you what you need and later, we'll see… When I get to Marseilles, I'll find *Papá*; he's probably found a group of Spaniards. The Red Cross will help us and…"

"Will you stay in France?"

"No… *Papá* is thinking of going to America, Spanish-speaking countries where life is easy for people from Spain."

"I want to go with you…"

"No, Guadalupe, it's not possible.When I've settled in, I'll call you."

As I speak to her, I'm convincing myself. Yes! I'm leaving… What can I do here all alone?

I go into the dining room where the sun shines in and the walls are covered with cloth, there's oak furniture, a crystal cabinet, a silver chandelier, a painting of the lakes in La Granja… and through the curtains, the fields look beautiful at a distance. I arranged all this for *Papá* when he arrives.

I tell María Luisa I have the passport.

"What? When did you get it?"

"Just four days ago… I have it."

"You won't be able to leave… soon Franco's troops will be in Madrid…"

"Well… Whatever God has in store…"

"There are no trains, no buses, no cars leaving Madrid. You'll have to walk!"

"Well if I have to..."

"Don't be so dramatic, *hija*!" You need to stay here because you have no choice; besides, nothing will happen to you when Franco takes over."

"I don't know about that… They killed my grandfather, and they could kill me."

"Sure… As soon as they take over, the first thing they'll do is look for you: 'Where is Celia Gálvez?' they'll say.'The one who was always telling stories to children. Where is she so we can devour her?'"

I have lunch in Aguilar's house. His dwelling feels like a nest to me, warm white with feathers. His wife is French; she's beautiful. His mother is elderly, enthusiastic and resolute, and he is as usual, serene, and understanding.

"Don't leave, dear girl! Spring is coming. Is there anything as beautiful as spring in Madrid?"

"How are you going to find your father in France? A needle in a haystack. You'll end up wandering in the streets like a beggar-woman. Marseilles is a port city filled with sailors, drunks, and people who are coming and going with no sense of morality…"

"Don't go, *hija*, don't go," says the mother. "A lady is safe alone in her house."

"Yes, I'm alone!" I say with tears in my eyes.

"But you have us. We love you. You can work as an editor for us."

"And my little sisters?"

"Your father will send your sisters here, and you'll continue as their *madrecita*. Don't be crazy. Don't leave!"

His words begin to make me doubt. Of course he's right. I'll be safe here, I won't be poor, I've got my house, and before a month goes by, my sisters will come here… and we'll be together as a family…, and Valeriana will be here too with all her tenderness and devotion, freeing us from all worries. But won't allow *Papá* in the country, he'll have to go to America alone, alone for the rest of his life without his children, without his wife, with no one to caress his face and bring him his newspaper. Poor *Papá*! No, he's not going to leave by himself! He'll leave with his children, with his home…or what's left of his home!"

It's getting dark. María Luisa and I are walking along Fortuny Street; I'm filled with an anxiousness that makes me hesitate. I sit down on the edge of the curb and cry, sobbing out loud. I'm crying for Jorge, for my granddad, for Aunt Julia and Gerardo… and my little sisters, as poor as rats, and my father stripped from his country… and from me… so unhappy… I'm crying because we've lost the war!

It's a very dark night, and I can't stop weeping. When a car goes by, the streets light up a little. It's cold; everything's dirty, ugly, and squalid.

"C'mon, *hija*, let's go. Are you going to stop crying anytime?" asks María Luisa.

"It's that… It's all true," I sob. "It's all true! I didn't believe it… I couldn't believe it. I thought I was living in a fairytale I was making up… I didn't believe it was real until now… until the Aguilar family told me."

"But what did they say?"

"That… that *Papá*…"

It's no use. My words don't reflect my thoughts, they delude them, they're weak, they have nothing to do with reality…"

We go to Julianita's house.

"Are you sure you want to leave?" asks her father.

"Yes, sir. I have a passport."

"Well, get ready. I got you a seat for Tuesday on the Casa Vasca bus line."

He looks for papers in his briefcase and hands me a pass.

"It departs at six in the morning… You'll have to spend the night in Madrid and bring something to eat for the ride. Then it leaves for Valencia and arrives around ten or eleven; then you'll go right to a designated house; they'll tell you how to get on the boat. There will be no time to lose. God be with you, *hija*."

He's distraught; he takes my hand tenderly, sadness in his eyes. Tears are about to stream out of my eyes, and I don't hold them back.

Then I say goodbye to everyone.

"Think it over!" says Doña Rosarito. She's so sweet, kind, and blond.

"Let her go. It's no use to think it over. She's already decided, or God decided. Let her go on her way!"

"But what if she finds no one to help her over there? That poor man with two little ones in his arms, and the only one around to take care of them is a girl who hasn't even graduated from secondary school…!"

"I tell you, Rosario, we don't have to think about the end of things. 'We do the work, but God determines the end.'" This girl's duty is to find her father and be with him in all his troubles… if they fail, if they don't find work, or if they drown in that bitter sea with all the others who've tried to escape…, that's not up to her, it's up to God."

Those words settle me. I'm sure now about what I have to do… and I'm going to do it.

February 27

I'm leaving. I open the closets to figure out what to bring.

"They're bombing us… all night long," Guadalupe says.

"Why? We've lost the war. Do they want to kill the only survivors?"

"I can only bring one suitcase, so I have to choose what I want to bring carefully… I don't know what I'm going to need… *Mamás* portrait… her slippers… the rosary Aunt Julia gave me… a little icon of Our Lady of Lourdes… Andersen's 'The Princess and the Pea,' …the little wooden figures of bears…my sewing kit…

It's not all going to fit. I have to choose… Jorge's letters… Poor Jorge… letter from *Papá*… the cookbook I bought in Santander… No, no, it doesn't fit, the designer dress, the leather jacket… shoes… *Mamá's* robe? They don't fit! But I can't leave these things behind because they make me remember when I was little…

Here is where *Papá* keeps all the baptism certificates: his parents', his grandparents', and ours. Should I take them along?

But am I really leaving? I feel like I might be fooling everyone around me. Yes, I am leaving! I'm leaving tomorrow, and tonight I'll spend the night in Madrid and get up early in the morning.

When my suitcase is ready, it won't shut. I have to decide which of these things I can leave behind… I'll leave out *Mamá's* robe and her slippers… All these books won't fit…

"*Señorita*, come to eat. Today we have something delicious; it's your goodbye dinner."

Guadalupe does all she can to prepare a decent meal… potato skins, garbanzo omelet, all flattened out with a tiny bit of oil in the frying pan.

At five I've managed to pack the things I need most into the suitcase. I shut the closets and give Guadalupe the keys. I go up to *Papá's* study, and I kiss the arms of the chair he sat in… it's where *Mamá* sat too.

Goodbye, goodbye, goodbye. I might not see you ever again.

Goodbye to the copy of *Don Quijote* with Moreno Carbonero's illustrations, and the other *Quijote* I read when I was a child; when I looked at the drawings, I imagined what Sancho and Don Quijote looked like. Goodbye… map of Madrid in the seventeenth century that *Papá* kept as a treasure!… Goodbye to the closet where I kept my toys when I was a girl…

Goodbye. I may not ever see you again… but you're in my thoughts; maybe I'll see you in a picture book My brother Cuchitrín's drawings, the ones he sketched with colored pencils! *Papá* tells me in his last letter that my brother is happy studying in London and that he sends me a hug. It's been so long since he's written me… I'm leaving now! I'm going to who knows where!

I go down the stairs caressing the handrail… Goodbye, goodbye! Guadalupe is waiting for me at the bottom of the stairs with my suitcase in her hand… I want to take a last stroll around the house and garden. Goodbye, poplar trees! Goodbye cypresses, you're getting dark… rose bushes… poor dry earth, frozen, just as spring begins to moisten everything! *Papá* says we are the earth where we were born. The earth of Madrid for me! I get down on my knees and kiss the ground…

Guadalupe and I go up the street to the road… Goodbye, house, goodbye!

February 28
By dawn I've fallen asleep.
"Celia, Celia, it's time. It's five o'clock…
It's María Luisa who's come to wake me up.
"It's five."
The whole family is up to see me off; they look astonished as they gaze at me.

"I don't know if I should tell you…" María Luisa's mother begins. "I don't know if I should… *Hija*, you still have time to think about it. What are you going to do all alone in that world? What will you do about money? Did you know that our money here isn't worth anything in other countries… What are you going to do in a French port city, with no money?… Think about it! Just think!"

"I'll find *Papá*."

"But maybe you won't. You don't know where he is… You don't even know if he left Barcelona."

"At the aviation offices they told me…"

"No matter what they told you, it might not be true; news today barely gets here…"

They all look at me. I drink a glass of saccharine malt, but it's hard to swallow. I'm nauseated, my stomach feels like it's shut up.

"More reason not to leave; you're sick. How can you leave this way? Do you want us to contact Casa Vasca to arrange for a special seat?"

I nod… I'm feeling horrible; it's impossible for me to leave like this… But then I think of what don César, Julianita's father, told me.

"No, no… don't say anything. I have to leave, I'm leaving. It's my duty."

Day breaks as María Luisa and I walk down Castellana carrying my suitcase between the two of us.

As we move toward the upper end of Alcalá, we see the Arc in a silhouette in the first rays of a red sun… and below Cibeles Plaza, grass growing between the flagstones… the Communications Palace, dirty, broken windows from the bombings.

All I can do is cry. I can't help it.

"There, there, now," María Luisa consoles me. "Don't cry… You'll be back soon."

"No, I won't be back. My heart tells me I won't ever be back. I know it… *Papá* won't be allowed to come back… the most honorable and generous man in the world… I'll always be with him."

Now we're walking toward La Puerta del Sol. There are very few people on the street, but as soon as we cross Nicolás María Rivero, we come across people carrying suitcases like us going to the same place.

There's the bus; we see more people walking toward it. María Luisa gets on and stays with me until it leaves; she fixes up the seat for me close to a window.

"It's not the best seat here in the back; it won't be a smooth ride, but there's nothing better."

Someone is tapping on the window. It's Guadalupe, who walked here from Chamartín to bring me one of the garbanzo omelets.

There's a heaviness in my heart and my stomach; it keeps me from seeing what's around me. María Luisa has stepped down after she kisses me…

I think she's crying. Guadalupe too. But not like the others. Her tears fall from her eyes in torrents, pouring out like a waterfall all over her dress.

"Goodbye… goodbye… goodbye!"

The bus rolls out toward Alcalá: I look out the window and see the two of them together in the middle of the street.

I look out into the streets; I breathe this fresh crystal air… *Adiós*, Madrid, my home city!

VALENCIA

A radiant sun allows me to forget the last sad hours in Madrid. The bus goes through towns in ruins without a single house standing, yet people are living in them. Ruins everywhere; I see a few women sewing and kids jumping and playing in the rocks and stones. One of the passengers says:

"They look like mice running among the stones!"

"What else are they going to do?" sighs a blond woman dressed in black. "What else? All they have is right here… If they were anywhere else, they'd be beggars."

In the bus everyone is silent, lost in their thoughts. The two blond women dressed in black are sitting in front of me. And next to me, a townsman and a soldier.

We arrive at Villaverde at midday. I'm familiar with this town because I've gone through here by bus three times.

"We're stopping here for an hour," says the driver. "Whoever wants to get off… go ahead. They're distributing sugarless malt in the Plaza."

We all get off. I follow several people as we step down in groups. I'm the only one traveling alone.

The streets are bathed in sun and smell like straw and manure… mixed with Spanish broom. It smells like a rural town, warm and pleasant.

I sense someone approaching me. It's a youngster who sits next to me.

"Excuse me, *señorita* Are you Celia Gálvez the one from *Blanco y Negro?*... the one who tells stories and...?"

"Yes, I am."

"They tell me you're a palm reader... Is it true?"

I laugh.

"How silly! Don't pay any attention... I just read a book one day that talked about reading hands, and from then on, I often stare at people's hands. But it was a joke, I don't believe in it!!"

"Would you care to read my palm?"

He extends his hands, palms up.

"No, not here. Are you going to Valencia?"

"Yes, I'm the driver's helper."

"Well, alright, when we get to Valencia, I'll look at them... But keep in mind that I don't know anything about this... it's only a joke."

The young man puts his hands in his pockets and says:

"I'll accompany you to the plaza... We can have a glass of malt. There's nothing else!"

We drink our malt in silence. He's a tall man; he must have been strong at one time, but now he's thin and pale.

"I've lost twenty-five kilos," he tells me when he notices I'm looking at him. It's because I've been hungry. I'm Basque!" he says proudly, "But I was born in Argentina. Argentina is home. Yet..."

He doesn't finish. We go back to the bus, and I don't see him again.

There are less ruins the closer we get to Valencia. Now it smells like orange blossoms.

When night falls, I hear airplanes and bombs exploding. Someone begins singing "The International," and we all follow along. It's a spirited hymn that livens us up. Then we sing "Himno de Riego" and we all ride along singing as we pass by more towns on a dark road barely illuminated by the bus's dim lights.

I go to sleep. When I awake, I see the streets of Valencia, dark and solitary.

Suddenly, the bus stops. Everyone steps down. Me too. We go through a door that leads to a lighted patio... I don't know what to do now... It's too late to look for a place to stay. There's no one around to help me with my suitcase, and I don't know where to leave it. So I look for the Basque man who's talking on the phone.

"The best thing to do is get back on the bus and go to sleep. It's a bad time to go looking for something."

I go back to the bus, and I see that some others have come back too. I put my coat on the seat to make a bed… off to sleep. My feet are freezing…! I take my shoes off and wrap my feet in a wool scarf. I sleep soundly. Please, God. Take care of me…!

At daybreak, a strong voice awakens me.

""Off the bus! It has to move along! Everyone off the bus.""

Without complaint, we all get off and bring our packages and suitcases.

"May I leave my suitcase here?" I ask a young lady half asleep watering her geraniums.

"Leave it," she says. "Does it have your name on it?"

"Yes…"

With the little strength I have, I drag the suitcase to a corner where I see other suitcases. I turn up my coat collar to cover my ears and go out into the empty street and try to figure out where I am.

Astonishing! I'm on the street where Fifina lives with her aunts. At that moment the doorman opens the entrance and I go in.

I knock, trying to wake Fifina up; she can't believe what she sees.

"Can it be you, love? You? How did you get here? The buses aren't running; nothing's functioning… it's…"

"I'm here; believe me, it hasn't been easy!" I say to her.

"My God. You're so thin! Like a shadow of yourself, *hija*! And your coat is all wrinkled!"

"I've had to sleep in it."

Her aunts are older, darker, and smellier than before. I give them a hug, and we have breakfast: malt with drops of milk and soft white bread. Then we go out into the street.

Fifina knows some ladies on the other side of town who might be able to put me up for a few days. It's the first of March, and what in Madrid was a promise of spring here is a promise fulfilled, a sweet-smelling reality.

"*Chica*, what light, what perfume!"

"Later we'll go to the flower market… You'll see."

But Valencia has changed since I was here a year ago. It's as if the city were sick, old, and poor, and it doesn't care anymore… women don't comb their hair, they don't even change their clothes.

There are lots of people on the street coming and going. The stores are closed with their metal shutters half-shut, the cafés are dirty, smokey, crowded, and the post office on Castelar Plaza is like a human anthill, people going in and out poorly dressed, nervous, worried… filled with frightened anxiety.

The house Fifina is taking me to is visible well before we get there. It's an immense red brick building in the middle of an abandoned block with rows of lifeless trees lining the streets.

The sunbaked earth has hardened since the last rain, forming a sea of dried mud.

Fifina can read my mind; she says:

"Ah… It's not going to rain now… You can be sure of that."

She tells me that the flats in this huge building are owned by the people who live there. Every resident has bought their dwelling, paying monthly installments. There's a patio as big as a city plaza with food stores, butcher shops, and a school.

"Everything was working before this inferno… after it all started, everyone did what they could to protect what they had… And now people say everything is falling apart."

A lady living in one of the apartments on the second floor greets me amicably.

"It'll be just like home here… there's a bathroom but no hot water because we can't light the pilot… Do you have a place you can go to eat?"

Fifina answers all her questions. She will get me a card that allows me to eat in a restaurant nearby.

"Right now, all I want to do is sleep.'

The lady shows me a small room; it's cheery and comfortable and sunny. There's a little bed, a closet, and a table.

Murillo's painting, *Immaculate Conception*, hangs on the wall… The virgin is in a natural pose; it's the same oil portrait as the one on the wall of my school. I stared at it for hours and hours.

Fifina promises to have my suitcase sent here. As she's on her way out, she says:

"*Señora*, a cup of tea will surely do her good."

I wash up in the bathroom; the water is cold, but there are towels. I dry up and go to bed.

As soon as I lay down, I hear knocking at the door. The lady comes in; she has white hair, unkempt. She looks sad. She stirs a cup of tea as she comes in.

"It has a couple of teaspoons of honey," she says. "It'll be good for you. I can't give you anything else."

I go to sleep looking at Murillo's painting. How beautiful the eyes of the Virgin…!

A sense of profound comfort engulfs me as I fall fast asleep.

I wake up in the middle of the afternoon. The first thing I see is Murillo's Virgin. The sun shines in her face, and a halo encircles her divine head.

"Dear Mother of God, help me, save me, guide me…!"

Someone is knocking at my door.

Señorita Gálvez… *Señorita*… Here is your suitcase."

"Come in…"

The lady comes in; she's accompanied by the young Basque man on the bus who's carrying my suitcase. I'm surprised at seeing him in my room. But he doesn't think anything of it.

"Are you sick, *Señorita* Celia?"

"No, just tired."

The lady doesn't close the door on her way out, and the Basque man pulls up a chair next to my bed without the slightest hesitation and extends his hands to me, palms up.

"Which one do you want to read, left or right?"

"Left," I respond immediately because if I don't, this man will not leave my room for the rest of his life. "You're going to take a long trip. Perhaps by sea."

"You got it right! Just right! How marvelous. I'm off to America!… Me. You know I'm Basque? It's because… well, my parents are Basque, but I was born in Argentina… in a country house they call *Ceibo*… I can ride a horse like a *gaucho*…, but now I can't because I haven't had anything to eat for a long time… I'm hungry…"

I interrupt him because if I don't, he'll never stop talking.

"You'll be very successful… no, maybe two triumphs…"

"That's it!" he yells. "Two! How did you know? And you told me you wouldn't be able to tell me anything… Look, *Señorita*, you're an angel from the heavens… That's what I told my friend… 'That girl over there with the braids… she's going to figure out my destiny.' I know it for sure!"

"Yes… two victories… You have two wishes that will come true."

"Of course! You see? That's it! And… I'm going to tell you… although I shouldn't tell anyone those things… but I can tell you… I sure can tell you… I'm not illiterate, *Señorita*, no ma'am, I'm not… I got to sixth grade in Argentina, and I studied here at The Polytechnical School for two years… I've studied physics, chemistry, and mathematics… weight and volume theory, electronics… and…"

The man tells me how much he has studied over and over again, his grades, and what his teachers have said about him.

"Just so you know… you're not dealing with an illiterate…"

I pull up the sheets to my chin and assure him that I never thought he was illiterate, not for a minute, and that I'm sure he's a genius.

The beams of the sun that were shining on the Virgin's head have moved to the golden frame, leaving a shadow over her figure. This fool has stripped me of the peacefulness I was feeling… who knows if I'll ever get it back!

Then he keeps on blabbing about muscular force and magnetic development of human vibrations… He talks to me in a low voice, as if he were telling me a secret that will change the world.

"Man can fly!" he says.

"Sure, we've flown in airplanes for some time…"

This irritates him, but he disguises it.

"*Señorita*, all I've studied leads to a conclusion that man can fly without the use of a machine…"

"Ah!"

He's convinced he knows what he's talking about.

"Have you tried it?"

No, he says, he's missing a detail, but once he finds it, he'll leap off the roof of his house.

"Lord!"

He laughs. I hope he doesn't kill himself. Bah! That's why he doesn't talk to anyone about his project, because people will think he's crazy. He'll scare them. But he's so sure about what he's saying. You just have to understand muscular force, he says, certain imperceptible movements and you must study arm and neck muscles… and magnetism… If we just understand all this, we'll be able to fly like birds.

"Can't we swim like fish? If we can swim like fish, we can fly like birds. It's a matter of studying it…"

He thinks he has it all resolved, just one small detail is missing. He's going to see if his findings can be used for the war. That's why he's going to offer his knowledge to Argentina. He would have offered it to the Spanish Republic, but now that we've lost the war, he won't.

He doesn't want money. He doesn't need it… The only thing he wants is to teach soldiers how to fly.

"Imagine… If just one man can fly, so can an entire army. They'll hold hands in formation, like a cloud coming down on a town or a whole nation."

I look at him. He's livid. His eyes open wide, as if he were looking at the flying soldiers sailing down like birds. Poor young man!

"I can't see anything else in your palm, and I have to go to dinner now."

"Oh, of course. Forgive my indiscretion, *Señorita*. I'm leaving. Look, I want to give you this. It's a voucher for a food supply room on Avenida Salmerón, 127, third floor. You'll eat well. Go there. They open every day at one. You don't have to thank me. I should thank you."

It's dark by the time he leaves. I get dressed and go to the dining room. I see the lady with a ten or twelve-year-old girl.

"Did you sleep well, *Señorita*?"

"Yes… But did you see the man who brought me my suitcase? He didn't leave until now. I think he's crazy."

"Almost everyone coming from Madrid is crazy," says the lady calmly. "They're all so hungry there. Here we have enough rice, oranges, oil... there's only been scarcity of tomatoes and onions, but that was for a short time. A cousin of mine got here a month ago, she hasn't gotten rid of a nervous tic... Don't be offended, *Señorita*, but I've heard you talking to yourself. My daughter and I noticed it... Please don't be offended; we know about certain ailments."

"You're right... I'm feeling very weak!"

When I say this, I feel my legs slipping out from under me. No, I'm not going out tonight. I'm very tired. Very tired!

I bring another glass of malt and honey to my room. I sleep deeply the entire night.

I'm awoken by kids making noise in the patio. I can see them through the window, it must be the school.

I go out into the street. It's a sunny, radiant morning. Warm. I go down a street with an enormous palm tree in the middle; then I stroll behind the station on a wide walkway. The last few days I was in Valencia, I met a couple who lived around here... Right here... It was this house with the big white-marble entrance. I ask the doorman if I can go in.

"Hey, it's Celia!" says the young married woman when she sees me in the vestibule. "It's Celia! Stay for lunch!"

She helps me find the ticket office that assigns passes for a ship out of Spain. But there are none available, and no one knows if there'll be anything. One of the officials in the office close to the station asks me:

"Which party are you in?"

I don't know how to answer. I look at Rosita, who says with a smile:

"Well, say something, *mujer*. You must be' in *Izquierda Republicana*, right?

"Yes," I say without much conviction.

"Alright..., leave your name... We're expecting English ships to arrive any day now... They're freight ships, but they transport refugees... I'll include your name."

"Where are they going?" asks Rosita.

"Oh, well. I'm not sure... Marseille, Oran, or... I don't know... No information... Do you have a passport?... Make sure you get a visa for

France or a country in America… Maybe Cuba… or Dominican Republic… Mexico… Up to you. Come here every day at noon, and be prepared to leave, because we won't know they're on their way for sure until three hours before embarkation.'"

Rosita's husband is sitting at the table and looking at me; his eyes tell me he's terrified for me.

"Please listen to me: it's crazy to leave… Those ships are just big barges carrying produce and a special cabin for the captain… What's more is that they won't even tell you where they're going. I think they're paid by political parties that want to save their fellow party members."

"But I must leave… *Papá* is waiting for me."

"I have to tell you, those ships are old, useless since the First World War, the hulls are in need of repair, they've painted them, which makes them vulnerable, so they might be bombed and likely sink. If the captain manages to arrive at a safe port, he gets a bonus; if not, the shipowner gets a payment of more than what the sunken piece of junk is worth. And that's what you want to board! Sure, the ones who know that when Franco takes power they'll be executed so to save their skin they… but you…!"

"I have no choice…"

Still, Doctor Terrada's words upset me, and I can't sleep… I toss and turn in bed. What if Father just waits…? What if he waits for everything to end, and then…

Another day in Valencia and I don't know what I'm going to do.

I go to a telephone booth at Plaza Castelar and try to get in touch with María Luisa.

"I don't know what I'm going to do… They're telling me that the ships are unsafe… If he waits…"

"The best thing for you, *hija*, is to stay. That's it. You've done all you can to leave the country, but things are not as easy as they look… Come back. Try to find transportation back to Madrid."

"You think I'll be able to leave when Franco's troops take over?"

"Of course not! Nonsense! How could I possibly think that? They're not going to let anyone leave Spain for months, maybe years. They're sure not going to let people leave just like that…"

"So…"

"So what?"

"So then I'll leave now. *Papá* needs me right now…"

"At least think it over."

"No… I've already thought it over Goodbye, María Luisa. Thank your mom and dad for their kindness to me… Go see Guadalupe… Tell her… and the trees, tell them…"

Both of us cry as we bid farewell… I'm thinking this might be the last time I hear her voice…

That's what's happening. Today there's been a communist uprising. Everything has been cut off, including the roads out of the city.

JUAN GARCÍA

I can eat lunch every day on Salmerón Avenue with the voucher that the young Basque man gave me. It's a tenement house. I go up to the third floor. There it is.

The entire house is filled with tables, from the vestibule to the hallways, all the way to the kitchen. They give out a dish of rice, a piece of meat, an orange, bread, and wine. For me this is a banquet. It seems I'm gaining weight. The diners look at me with curiosity. They're probably country folk or drivers who haul provisions from the farms. No one talks to me, and I don't talk to anyone; I'm absorbed thinking of all the hardships making my life miserable.

I get up late. I'm waiting to use the bathroom because Doña Carmen and her daughter are taking a bath. I get dressed slowly, and at eleven-thirty I go to the consignment house. As I approach, I shorten my steps… What if they sail today? I feel an uncomfortable vibration of anguish in my stomach and entire body.

The door with the polished windows is open; I look inside and I see women and girls. I walk over to their table.

"Any news of ships?"

"Nothing. Still nothing. Be sure to have everything ready."

When I go out into the street, the sun is out, the air is clear, and the city looks happier. I go to the French Consulate on Colón Plaza. It's a two-storey building; in the entrance there are men speaking to one another in hushed voices; it seems they're in mourning. There are lots of people on the stairs going up to the first floor, and on the first floor, more people are crowded together in the entrance to the vestibule… It's difficult for me to make my way in. It's strange that with so many people in the room, no one is speaking. It's very quiet, which is what makes me think they're in mourning.

"What would you like?" a man asks me. He has a pencil and notebook.

"I want someone to check my passport for a visa to leave the country after I get there."

"So your final destination isn't France?"

"Yes, sir."

"Are you sure you want to leave France immediately after you arrive?"

"Yes…"

"Where are you going?"

"To America."

"Yes, but what country in America?"

"I don't know. My father is in France, and he'll know where to go."

The man takes my passport. Many people have left, so I can sit down. America? Why are we going to America? What are we going to do in America? I don't know where I got that idea about America? I don't even know who told me that America would mean the end of our woes… Did *Papá* ever talk about it? I don't know. I don't want to go there… I don't like the idea of America. The people who were born in those modern countries can live there all they want, but not me. Me, the one who comes from my grandfather's home next to the Segovia Aqueduct… I don't want to go there. If we have to get away from Europe, we'll go to Africa, Oran, or Algeria… Who knows if they'll allow us to live in a French country?

The man who took my passport comes back with the visa that allows us to stay in France for twenty-four hours.

I go to lunch. When I step out, there's a crowd in the plaza listening in silence to a blaring loudspeaker:

Spaniards. Defenders of the Republic. The final hours have arrived. We shall lose with dignity. We shall face death with serenity. We need more strength to die in defeat than to fall in battle. Spaniards. Defenders of the Republic…

The woman next to me is crying. When the words of the loudspeaker fall silent, we hear the hymn of the Republic, and everyone continues on their way in silence. At Plaza Castelar, little pieces of paper flutter down from the sky with a note announcing greetings from Franco, who offers protection.

Someone was tossing down papers with Franco's message from the roof of a balcony. But no one pays any attention.

On Blasco Ibáñez Street, there are signs with big letters denouncing the ministers of the Republic, that they're traitors, that they're easily knocked down in a matter of minutes.

"If the ship doesn't get here in two days, you won't be able to leave," Rosita's mother says to me.

The next days I wait calmly in the middle of swarming anguished people. I'm able to sleep well into the morning, and in the afternoon, the sun shines again on the face of Murillo's virgin. I hear the sounds of children screaming happily on their way to school, the blissful ignorance of children indifferent to the destruction that surrounds them.

The only thing disturbing my serenity is my daily visit to the consignment office. Is it today? No, not today.

"*Señorita* Celia! Don't you recognize me?"

A military officer is waving to me from his car… No, I don't recognize him.

"I'm Juan, the gardener of your place in Chamartín. Don't you remember?"

It's true! This is the youngster who took care of our garden the days just before the war. It was 1936. When the war broke out, he went to the mountains to join the revolution… How could I recognize him? He's taller, stronger… He looks confident, elegant with his captain's uniform. He looks distinguished!

He gets out of his car to greet me with a military salute.

"What are you doing here?"

We talk. He's affable and addresses me with respect, but with an air of superiority. He's caught me off guard.

If I need anything, I am to let him know. Where do I live? Far? No, that can't be. He lives in the Victoria Hotel, and I should go there. That way I can use his car, and he'll take care of me. Have I forgotten that I'll need a car to get to Port Grau when the ship disembarks, it's fifteen kilometers from here?

He takes me to the hotel, a beautiful room with a view of a narrow street.

Here they'll serve me a meal a day... Everything's settled in a matter of minutes, and off we go in his car to retrieve the suitcases I've kept in the brick house in the middle of an undeveloped area where I've been living until now.

Doña Carmen says goodbye to me. Have a good trip, she tells me. Hoping you find your father. And that she hopes we find happiness in that land across the ocean.

Fifina looks alarmed when she finds out about my departure.

"Do you think you'll be better off there?"

At least I'll avoid those long daily walks jumping over the cart tracks... Also, Juan is a good man, refined and respectful, and he could help me to get to where I need to go.

"I guess you know," she says to me unconvinced. "He's your gardener."

March 12

Juan disappeared from the hotel after having arranged my stay, and he hasn't returned. I ask the concierge:

"The captain? He isn't here often. He's rented his room for more than six months; he's always traveling... He's closely tied to the government... He could be a general if he wanted to, but he's not ambitious."

This morning a phone call wakes me up.

"*Señorita* Celia? It's me, Juan García. I'm here alone for a few hours. Would you honor me by accepting my invitation to lunch?"

"Well, I'd love to, Juan."

"You told me you have a friend here... would you like to invite her?"

"Yes... yes. Where and at what time?"

"At one in the hotel dining room. I talked to the concierge and it's all settled. They've reserved a table for us next to the big, stained-glass window. Until then, *Señorita*. At your service."

I need to dress well for this meal. My gray designer dress, well-brushed, black shoes… And later I'll tell Fifina; she's bound to laugh at me for the invitation.

"Are you really falling for the gardener? Likely you're talking about all the ways of grafting roses, or the variety of geraniums. Your conversations with Juan will probably be more interesting than the ones with those pretentious university students…"

I see she's putting on makeup and carefully puffing her nose. When we arrive at the hotel, it's one o'clock. The waiter greets us no sooner than when we enter the dining room.

"This way, *Señoritas*… That table is right there."

The dining room is crowded, and everyone stares at us as we approach the table. Maybe it was the elegance of the table close to the stained-glass window, or the rose-colored tablecloth and fancy linen napkins that made everyone take notice.

Before we are seated, Juan appears. His stature, noble appearance, elegance, and serious demeanor attract the gaze of the diners whispering about us.

I introduce Fifina to him.

"Captain Juan García, this is my friend Fifina Estremeras."

As soon as we sit down, Juan's chauffeur, who appears to be his assistant as well, brings us a tray of cold cuts.

"Ah, this is a banquet," says Fifina.

"It's not worthy of you, but I was unable to get anything better," says Juan decorously.

After the hors d'oeuvres, we're served rice with shellfish and chicken in almond sauce, accompanied by white wine.. Fifina and I are too excited to speak. Our palates had forgotten the taste of these delicacies. For dessert, peaches in their juice and coffee… real coffee with sugar.

When Fifina finishes gobbling up everything (or when we both finish gobbling), she sighs:

"This hotel is a real find. Where did they get such fresh ingredients?"

Juan laughs without losing his air of gravity.

"No, *Señorita* Fifina, the hotel has nothing to do with this. Look at the difference between what we're eating and what the others around us are eating. I… and above all my assistant Paco, have acquired the chickens… and…"

"How marvelous!" Fifina, who has been doing nothing but swallowing throughout the meal, looks at the captain admiringly. "Do you military men eat like this every day?"

Paco is the one who answers as he clears the dishes before he serves the coffee:

"No, *Señorita*, no… The captain and I eat rice when there's enough. But many of us don't get to eat every day."

"Eat as much as you want today," Juan says, "and don't speak of it." Fifina, who has imbibed a good amount of wine, speaks out of turn.

"Are you on the front… or working in an office… or…?"

"There is much to do everywhere," he answers evasively.

"And is it true that soldiers on the front demand books? Do they read?"

"Yes, they read constantly. They read as they've never read before. There are many who have never even held a book in their hands and now read voraciously… as if they were making up for lost time."

"Do they read Galdós?"

"Yes and Valera, Pereda, Gómez de la Serna, Pérez de Ayala, and Azorín and they love Pío Baroja Also, lots of foreign books in translation All the books in demand among the soldiers. It's possible that the war has accomplished something that no one saw coming, because…"

Abruptly, he stops speaking and stands up.

"I'm very sorry, but I must leave you; I'm going to Valencia… I believe I'll be back in three days. It's been a pleasure to have been in your company…"

He shakes our hand, gives us his military salute, and leaves.

Fifina can't take her eyes off him until he exits the dining room.

"*Chica*, what a guy! Are you sure he's your gardener?"

"Of course… That's Juan García."

"Well, I'd swear he was a Castilian lord. The Duke of Alba wouldn't have paid us as much respect, or with such elegance. Did you notice how he served the wine? Magnificent!... and later that conversation he started about literature and philosophy…"

"It's a case of adapting to one's environment…"

"Adapting? No, it's triumph over your circumstances! He's unique…"

Fifina reflects in silence. But then she asks me:

"Is this man thinking of escaping from Franco?"

"It doesn't look that way…"

"Well, Franco will surely execute him when he takes over…"

"That's the best that could happen to him. Imagine what they'd do if they didn't kill him… Surely, strip him of his captain's rank… He doesn't have a degree and he's too old to start now."

"How old do you think he is?"

"Thirty-five… don't you think? All that pretense of a well-educated man won't be of use in making a new career. I bet he doesn't even know how to write. He'd have to go back to gardening… three fifty a day in overalls."

"What a pity!"

"Yes… materially and spiritually he's an exceptional man, but his upbringing hasn't provided him a decent future."

Fifina is upset.

"It's horrible! I'm telling you, it's outrageous he has to suffer such injustice!"

"But what can we do?"

"What can *we* do? You mean women? I don't know about you, but I'm going to keep my eye on that man. I'm going to try to help him in any way I can so that he gets the necessary means to a decent job, a military officer, a doctor, or…"

"Fifina, you've fallen in love with him!..."

ADIÓS

March 18

I go back to the consignment office as I do every day. There's an unpleasant wind blowing on the earth and dust off the unswept streets. Every now and then the sun hides behind the clouds.

Just before I arrive, I see many people at the door. I approach the counter to talk to an office worker.

"A ship sets off today at four."

A deathly coldness crawls up my body to my neck.

"Where is it going?"

"You'll see when it arrives… Name? Ah, yes. Here is your pass. Be at customs on the wharf at three sharp. No typewriters, cameras, jewels, or money…"

"But how am I going to live when I get to the port?"

"That's your problem. Next?"… he yells out to the people behind me in line.

I find myself standing at the door with the pass in my hand. It just has one number on it, nothing else: one-hundred-fifteen. A man comes up to me.

"Does your passport have a visa?"

"Yes, for France."

"But you need it for a country in America. The only possibility is Nicaragua. Over there... by a pharmacy on Barcelona Street. Also, you've got to get it stamped by the police."

I ask everyone where this place is, I find a narrow street and an ancient stone building where they stamp my passport... It's one o'clock.

The Nicaraguan embassy approves my visa, but I'm told it's just a formality because Nicaragua doesn't accept Spanish refugees...

I go back home. Everyone has eaten; there's nothing left.

"Can you tell me where Captain García is?"

"He came back this morning... Maybe he's in his room."

I phone him.

"It's me, Celia. A ship leaves today at four but I have to be at the port at three."

"Alright... I'm sorry I can't take you, but Paco will drive you there... He'll be waiting for you at two-thirty at the door. *Salud, Señorita*... At your father's service... Goodbye."

I hang up. I had felt so safe since the day I found Juan, but now...

I pack my suitcase. I'll bring all I'm going to need for three days on the ship... Where am I to go? What will happen to me? I'll be lost in the world.

I don't want to think about it. I'm in God's hands. I want to say goodbye to Rosita and her husband.

They're sitting at a table in the dining room; the doctor looks at me, he can't believe I'm leaving.

"What? You say the ship leaves today?"

"Yes... At four."

They continue to eat in silence. The doctor says:

"It's crazy!"

They serve me a cup of malt. I'm so nervous that the cup shakes in my hands.

They speak of insignificant things: the little house they bought, the marble table in the house...

"It's too bad you can't see it, Celia. It's in a beautiful place, on a plateau... Imagine, it's an area completely desolate since the beginning of the revolution... but now that it's all ending, thank God, we're going to fix it up, and it'll be divine. Right, Rosita?"

It's as if these words were coming from dying people talking about life... I'm at the margin of all this... I'm not of this world... In a few hours, I'll be in a ship going to God knows where... without money... all alone.

Rosita interrupts my reflections:

"Do you have a blanket for your trip?"

"No."

The doctor adds:

"I can't believe it! Don't you know that you'll be in the lower deck of the ship with a crowd of passengers all hunched together, and the only place to sit will be your suitcase, and the only place to sleep will be the floor?"

"No... I didn't know."

"Well, now you know..."

"No matter... It'll just be two or three days and then..."

"Then? Well, *hija*," he says impatiently, "why argue? You've made up your mind. I'm going to give you the military blanket they gave me when I was thinking of going to the front... and a book to read along the way... Well, not exactly... it's not my book, it belongs to Luis; he'll be here any minute."

"But I have to go now..."

"No hurry yet, rest here for a while."

My clock says it's two. They speak of their friend Luis, the one they've called on the phone, he's a member of Clara de Monteverde's family...

"She too wants to bid you farewell. She talks about you all the time."

"Me?"

I'm thinking of Fifina. She doesn't know I'm leaving. I can't go without telling her. We may not see each other again. Their servant delivers a note I've written to Fifina: "I'm leaving in an hour. Say goodbye to your aunts. I'm at Doctor Terrada's house. Come say goodbye."

Luis arrives with his wife Marcela; they're the other couple I met on my first trip to Valencia. Luis is kind, affectionate and friendly. He gives me the book, telling me not to try to separate the two pages that are stuck together....

Then they all start talking about my situation.

"The communist revolution in Madrid failed. It's a matter of days... or maybe hours before Franco's army takes over. They're going to execute about half the population."

They seem pleased about it. My God! What would *Papá* say? And Jorge...! Poor Jorge! It's all over... All we can do is flee... And that's what I'm doing... The others are happy. Did they ever believe in democracy like *Papá*? Who was right? *Papá*, for sure. I'm certain *Papá* and granddad are the only ones who got it right...

They continue to talk and talk, but I don't pay attention... Tonight I'll sleep on a ship in the middle of the sea on my way to a port I've never been to... a French port...

When I get there, I'll ask the Spanish people fleeing from Barcelona if they know my father, and then I'll find him... Ay *Papá*! My dear *Papá*!... We'll find Valeriana for sure, and the girls, and then...

Doña Clara arrives grasping her two daughters' arms and says in her severe voice:

"I feel it's my obligation to bid you farewell and wish you a good trip... As a Spanish Christian I forgive my enemies, although I don't excuse them..."

Luis lets out a kindly laugh.

"Celia is a lovely enemy."

"Lovely or not, she does well to leave. Franco would have her executed if she stayed... and for good reason."

I'm dumbfounded by this lady's words, but I try to take them as a joke.

"Why doña Clara, I thought you'd hide me in that beautiful cabinet you have..."

"You're wrong, *Señorita*! Wrong! For reasons I won't say, I wouldn't hide you... I swear I wouldn't. You are an enemy of our sacred institutions and the social order!"

"Me?"

"Yes, you, the very one... I've suffered so much from your henchmen's slander. My heart's still bleeding from wounds that haven't healed... Now I see that I shouldn't have come here... You can't look at one's enemy in the face without hating him. May God be my witness... I'd love to forgive you! I want to forgive! I want to forgive!"

She goes down the hall with her daughters in tow, uttering those words

256

over and over again. The rest of the family accompanies her, except Luis and Marcela…

They're laughing at my astonishment.

"Don't pay any attention to that crazy woman, *hija*. Of course you're our enemy…"

"Me?"

"Yes, you, poor innocent girl," laughs Marcela. "Aren't you an enemy of Franco? Well, we're his friends… and of course much more so since he's about to win."

They're still laughing in my astonished face.

"Terrada is much worse than us because he was always on Franco's side. He's a falangist."

"I don't believe it!"

"Yes, dear. But that doesn't mean we don't love you or wouldn't hide you if we had to. But that won't happen…"

"But *Papá*… my father…"

"Your father, my love, is a starry-eyed idealist…"

I look out into the street through the wide window… The sun is shining on the sidewalks and pedestrians walking along these sidewalks… I won't see these people again…! But I'm glad about it! Now I'm happy about leaving…

I used to be like a sailboat at full mast propelled by the wind… But now one by one, the masts fall… They all tell me they love me, but they're convinced I'm an enemy, and even worse, my father's an enemy. They lied during the war because they were scared. So they were executed because they were lying.

I say goodbye to all of them when Fifina arrives.

"Are you really leaving?" she asks.

"Yes, just this minute… The driver is waiting…"

When we're on the street, I say:

"They're right-wing!"

"Who?"

"Rosita and her husband… Even Luis and Marcela."

"Luis? I can't believe it… But it makes sense. The middle class is filled with right-wingers… and now everyone who said they weren't fascists has switched to Franco's side. The ones who lost now have few friends."

"Doña Clara came by"

"Don't pay any attention, *hija*... They're staying here and they have to live... Look, my aunts have begged me... 'for God's sake,' they say, 'stay away from Celia...' they say that someone could accuse me later on and... but I want you to know that if I don't accompany you to the port, it's not because you're one of them, it's because I don't want to see you leave..."

We pass by a small plaza with benches and trees surrounding a statue. I have to sit down because my legs are trembling.

"I'm tired!"

"Me too," says Fifina. We can't face each other; we don't speak.

It's almost time. I stand up. I have to leave now.

"I'm staying here," says Fifina, and she kisses me.

Her eyes are filled with tears.

"I'll see you when I get back," I say.

"God's will..."

I rush out of the plaza to the other side of the street and look back at her. Fifina remains on the bench without looking at me and dries her eyes...

"Goodbye," I whisper...

When I get to the boarding house, I see Paco in the car looking out the window.

"Should I fetch the luggage?"

"Yes... let's go."

"I ask for the bill and leave a huge tip. The little money I have left will be of no use to me since they'll take it away in customs.

The car passes Plaza Castelar and then the outskirts of the city. People standing in the doors of their houses waiting anxiously for something. They wait! They're all waiting for what's about to happen... For some nothing will change, others will go to jail, and many will be executed...

"So no one is seeing you off?" asks Paco, Juan's assistant.

"No..."

"Of course! No one wants to get involved."

"Yes, everyone suddenly is a Franco supporter..."

"Or they've all had a sudden change of heart... Look, a few days from now, I'd do the same… The captain used to be one of Franco's soldiers, and I hope they remember that…"

We're on a long, tree-lined street. Everything looks dirty to me, all covered with dry gray mud..

The little sailboat I was on has lost its last sail. Even Juan García changes his allegiance.

I catch a glimpse of the blue sea at the end of the street. The sea! The sea! That's the path to *Papá*!

The car stops.

"Here's customs," says Paco.

I take my handbag and follow him as he carries my suitcase to the ship's luggage compartment. There's a group of ill-clad soldiers with their peasant overcoats over their shoulders and military caps on their heads. Women and children bunch together close to the door.

"I'm going back to Valencia right now," Paco tells me. "Have a good trip!" And almost without looking at me, he goes back to the car, backs up, and off he goes. I'm alone under the bare trees that line an ample sidewalk leading to the ship… Alone…! All of them, one after another, have left me here just before I leave…

"But I'm not alone!" I say over and over again to lift my spirits. "I'm in the hands of God!"

July 13, 1943

Swan Isle Press is a not-for-profit publisher of literature
in translation including fiction, nonfiction, and poetry.

For information on books of related interest
or for a catalog of Swan Isle Press titles:
www.swanislepress.com

Celia in the Revolution
Book and cover design by Marianne Jankowski
Typeset in Adobe Jensen Pro